"So, did you see a bull you liked out there?"

"Maybe." Tess didn't want to sound too eager. "I wouldn't mind seeing that big black one."

"The black one, eh? I had a feeling that son of a gun would catch your eye."

"Is something wrong with him—besides the missing horn?"

"There's nothing wrong with him. But if you were to take him, you'd have your hands full. When they say a bucking bull is rank, it's usually a compliment. But that black bastard—he's RANK, in capital letters—smart, unpredictable, and full of the devil. Just when you think you've got everything under control, he'll take you down—like stepping in quicksand when you don't know it's there."

"Quicksand." Tess rolled the word off her tongue. "You like him, don't you?"

Brock's breath caught. Then the laughter exploded out of him, rumbling through his body. "Like him? You're damn right I do. He reminds me of me at my worst."

Don't miss any of Janet Dailey's bestsellers

JANET DAILEY

QUICKSAND

ZEBRA BOOKS
Kensington Publishing Corp.
www.kensingtonbooks.com

QUICKSAND

CHAPTER 1

Southern Arizona, March

As the sun climbed toward midmorning, a golden eagle rose from its perch atop a hundred-year-old saguaro. Its beating wings, wider than a man's reach, lifted the bird skyward, where it soared and circled on the updrafts, its golden eyes scanning the desert for prey.

Brock Tolman shaded his eyes to follow the eagle's flight. He felt a certain kinship with the great bird—both of them apex predators, both of them powerful. But the eagle's power came from its wings. Brock's came from his ambition.

As the eagle rose, its moving shadow passed over foothills painted with the bright gold of flowering brittlebush. Crimson-tipped spears of ocotillo and lemony clouds of blooming paloverde dotted the landscape with the colors of Sonoran spring.

In the weeks ahead, blossoming cactuses would blaze with hues of rusty yellow, pink, and magenta. Then white blooms would crown the giant saguaros that stood like guardians over the desert. Finally, the women of the Tohono O'odham who called the desert home would come with their long poles and harvest the seedy red fruit.

Brock had made enough money with his investments to live anywhere he wanted. But he had chosen this place, in the foothills of the Santa Catalina Mountains outside Tucson, to build his private kingdom. The Tolman Ranch was a patchwork of pristine desert and fenced pastureland where genetically bred bucking bulls—close to 100 of them not counting the cows and calves, along with a herd of Angus beef steers—grazed on native grass watered by mountain springs. The ranch's setting was beautiful, and Brock was not immune to beauty—whether admiring it, coveting it, or possessing it.

Today, as Brock sat astride his big sorrel gelding and watched Miss Tess Champion ride out across the pasture, Brock reflected that most men would be satisfied with what he had. But for him, it wasn't enough. To Brock's way of thinking, *enough* didn't exist. There was always more to want, always more to get.

And more to lose.

Brock shifted in the saddle, feeling the crackle of the folded envelope he'd stuffed into his hip pocket. It had arrived in yesterday's mail, but he hadn't opened it until this morning. What he'd found inside had jerked a noose around his heart. He'd recognized the yellowed newspaper clipping at once; but what did it mean? Was it some kind of warning? Maybe an attempt at blackmail? Was his whole perfectly ordered world about to come crashing down around him?

He'd been reading the text when Tess's truck had pulled up outside. There'd been no time to do anything but replace the clipping in the envelope, fold it, and stuff it into the deep hip pocket of his Wranglers, where it wouldn't be seen by any eyes but his. He would worry about it later. Right now, he had more pressing matters on his mind.

A few months earlier, he'd bailed Tess's family's ranch

out of foreclosure and forced a reluctant Tess to take him on as a business partner. He might have had other ideas for Tess—like getting her into his bed. But if there was one thing he'd learned in life, it was that mixing business with pleasure was a recipe for disaster.

So, for as long as they were partners, the rule would be hands off. And that was a damned shame, Brock mused, admiring the way her slender body sat the horse and the way the wind played with the long dark hair that fell loose below her hat. Tess was well past girlhood, but she was a beautiful, smart, sexy woman. The fact that she was the most stubborn, muleheaded, prickly female he'd ever known only sweetened the challenge.

But Brock knew better than to cross that line. He was a man who made his own rules and played by them. With Tess, for now at least, the rule was strictly business.

This morning Tess was here to choose the bull he'd offered her in exchange for Whiplash, the rank bucker who'd been ruled too dangerous for the arena. Brock had long dreamed of breeding a world champion bull. It was his hope that Whiplash's fiery bloodline might make the magic happen.

In return, Tess had been given her choice from among Brock's three- and four-year-old bulls, who were just starting their careers in the rodeo arena. There were twenty-three of them in this pasture, all trained, tested, and ready for the big time.

Tess had a keen eye for bulls. She would no doubt pick one of his best. Brock was fine with that. As her partner, he would retain part ownership of any bull she chose. He had nothing to lose.

But curse the woman, why had she insisted on riding out alone to inspect the herd? Brock had saddled up, planning to go with her. However, after declaring that she wanted to view the bulls without the distraction of his company, she'd ridden off and left him fuming at the pasture gate.

Something told Brock that chasing after her would only add to his humiliation. He would let her go. But he couldn't help worrying. Tess was an expert rider, and she knew her way around bulls. But if anything were to go wrong, she'd be unprotected out there.

He would keep his distance, Brock resolved. But he wasn't about to let the woman get too far ahead of him.

Tess paused her mount to scan the pasture. The grassy expanse, scattered with creosote, ironwood trees, and clumps of sage, seemed to go on forever. But why should she let that surprise her? Everything Brock Tolman owned was too large, too grand, and too fine for ordinary folk. Even the horse he'd lent her, a registered Appaloosa, was probably the most superb animal she'd ever ridden.

Not that she was impressed. Brock was a show-off who lived for the power and possessions his money could buy. Tess couldn't abide the man. What was more, she didn't trust him.

True, he'd saved her family's Alamo Canyon Ranch from foreclosure, but he hadn't done it out of kindness. He wanted the ranch for himself. And now that he had a foot in the door as her partner, he wasn't about to back off.

Right now, she knew that Brock was watching her. If she were to look back—not that she'd give him the satisfaction—she would see him sitting his horse like John Wayne, just as big and rugged as the late actor—except that Brock was no movie hero. He was more like a scheming, avaricious villain.

But she wasn't here to judge him. She was here to pick out a promising bull—one that would dominate in the arena and strengthen her family's own small herd with his bloodline. The future of the Alamo Canyon Ranch could be riding on the choice she was about to make.

She could see the bulls now, loosely scattered at the far

end of the pasture. Brock had shown her the stud book at the house, but looking through it had scarcely been worth her time. The young bulls appeared to have solid pedigrees and had been tested in the bucking pen. Any one of them could earn his keep in the PBR or PRCA rodeos. But would any of them have that fiery spark—the spark she'd witnessed in Whiplash before fate had led the big brindle to kill an intruder on the ranch?

Brock's intervention had saved the bull's life and given him a home. But Whiplash, so strong and full of promise, would never compete again.

The young bulls had caught her scent. They'd raised their heads and turned in her direction, watching her approach. Tess held the horse to a measured walk. She'd been dealing with cattle all her life, and she knew better than to alarm them, especially bulls.

She also knew better than to get off her horse for a closer look. Here, as on her own ranch, bulls in the pasture were handled on horseback or from sturdy vehicles. They were accustomed to mounted riders. But a human approaching on foot would be asking for trouble.

At a distance of about thirty yards, she paused again to study the bulls. They were splendid animals, sleek and muscular, their horn tips newly blunted for the arena. Green metal ID tags, inscribed with numbers, dangled like jewelry from their ears. Most of the bulls were a solid color, ranging from fawn to red to dark chocolate. Two of the bulls were pale cream speckled with black. One bull, the biggest of the herd, was as black as sin with a white slash, like a lightning bolt, running down his face. His left horn was missing—likely due to injury or infection. The other horn, even blunted, was long enough to do plenty of damage.

As Tess ventured closer, the bulls tightened their ranks, snorting and lowing in a way that clearly meant, *That's far enough, stranger.* The big black lowered his head and scraped at the grass with his single horn—a clear threat.

Tess backed off a few steps, keeping an eye on the bull who'd already captured her interest. It was too soon to make a decision. But her instincts were calling for a closer look at this tough brute.

"You're certainly no beauty." She spoke in a soothing voice. "But then, this isn't a beauty contest, is it, big boy?"

She should at least look at the others—and of course, she'd want to see some of them buck. It would be rash to make an on-the-spot decision. She needed time—days, even weeks, to choose the right animal.

The black bull tossed his head and pawed the ground. Tess didn't believe he'd charge, but just to be sure, she backed the horse farther away, onto the low, brushy rise where she'd stopped earlier. The Appaloosa responded to her lightest touch.

The bull stood his ground, eyeing her suspiciously. "It's all right, big boy," she said. "I'm not coming any—"

A sinister buzzing sound from the high grass chilled her blood. Her pulse lurched; but before she could act, the horse leaped straight up and twisted to one side, flinging her out of the saddle like a marble from a slingshot.

Tess hit the ground so hard that the wind whooshed out of her lungs. As she gasped for breath, struggling onto her side, she came almost eye to eye with the snake. The six-foot diamondback, its thick body coiling to strike, was only a few steps from her face. She could see its delicate forked tongue, testing the air. Testing her.

Terror fueled her reflexes. With no time to scramble to her feet or even get her breath, she tumbled backward and rolled like a log, letting her momentum carry her partway down the rough slope. Her back crushed something sharp. Pain shot through her ribs, but she didn't stop until she was out of striking distance.

Shaken, scratched, and sore, she forced herself to sit up. Glancing back, she could see no sign of the rattler. As she hugged her knees and took deep, gasping breaths, she recalled the words of Ruben Diego, an elder of the Tohono O'odham tribe and the longtime foreman of the Alamo Canyon Ranch.

"The rattlesnake doesn't want to kill you. He only wants to live. That is why he gives a warning. Let him go in peace."

After testing her limbs, Tess pushed to her feet. The horse had bolted and was gone. She was feeling some pain, but as long as her legs worked, she should be able to walk back to the gate, where she'd told Brock to wait for her.

Her hat lay nearby. She picked it up and jammed it onto her head. Only then, as she looked around, did she realize that she had another problem.

The bulls had moved in closer. They were staring in her direction, snorting, lowing, and tossing their horns. The black brute, standing in front like the lead tough in a street gang, scraped the ground with his horn, tossing up clumps of dirt and grass. If the bulls were to charge, she wouldn't have a chance.

Scarcely daring to breathe, Tess backed away a few steps. If she could duck out of sight behind a nearby sagebrush clump, the bulls might calm down—but the snake could be there, and there was nothing else close enough to serve as a hiding place.

"It's all right, boys. I'm not here to make trouble." As she inched backward, she spoke in a low tone—not so much to calm the bulls as to soothe her own nerves. Her heart was pounding. Bulls weren't stupid animals. They could sense fear.

The black bull bellowed and lunged, then stopped—another threat, nothing more. But there was no way she could outrun a real charge. For now, all she could do was retreat, step-by-step, making no sudden moves.

A memory flickered in her mind—tales of the old-time cattle drives and the cowboy songs that would calm the herd when it was time for them to bed down. Driven by desperation, she began to sing.

"'Down in the valley . . . the valley so low . . . Hang your head over . . . hear the wind blow . . .'"

Tess had never been a singer. Her untrained alto was off-key, her voice unsteady. The bulls didn't seem to like her song. They continued to snort, blow, and follow her as she tried to widen the distance between them. She wasn't making much progress. The pasture gate was still a long way off.

Coming out here alone had been a bad decision, made in a moment of pride—as if to show Brock she could manage without him. He'd probably been amused. He was probably laughing behind her back.

With her gaze fixed on the bulls, she started another stanza of the old song.

"'If you don't love me . . . love whom you please . . .'"

Step-by-step, her feet carried her backward over the uneven ground. A raven flapped out of the sky and perched on a stump, watching her with curious eyes. Even to the bird, she probably looked like a fool.

One more step, then another. Suddenly her boot heel caught in a tangled root. Stumbling backward, she lost her balance and went down hard on her rump.

That was when she heard a voice behind her—a deep voice, edged with amusement. Brock, on his big red horse, was perhaps a dozen yards behind her. "Don't stop," he said. "I was enjoying the entertainment."

Blazing with humiliation, she scrambled to her feet. "How long have you been there?"

"Not that long. When your horse came back, I figured you might need some help. I was riding to your rescue, but when I saw the show you were putting on, I couldn't resist watching. I should've known you could take care of yourself."

The man was gloating. He didn't care that she could've been snake-bitten or trampled. If he'd been within reach, Tess would've punched him.

As he looked her up and down, taking in her scratched,

dirt-smeared face and hands, his sardonic smile faded. "Are you all right, Tess?"

"I'm fine. How's the horse?"

"Just spooked. We need to put some salve on those scratches. Come on, I'll take you back to the house. You can tell me what happened on the way."

He leaned down from the saddle and offered a hand. Tess took it and let him swing her up behind the saddle. The bulls watched but made no more aggressive moves as Brock turned the big sorrel back toward the gate.

To keep from sliding off, Tess had to grip Brock's waist. He was rock solid beneath the denim shirt he wore. The aromas of man sweat and sagebrush teased her senses, stirring tugs and tingles in forbidden places. Not good. She cleared her throat.

"You wanted me to tell you what happened. The horse spooked at a rattler. By the time I came to my senses, the snake was gone and so was the horse. The bulls kept moving toward me—maybe just curious, but I couldn't be sure."

"So you decided to serenade them. Good thinking." He chuckled. Tess could feel the vibrations through her fingertips.

"I can't say much for my voice," she said. "I probably scared the poor things."

"So, did you see a bull you liked out there?"

"Maybe." Tess didn't want to sound too eager.

"If you want to see any of them buck, I'll have the boys set them up in the chutes."

"You know I don't want to make a hasty decision. But I wouldn't mind seeing that big black one."

He was silent for a moment, his gaze following the contrail of a military jet streaking across the sky. "The black one, eh? I had a feeling that son of a gun would catch your eye."

"Is something wrong with him—besides the missing horn?"

"There's nothing wrong with him. But if you were to take

him, you'd have your hands full." Brock opened the steel-railed pasture gate with the remote control in his pocket. It closed behind the horse as they rode through. "When they say a bucking bull is rank, it's usually a compliment. But that black bastard—he's RANK, in capital letters—smart, unpredictable, and full of the devil. Just when you think you've got everything under control, he'll take you down—like stepping in quicksand when you don't know it's there."

"Quicksand." Tess rolled the word off her tongue, liking the sound of it and the way it fit the bull. "You like him, don't you?"

Brock's breath caught. Then the laughter exploded out of him, rumbling through his body. "Like him? You're damn right I do. He reminds me of me at my worst. But believe me, you don't want to choose that bull."

"I'll be the judge of that," Tess said. "At least I want to see him buck, along with a couple of others. You can decide which ones to show me."

"You've got it. I'll alert the boys to get them ready for the chutes. It'll take about thirty minutes to set up. Meanwhile we'll get those scratches doctored and maybe have something cold to drink." He spoke into the walkie-talkie he carried in a leather holster clipped to his belt. "There, it's taken care of. Now let's get you up to the house."

Brock's home was an imposing cube of glass, stone, and timber, with a broad, covered porch that offered a panorama of the ranch and the desert beyond. As far as Tess knew, he lived here alone with only a retired range cook to prepare meals and keep the house in order. If there was a woman in his life, Tess wasn't aware of it, but Brock was a private person. Apart from the side he chose to show her, she knew very little about the man.

All the more reason not to trust him, she reminded herself as he helped her dismount and turned the horse over to a waiting stable hand, a good-looking young man with blond curls and hazel eyes.

Sharing the yard with the house were two guest cottages, a bunkhouse, barns, pens, and sheds, and a small arena equipped with bucking chutes. Somewhere beyond the pastures was an airstrip with a hangar where Brock stored the airplane he piloted himself.

Everything about the place was spare and simple, but constructed with the finest materials and workmanship money could buy. Knowing Brock, Tess wouldn't have expected anything less.

Walking beside him, she could feel the soreness from the fall she'd taken. As she took the first of the broad steps to the porch, her knee buckled.

"Take it easy." He caught her arm, saving her from a stumble. "You just got thrown from a horse. You're lucky to be walking. Let's get you to a chair."

In a move to steady her, he laid a hand at the small of her back. Tess yelped as the contact shot pain up her spine.

"What the devil—?" He moved behind her. "You must've tangled with a prickly pear. You've got a nasty spine stuck right through your shirt. You're bleeding. Come on in. We'll have you patched up in no time."

Inside, the house was sleek and immaculate, with tile floors and heavy wooden vigas supporting the ceiling. Plants in giant Talavera pots stood here and there. Massive leather furniture pieces were grouped on a thick alpaca rug. Touches of art enlivened the space—a genuine Charles Russell painting above the stone fireplace, a Frederic Remington bronze of stampeding buffalo on a sideboard.

"Impressive," she murmured, forgetting her pain for the moment.

"Thanks. I draw the line at mounted animal heads," he said. "Have a seat on the sofa."

"You said I was bleeding." She lowered herself carefully to the edge of the cushioned leather seat.

"You're fine. But it might help to drink something before we get started. We've got cold Coronas, or if you need something stronger, there's some good Kentucky bourbon in the cabinet."

"A Coke would be nice if you've got some," Tess said. "I wouldn't mind a beer, but with my sister a recovering alcoholic, I'm doing my best to support her. That includes following her rules—with no cheating, even when I'm away from home."

"Coke it is. Hang on. I'll be right back."

He returned a few moments later with two Coke cans and a large red cooler—some kind of medical kit. Opening the cooler, he took out a dispenser of antibacterial handwipes and handed one to her. Taking her cue from him, she cleansed her hands. The scrapes and cuts from the fall stung when the alcohol touched them. "We'll put some salve on those after I get that spine out of your back."

He popped one of the Coke cans and handed it to her. "Drink up. When you're ready, lean over the arm of the sofa. Getting the barb out is going to sting pretty bad. Can you handle that?"

"You'd be surprised what I can handle." Tess took a deep swig of Coke and put the can on the glass-topped coffee table. "As a kid, I was always getting stuck. My dad pulled the spines out with pliers. It hurt like hell, and he didn't hold with girls crying."

Brock would remember her late father, of course. Years ago, after Bert Champion had arranged to buy a desirable piece of land, Brock had bought it out from under him by offering the owner more money. The Champion family had needed that land for their cattle. They hated Brock to this day. Even in light of the new partnership, that hadn't changed.

CHAPTER 2

*T*HE CACTUS SPINE, ITS TIP BARBED LIKE A FISHHOOK, HAD passed through Tess's thin white shirt to become imbedded in the flesh of her back. Her struggles after the fall from her horse had driven it deeper. Brock knew that a too-hasty pull on the shirt would break the spine and leave the barb, leading to more pain and a nasty infection.

"How does it look?" Tess was leaning over the rounded arm of the sofa to better expose her back. Brock would have to peel her shirt up until he could see where the spine had pierced her skin.

This was not the way he'd imagined undressing her.

"It'll take some care," he said. "You'll have to hold very still."

"I know. Get it over with."

Brock turned on the reading lamp above the sofa for more light and pulled up the ottoman to give him a low seat next to her. The slight crackle as he sat reminded him of the envelope he'd stuffed into his pocket with the clipping inside. If its arrival meant what he feared it might, everything he'd worked for could be at risk.

But he would have to deal with that later.

He used an alcohol wipe to sterilize the tweezers from the kit. "Ready?"

"Ready." Her body tensed as he pulled the hem of her shirt loose from her jeans and eased it upward to expose the cactus spine. Tess's face, neck, and arms were golden brown from years of working in the sun. But the skin on her back was soft ivory, glistening with sweat. The urge to see the rest of her triggered a stab of arousal. But he forced it away as he plied the sharp-tipped tweezers.

"You mentioned your sister," he said, making small talk. "How is Val doing?"

"All right. Now that Casey's back on the circuit, she's home again. She's been urging him to quit bullfighting and get a different job, maybe as a trainer. But you know Casey. He loves being where the action is."

"So they haven't set a wedding date?"

"Casey would marry her tomorrow. But Val's still gun-shy. Whatever's going on in her head, she isn't telling me about it."

"And Lexie?" Brock probed around the imbedded cactus spine, checking the angle of the barb.

"Her baby's due in May. It's a boy. She and Shane are over the moon."

"Tell them I'm over the moon for them."

Shane Tully, who'd lived on Brock's ranch since his teens, was one more source of conflict between him and the Champions. Brock had offered the young man a brilliant future as his manager and eventual heir. Shane had chosen Lexie and independence. Brock could only hope that fatherhood might change his mind.

"I'll tell them that you—*ow!*" Tess yelped as Brock worked the barb free.

"Got it." He held up the tweezers for her to see. "Don't move yet. You're bleeding." He stanched the blood with gauze, then applied salve and an oversize adhesive bandage before pulling down the back of her shirt. "I'm guessing you've had a tetanus shot."

"Hasn't everybody?" She sat up. "If you'll give me the salve and point me to a bathroom, I'll manage the rest of my wounds."

"Here you are." Brock felt a twinge of disappointment as he handed her the tube of Neosporin. He'd enjoyed taking care of her. "The bathroom's down the hallway, first door on your right. You'll find fresh washcloths in the cabinet. I'll clean up here and meet you on the porch."

Tess cleansed her face and hands and dabbed salve on the scratches she'd gotten from rolling through brush and cactuses. The red line slashing across her left cheek was the worst. But it wasn't deep. It would heal.

She finished and gave herself a quick inspection in the mirror. She looked as if she'd tangled with a bobcat. But she'd long since given up fussing over her appearance.

If she had a dime for every scrape, cut, bruise, and sprain she'd suffered on the ranch, she'd have a pile of money. And she'd likely have an even bigger pile by the time she was an old woman. But since her fiancé's death in Afghanistan almost ten years ago, she'd never expected anything more from life than days on the Alamo Canyon Ranch with her family, the animals she loved, and the endless routine of hard work. The ranch was her everything. She would fight to her last ounce of strength to keep it.

After tucking her shirt into her jeans, she found her hat, crossed the living room, and stepped outside to the porch. Brock was seated at a teakwood table with a half-finished Corona in his hand.

"You caught me," he said. "Cyrus left us some sandwiches in the kitchen. If you're hungry, we can eat before we watch the bulls buck."

"Are the bulls ready?"

"The first one's in the chute. The other two are lined up."

"Then let's go. We can eat later."

She strode ahead of him to the arena, built with two bucking chutes and a row of elevated bleachers along one side. The pen was thickly layered with sawdust and surrounded by a six-foot steel rail fence. A series of gates and passageways allowed the bulls to be herded into the chutes without open contact.

Two cowboys manned the gated chutes. They worked as a team, preparing the first bull to buck. Tess recognized one of them as the blond young man who'd taken Brock's horse earlier. Another cowboy waited in the pen, mounted, with a rope ready.

Tess moved over to make room for Brock beside her on the bleacher seat. The bulls would be bucked with a remotely controlled dummy—a weighted metal box with a strap—on their backs. The remote in Brock's hand would release the strap when the bull had bucked for eight seconds.

"I'm surprised you don't have one of those new human-shaped dummies," Tess said as they waited for the cowboys to rig the flank strap, and then the dummy, to the first bull. "I wouldn't mind having one to train our bulls, but they're expensive."

"I've looked at them," Brock said, "but I'm not sold. The traditional dummies always worked fine."

"Tell me about the first bull." She leaned forward on the bench, resting her elbows on her knees. She was at ease now. This was business—and also something they both understood and shared, a passion for bucking bulls.

"He's a good, solid bull," Brock said. "I've taken him to a couple of local rodeos. He bucked off both riders with decent scores."

"Do you think he's PBR material?"

"Maybe, with more experience. Take a look. Here he comes now."

The gate swung open. The bull, one of the white speckled ones she'd seen, flew into the pen, kicking and spinning to fling the weight off his back. "Good kick, and he's spinning left. Lots of energy, but I want to see more."

At eight seconds, Brock pressed the remote, releasing the strap. The dummy flew off the bull's back. The bull, accustomed to the routine, gave a couple of kicks and trotted out through the open chute. As the gate closed behind him, one of the cowboys retrieved the dummy from the pen.

"So what do you think so far?" Brock asked.

"He looks like he'd be easy to handle. But I'm looking for more fight," Tess said.

"Take your time. If you're aiming for the PBR, you know the kind of competition your bull will be facing."

Tess did. Some of the all-time great bulls, like Smooth Operator and Sweet Pro's Bruiser, had retired or were nearing the end of their careers. But the younger bulls moving up were stunning. The current bull to beat, a massive red beast named Woopaa, had won Bull of the Year honors at last November's PBR finals in Las Vegas. Veterans like Chiseled and Lil 2-Train were still going strong. And breeding had become an exact science. Each new generation of bucking bulls seemed more spectacular than the last.

Whirlwind, the first Alamo Canyon bull to make the PBR, was doing well on the circuit. Whiplash, his full brother, might have done even better. But his glory time had ended almost before it began.

Where was she going to find another bull with that kind of talent?

The bull in the second chute was ready to buck. Tess caught a glimpse of mahogany-colored hide before the gate opened and the bull burst out.

Bucking bulls had three basic moves—kicking high with

the rear legs, spinning while bucking, and leaping straight up with all four feet off the ground. A high-scoring bull could combine all three moves with surprise twists and direction changes.

This bull kicked high and spun fast. He'd probably earn some prize money on the rodeo circuit. A sensible choice, Tess told herself. But she had yet to see the rank bull who'd caught her interest.

Brock had been watching her reaction. "You couldn't go wrong with this one. He could even be PBR material."

"He's sharp. But we'll see," Tess said as the mahogany bull, shooed along by the roper, exited the pen. Her eyes were on the opposite chute, where the cowboys were struggling to rig the black bull for bucking.

Even with a calm bull, attaching the dummy wasn't easy. One end of the strap had to be dropped to the bottom of the chute, caught with a hook, then pulled under the bull and up onto the other side before it could be inserted into the dummy.

An uncooperative bull could make the job difficult, even dangerous. And this bull was in no mood to cooperate. He was slamming the sides of the chute, his single horn clattering against the steel rails.

"What happened to his other horn?" Tess asked Brock.

"Infection at the base. The vet had to remove it. He was just a yearling at the time. But I can't help thinking that having only one horn is what's made him so damned ornery. It might have been a good idea to take them both off. Believe me, Tess, you don't want that bull. He's not worth the trouble you'd have."

"I'll be the judge of that. Look, he's ready."

The black bull exploded out of the gate, leaping and twisting in midair to rid himself of the hated dummy. After a flash of spinning kicks that raised a cloud of sawdust, he was off again, jumping as if he had springs in his legs. By the time Brock pushed the release button on the remote, Tess was on her feet. She clapped and cheered as the bull circled the pen at a gallop, tossing his head before the roper herded him out.

"He's amazing!" She took her seat again. "What makes you think I wouldn't want him?"

Brock shook his head. "You just saw him at his best. But the black bastard is too smart for his own good. He's got tricks that would make you wish you'd never laid eyes on him. For one thing, he's hell to handle in the trailer and in the chute. Worse, we took him to one rodeo, and he wouldn't buck. He had to be prodded out of the chute. The rider was given a reride. I could keep him as a breeder, like Whiplash, but that could be a problem, as well."

"I'm still tempted to take him. He has so much potential. But I don't remember seeing his pedigree."

"That's because he doesn't have one," Brock said. "A couple of my cowhands found this six-month-old calf alone in the desert, half-starved and fending off a family of coyotes. He had the look of a first-class bucking bull, but no brand or tags. I contacted the police and put out notices online and in newsletters, but nobody claimed him. My guess is that he was stolen, and the rustlers dumped him when the law got too close."

"So you don't know anything about his bloodline?"

"I don't. That's another reason for you not to take him. There's always DNA testing. I'd have it done if I were going to sell or breed him. So far, it hardly seems worth the trouble."

"I still like him. I like him a lot—just a feeling I have."

Brock sighed and stood. Tess was five foot eight, but he loomed over her. She always felt small beside him. "I'll tell you what," he said. "Go home. Talk to your family. Sleep on the idea for a night or two before you make up your mind. I'll have some bulls in the Cave Creek event this weekend. We can talk there. If you really want that bull, I'll load him in a trailer and have him delivered to your ranch. But if you come to your senses and decide not to take him, you can come back and choose a different bull. Fair enough?"

"Fair enough. I'll let you know." She accepted the hand-shake he offered, her slim fingers lost in his big, leathery palm. Had he told her the truth about the black bull? The story seemed almost too fantastic to believe. Maybe he wanted to keep the bull for himself.

"I hope you're planning to stay for lunch," he said. "It's a long drive. You'll be hungry before you get home."

"Actually, I should get going," she said. "Don't worry about lunch. I'll grab a burger and fries somewhere."

"You're sure? The sandwiches are already made."

"Quite sure. Thanks."

To be truthful, she was hungry. But Brock Tolman's presence was so overpowering that, after being with him, she had to go off and decompress. That clock was ticking now.

She fished the keys out of her shoulder bag and strode toward her beat-up Ford pickup truck. "I'll let you know about the bull," she said. "Thanks for patching me up, and for your time."

Before he could respond, she climbed into the truck and started the engine. As she headed down the long driveway, she gave him a wave. But she didn't look to see if he was waving back.

Reaching the highway, she shifted gears and turned right, toward home. The radio was blaring an old Patsy Cline song, "Crazy." She turned it up and sang along.

Maybe she was crazy for wanting that black bull. Despite Brock's warning, she couldn't stop thinking about him. If she could get around his behavior problems, he could go all the way to the PBR—even all the way to the top.

As the song ended, she murmured the name she'd already chosen for him . . . *Quicksand*.

* * *

Brock stood watching Tess's red pickup until it vanished in the direction of the highway. The Alamo Canyon Ranch was a three-hour drive from here. He could only hope that the rusting piece of junk she drove could make the trip. Brock had offered to buy her a new vehicle to celebrate their partnership. She'd turned him down, of course. That old red truck had belonged to her brother, Jack, who'd died falling under a bull at the National Finals Rodeo two years ago—or was it three years? Brock was too distracted to remember.

She'd be saving herself a lot of grief if she didn't take that black bull. But knowing Tess, his warnings had only piqued her interest. He'd bet good money that she'd already made up her mind—and Brock knew better than to try to change it. Besides, right now, he had more pressing concerns.

Dark thoughts gathered like storm clouds as he mounted the porch and went back into the house. He could hear Cyrus, who cooked and ran the place, puttering in the kitchen. Brock had always trusted the old man to be discreet. But even Cyrus mustn't know what was troubling his boss today.

This lightning bolt had struck from nowhere. And he was still reeling from the shock.

Entering the walnut-paneled room that served as his study and office, he closed the door and locked it behind him. Only then did he take the folded envelope out of his hip pocket and lay it on the desk. Sitting in his oversize leather chair, with his back to the window, he reopened the envelope and let the newspaper clipping flutter onto the polished surface of the desk.

For a moment he was tempted to touch a flame to the thin, yellowed column of paper and burn it out of existence. But that would accomplish nothing. Whatever the intent of this message from the past, he would have to deal with it.

Smoothing the paper flat on his desk, he focused his gaze on the small print and forced himself to begin reading.

Local girl dies in auto wreck. Driver
charged.

Tess had planned to pass the turnoff to the ranch and
drive into Ajo for groceries and mail. But she was tired and
hadn't eaten anything except the protein bar she'd wolfed
down at the fuel stop in Sells. When she reached the place
where the graveled ranch road met the asphalt, she gave in
to temptation and swung the truck toward home. Ajo could
wait.

The rutted road cut across the desert for several miles before making a slow climb to the top of a ridge. From there,
the road descended to the ranch in a series of steep, sharp
switchbacks that Tess had driven so many times she could
almost have done it in her sleep—even pulling a trailer
loaded with bulls.

At the top of the ridge, she idled the truck, taking a moment to look down on the ranch where she'd spent her entire
life. She could see the rambling Spanish-style house, with
its roof of red Mexican tiles, and the two mobile homes
where Ruben, his married daughter, Maria, and her husband,
Pedro, lived. Sprawling around it were the sheds and barn,
the chutes and corrals, the bucking pen, and the pastures.
The ranch was less than a quarter the size of Brock's lavish
spread. But it was home, and Tess loved every acre of it.

In the north end of the mountain valley lay a stretch of
hayfields, sprouting green, watered by a sprinkling system
hooked up to an artesian well. These fields, and the vacant
house on the edge of them, were not part of the Alamo
Canyon Ranch. The property was run by a management
company. But Tess knew for a fact that the hayfields had
been recently bought by Brock Tolman.

Driving down the switchback road, she pushed thoughts
of Brock to the back of her mind. She was coming home.

Several vehicles were parked in the yard out front. She
recognized the heavy-duty trucks used to pull the stock trail-

ers, the beat-up Chevy sedan that the family used for light errands, the older pickup that Ruben and Pedro shared, and the specially equipped van designed to transport Shane in his wheelchair. The customized truck parked next to the loading chute was unfamiliar—until she remembered that the farrier had been scheduled to trim the bulls' hooves. He was already at work. Tess shifted the truck into low gear and drove down the switchbacks to the ranch.

Several people stood outside the corral fence watching the farrier. The bull to be trimmed—Whirlwind now—was herded up a ramp into a cage-like device mounted on a trailer. Once the bull was in place, the cage's side walls were cranked inward until he was held fast between them, unable to move. Then the whole device was turned onto its side, holding the bull like a sandwich ready for grilling, with his four feet sticking out of what had been the bottom.

For a massive animal, a bull had surprisingly delicate legs and hooves. Whirlwind bawled and complained, but it was more due to the indignity than any pain involved. The farrier—a bearded man with a flag tattoo on his left shoulder—used a clipper and an electric grinder to trim and smooth each hoof. The whole efficient process was done in minutes. Then the cage was righted and the front gate opened to let Whirlwind trot down the exit ramp to freedom.

Ruben stood next to the corral fence directing the operation, while Pedro, on horseback, herded the next bull into the chute and up the ramp.

A short, muscular man in his sixties, Ruben had been part of the ranch family since Tess was a child. In his youth, he'd been a bull rider on the small-town rodeo circuit. Broken bones, badly healed, had left him with crooked shoulders and a limp. But his kinship with bulls had grown even stronger over the years. If any man could be called a bull whisperer, it was Ruben Diego.

"So did you choose a new bull?" he asked as Tess joined him.

"Maybe. But I need time to think about it. The bull I like would be a challenge." She gave him a brief description of the black one-horned bull. "He's got handling problems. His first time at a rodeo, he refused to buck. Brock says I'd be a fool to take him."

"But you saw him buck?"

"Yes, in the pen, with a dummy."

"And how did he buck?" Ruben's wise dark eyes narrowed.

"Like the devil with wings."

A smile creased the foreman's weathered face. "Then I think you have found your bull, *hija*. Your head may tell you different, but your heart will not change."

"We'll see." Tess turned away. Ruben had known her since she was a baby. He was more of a father to her than the distant, driven Bert Champion had ever been—and he understood her, maybe even better than she understood herself. She would sleep on the question of the black bull, but in her heart, she had already made her choice.

After making herself a peanut butter sandwich and pouring a glass of milk, Tess joined her two sisters on the front porch. They sat in plastic lawn chairs, Lexie with her feet elevated and her hands resting on her swollen belly. The new dog, a year-old shepherd-collie mix, leaned against her chair, eyes closing as she scratched his ears.

Val sipped her Diet Coke. "So how did the morning go? Did you see Whiplash? Is he all right?"

"I didn't see him, but I asked about him. Brock said he's settled in and is doing fine." Tess understood Val's concern for the bull. Whiplash had saved her life when he'd killed the mobster who was stalking her. Only Brock's intervention had saved the bull from being put down.

"I'm surprised to see you back so soon," Val said. "I can't believe Brock didn't ask you to lunch, or even to drive into town for an early dinner. I know the man has a thing for you."

"You're way off base, Val. The only thing Brock wants from me is this ranch. Today was all business, and I left as soon as the business was over. He did invite me to have a bite in the kitchen, but I didn't want to take the time."

Lexie stared at her. "Heavens, you look like something attacked you. How did you get those awful scratches?"

"Relax. They're not as bad as they look." Tess gave a brief account of what had happened, leaving out the part where Brock had doctored her back. Val would tease her mercilessly about that.

Lexie's innocent blue eyes welled with tears. Pregnancy had pushed her emotions to the edge. "Tess, that snake could have bitten you. You could've been trampled by the bulls, or you could've broken your neck falling off the horse. You're lucky to be alive!"

"She's fine, Lexie. You're too young to remember how Tess was always getting bumped and scraped and stuck by cactuses when she was a kid. When it happened, she'd just jump up and keep on playing. Some things don't change." Val finished her Diet Coke and crumpled the can in her fist. "What I want to know is, did you find a bull to replace Whiplash?"

"Maybe. But I'm still thinking it over. You'll know soon enough. Thanks for trusting me on this."

"You're the expert. Everybody trusts your judgment, even Ruben. Except maybe when it comes to men. Brock's a good guy. He's handsome and he's got money. If you had any sense, you'd fall into his arms."

Heat blazed in Tess's cheeks. "That's enough, Val! You don't know Brock Tolman like I do. The man would sell his own grandmother if he thought he could make a profit on her. Besides, I found the perfect man once and lost him. There'll never be anyone but Mitch for me."

"We've been talking about this, Tess," Lexie said. "Mitch

has been gone almost ten years. He would want you to fall in love again and have a happy life, maybe even have a family. You know he would."

Tess stood, leaving her milk and sandwich on the table. "This conversation is over," she said. "I already have the life I want. I won't stand for your trying to push me toward some man—especially a man I can't stand!"

She stalked into the house, letting go of the screen door so the pull of the spring would slam it shut behind her. She knew she was being childish, but nothing less than a show of temper would get through to her sisters. Why couldn't they just mind their own business? She didn't need a man in her life—especially a man as power-hungry and domineering as Brock Tolman.

From the ranch office down the hall came the sounds of someone working. The hum of the printer and the muffled twang of country music from a local radio station grew more distinct as she stepped through the open doorway.

Shane Tully, Lexie's husband, sat at the desk, which had been moved against the wall to accommodate the light-weight wheelchair he used around the house. He turned off the radio and swiveled to face her as she walked into the room.

Darkly handsome, Shane had been a top bull rider before a fall under a bull had damaged his spine, leaving him without the use of his legs. In his role as business manager of the ranch, he'd proven so invaluable to Tess that she could no longer imagine doing the job without him.

But that was what she feared might be about to happen.

"How's it going?" She took a seat in the chair opposite him.

"Fine. Just updating the books and paying some bills." He lowered his gaze, then met her eyes again. "I hear you may have found a bull."

"So you've been talking to Brock." Tess forced a smile.

"I have. He called while you were on the road. You know I promised to be up front with you, Tess. That's what I'm trying to do."

"Yes, I know. And I appreciate it, knowing that you'd never lie to me or go behind my back. I take it he's pushing you hard for a decision."

"Harder than ever. Today he almost sounded worried, which isn't like Brock at all. He was talking about putting the ranch in a trust, with me as the beneficiary. He's never mentioned that before. I can't help wondering if something has happened. But as you know, Brock plays his cards pretty close to his vest."

"Tell me about it. The man's my business partner, and I hardly know anything about him. Like, how did he make enough money to build that ranch? The place has to be worth millions."

"Smart investing, that's all he's ever told me. He has no family that I know of. Early on, he was married, but it didn't last. No children. As he tells me, I'm the closest thing to a son he's ever had."

"How does that make you feel?" Tess asked.

"Pressured, more than anything. Any man would be a fool to turn down what he's offering. But if I go back to Brock, he'll own me for life. That was why I left him in the first place."

"And Lexie? What's she got to say about all this?"

"She's torn, like I am. With Brock, we could give our children the best education, travel, security for life. But Brock would own them, too. That's why we've agreed not to make any decisions until after the baby's born. She definitely wants to be with her family for that."

Tess stood. "Well, I'll let you get back to work. If I take that black bull, he'll be here in the next few days. I'll be depending on your help and Ruben's to settle him in."

"You've got it." As Tess moved toward the door, he

swiveled his chair partway toward the desk, then paused. "Tess, whatever happens, you'll always be family. We'll always be there for you."

"Thanks. I know." She walked out of the room, fighting tears she didn't want him to see. She could understand Shane's concern about providing for his family. But if he were to join Brock, she would be losing half of her family—including the future children who would carry on the ranch. Val was unable to have a child. And Tess herself, past thirty and single, had long since given up on the idea of having a family of her own. Looking ahead, she could see the Alamo Canyon Ranch being taken over by Brock and his minions, whoever they might be. Everything her father, and his father before him, had built—and everything she had fought so hard to keep—would be gone.

How long could she keep fighting? How long before she wearied, surrendered to fate, and lost it all?

CHAPTER 3

**Local girl dies in auto wreck.
Driver charged.**

Ridgewood, Missouri, June 6, 1998

Mia Carpenter, 15, daughter of prominent Ridgewood businessman Chase
Carpenter, died in a one-car rollover
around midnight on June 4. The driver of
the car, a 1995 Porsche 928, was Ben
Talbot, 20, an employee of Carpenter
Motors.

Miss Carpenter, a passenger in the
back seat, suffered fatal head injuries
when the vehicle rolled off a steep
embankment. She was not wearing a seat
belt.

Jeff Carpenter, the car's owner and
brother of the deceased, was a passenger
in the front seat. He and Talbot have been

released from the hospital. According to
the police, both men had high levels of
blood alcohol. Talbot is expected to plead
guilty to charges of DUI and negligent
homicide.

Dread crawled along Brock's nerves as he reread
the clipping. It had to be genuine—no question of that. But
who would have known enough to send it?

For years, he'd felt certain that the damning secret was
buried. Of those who knew the truth, Chase Carpenter was
long dead of cancer. His wife, Johanna—not that she'd ever
known—had suffered a stroke and was confined to a nursing
home. By now, if she was even alive, she'd be elderly and
maybe senile. Jeff Carpenter had disappeared off a sport
fishing boat nine years ago, leaving nothing behind but an
empty bottle of Jack Daniels and a .38 Smith & Wesson with
one bullet missing. As for Ben Talbot, he'd vanished through
the gloomy doors of the Missouri State Prison in Jefferson,
never to be heard from again.

Who else would know? A spouse? A child? It might be a
good idea to have an investigator track down the rest of the
Carpenter family. He would think about that tomorrow. The
question now was, what did the mysterious sender want
from him?

Money, most likely. That anonymous clipping had blackmail written all over it. Sooner or later the call would come.
He would have to be ready for it. Meanwhile, the smartest
thing he could do would be to protect his assets. The blackmailer might not be able to touch him legally. But the damage to his reputation could be catastrophic—and expensive.

Putting the ranch in trust for his heirs would make sense.
But his call to Shane had ended in frustration. Didn't the

young fool understand what he was being offered—and that the offer might not be there forever?

Picking up the envelope, he stared at it. No return address, but it was postmarked Tucson—close. His name and address were hand printed in blue ballpoint pen. There was nothing else except the stamp—an American flag, available anywhere.

Battling the urge to pick up a chair and hurl it at something, he slipped the clipping back into the envelope, sealed it with tape, and locked it away in the wall safe that was hidden behind a Charles Russell painting of a cowboy roping a longhorn steer. He needed to get out of here. If he didn't, he would explode.

Maybe he could take his new Cessna TTx and fly up to his Montana fishing cabin for a few days. But no, he needed to be here, in control, especially if the unknown blackmailer showed his hand.

He could always call one of the women he knew—attractive ladies who'd be happy to share a pleasurable evening with no strings attached.

But he wasn't in the mood for that kind of entertainment. He needed to come up with some kind of plan. But how could he make a plan when he didn't know what he was facing? For now, all he could do was stay alert and go on as if nothing had happened.

Tess would be calling him about the bull. He'd told her to take her time, but he'd seen the hunger in her eyes—a hunger he recognized and understood because he'd experienced it himself. She wanted that bull, and she would have it. Consequences be damned.

Tess would deny it, but Brock sensed that the two of them were alike in many ways—in their ambition, their passion, and their determination to get what they wanted.

But she was no match for him—not when what he wanted was the Alamo Canyon Ranch, Shane, and Tess herself, all wrapped up in one neat package.

Meanwhile he had to deal with an invisible threat that could topple his world. And trying to fight it was like flailing away in the dark.

After supper, the sisters gathered on the front porch to unwind from the day and watch the stars come out. The time-honored practice had started with Callie, their beloved stepmother. Now that she was gone, the three Champion women kept the custom whenever they could. Some evenings, it was almost as if they could feel her presence beside them and hear her warm Southern laughter.

Tess inhaled the night air, filling her senses with the rank aromas of the ranch—road dust, diesel fuel, horses, and cattle. Roasting chiles from Maria's kitchen blended with the fragrance of blooming paloverde. A burrowing owl called from the hillside. A band of javelinas rooted in the darkness beyond the paddock.

After the warm spring day, the light breeze was refreshing. Tess leaned back in the chair and let it cool her face. When the dog pressed a damp muzzle into her hand, she scratched his ears. Lexie and Val were chatting, but Tess was too tired to pay them much attention. She'd be smart to break away and make it an early night.

This weekend she would be driving Whirlwind to the PBR event at Cave Creek, just north of Phoenix. Brock would be there. He wouldn't be surprised when she told him she'd decided to take the black bull.

Once they'd worked out the details, Quicksand should be delivered in the next few days. Then the real work of readying him for the arena would begin—and it would have to happen fast. The ranch couldn't afford to keep the bull if he wasn't earning his way. Even as a breeder, with no pedigree or registration, his value would be in doubt.

"So, what have you heard from Casey?" Lexie asked Val.

"Nothing since yesterday. He was supposed to call me

after that event in Gallup last night, but I haven't heard a word. For all I know he could be lying in a hospital bed, or on a slab in some morgue. Every time he steps into the arena, I have nightmares about him getting tossed or trampled. But Casey doesn't seem to care. For him, jumping in front of a mad bull to save some fool cowboy is just another day at the office. I can't get it through his thick head how much I worry about him. Sometimes I wonder if sticking around is worth the pain."

Lexie shifted in the lounge chair to ease the discomfort of her swollen belly. "You signed on for this, Val, just like I did. After Jack died in the arena, I swore that I'd never fall for a bull rider. But then I met Shane. And when he got hurt, I knew I had to be there for him. You'd do the same for Casey. The two of you belong together."

"You're not helping, Lexie," Val said. "I'm not strong like you are. If anything were to happen to Casey, I'd go to pieces. I'd probably drink myself back into the gutter. If you ask me, loving somebody is a one-way ticket to hell."

The conversation faded as Tess drifted into a light doze. Only when Val nudged her and pointed toward the road did she come to full attention. A pair of bright truck headlights had come over the ridge and started down the first switchback.

"Was anybody expecting company?" she asked, wondering if she should go for the rifle mounted inside the front door, above the frame.

Val was on her feet. "I recognize those lights. That looks like Casey's truck." She lowered her voice to a hoarse whisper, as if thinking aloud. "But he was supposed to be in Gallup this weekend. What if something's gone wrong, and somebody's come in his truck to tell me?"

The security lights came on as the black pickup rolled into the yard. Yes, the truck was Casey's. Val stumbled down the front steps and raced out to meet it. From the porch, Tess could see into the cab as the door opened and the dome light came on. It was Casey. At first glance, he looked fine—husky, handsome, and fit as ever.

But as he eased painfully out of the truck, using a crutch for support, Tess stifled a groan. Even a minor injury would be enough to keep him from doing the work he loved.

Val was running toward him, but when she saw the crutch and his thickly wrapped ankle, she stopped as if she'd run into a wall. "What . . . ?" She gasped out the word.

"It's nothing. Just a bad sprain—maybe more." He gave her a tired smile. "But I need to stay off it for a few weeks until it heals. At least it's my left side, so I can drive an automatic shift. Otherwise, I'd be in a bad way."

"So how did it happen?" Tess had trotted out to retrieve his duffel bag from the rear seat.

"Just bad timing. I got tossed by Cactus Jack and landed on my feet, a little off-balance. The ankle twisted under me. I should've seen it coming and rolled instead. It's a good thing you couldn't hear me cuss. I know guys who would just wrap the ankle and get back out there, but if a rider were to get hurt because I wasn't a hundred percent, I couldn't live with that."

Val came to him then, wrapped her arms around his ribs, and held him fiercely tight. "Damn you, Casey Bozeman, when are you going to learn some common sense? You're getting too old for this adolescent boys' sport!"

"When I get too old, I'll know it." Casey held her with one arm, steadying his balance with the crutch.

Tess sensed the tension building between these two people who loved each other so much. "You must be hungry, Casey," she said. "Come on into the kitchen. I'll warm you up some leftover enchiladas."

Brushing off Val's efforts to help him up the steps, Casey made his way across the porch and into the kitchen. Tess had gone ahead to scoop two beef enchiladas with beans onto a plate and slide them into the microwave.

The house, which had no air conditioning, was still warm

from the day. Ceiling fans stirred the tepid air. Casey sank onto a chair with Val next to him. Lexie had chosen to stay outside. From the spare bedroom came the sound of Shane working out on his weight machines.

"How about something to drink?" Tess asked. "Another Coke, Val? And you, Casey?"

"Water's fine." Casey stretched his leg to ease the weight on his ankle. Val waved her hand to decline the offer of a Coke.

"So how long do you have to stay off the ankle?" Tess dropped two ice cubes into a glass and filled it with cold water.

"Thanks." Casey took it from her. "Total rest for the first two weeks. Then a couple more weeks of physical therapy. After that I'm hoping I'll be fit to go back on the circuit. Any longer and I could miss the finals in May."

This had been a year of change for the PBR. The next national finals, usually held in Las Vegas, in November, had been moved to Fort Worth in May. That meant one short, strenuous season to accommodate the change. On the new schedule, bull riders and other personnel, like Casey, would have summers off to rest, train, or take part in traditional rodeos. But until after the May finals, the pressure was on.

"Why not skip the rest of the season and start fresh next fall?" Val asked. "That would give you plenty of time to rest and heal."

"It would give me plenty of time to get fat and lazy." Casey dug into the plate of food Tess had set in front of him. Tess knew that Val was his first and only love. But a man needed more than love in his life. It had been the same with Mitch and the Marines. He had willingly gone into combat, and in the end, she had lost him.

The poet Lord Byron had said it best: "Man's love is of man's life a thing apart, 'tis woman's whole existence."

But that bit of wisdom would be lost on Val.

"Actually, Val," Casey said, "I was hoping you could

come back to Tucson with me and stay in the condo while I mend. I can manage all right on my own, but it would give us some time together—something we haven't had enough of this season."

Tess could sense Val's resistance. A month of watching ESPN in Casey's drab bachelor condo would try the patience of any woman. To the restless Val, it would be more like a jail sentence than a romantic getaway.

"I've got a better idea," Tess said. "Why not stay here with us, Casey—at least until you're ready for physical therapy. We've got plenty of room, and I could use your insight with the new bull that's coming. He's young and has some issues."

"This is Brock's bull—the one that's replacing Whiplash?"

"Right. I saw him buck today. He's going to be a handful. But if we can get him under control, he could be a moneymaker."

"I'm willing to help, but I'm hardly in shape for bull wrangling."

"I'm aware that you can't get in the pen with him, but your advice would be worth a lot. You know how bulls think."

Casey shook his head and smiled. "Nobody knows how bulls think except bulls. But as long as I can eat Maria's cooking, I'll stay anywhere. Is that all right with you, Val?"

"Sure. Just don't leave your dirty undies on my bedroom floor." She rubbed her head against his shoulder in a clear invitation.

"Well, at least I'll know where to drop off your duffel." Tess stood and began clearing the table. "Chocolate cake? Val made it."

"Don't tempt me. I'm stuffed. I'll need to figure out how to keep in shape while I'm mending."

"Jack's old exercise equipment is still here. Shane uses it every day. I'm sure he won't mind sharing." Tess rinsed the dishes and added them to the load in the dishwasher. "Early bedtime for me. I'll see you two in the morning."

Picking up Casey's bag where she'd left it on the couch, she carried it down the hall, opened the door to Val's room, and tossed it on the bed. Having Casey here would be good for Val. Maybe with time together, away from the arena, they'd be able to make some solid plans.

Hopefully, those plans would include a wedding. But if her sister and Casey married, she couldn't expect them to make their home here with her. They would go where Casey's work took him—whatever that work might be. And if Brock managed to lure Shane and Lexie to a life of abundance on his ranch, what then?

Tess knew the answer to that question. Her entire family would be gone. Except for the hired help, she would be here alone—the last of the Champions on the Alamo Canyon Ranch.

As the full moon climbed the late-night sky, Val lay curled against Casey's naked body, warm and utterly content. It seemed that there was always an abundance of things to argue about. But when they made love, they became one. Nothing mattered but this sweet, burning passion that never failed them. She was his woman, heart and soul. He was her man.

He chuckled, his lips brushing her tangled hair. "You're quite the rider, lady," he whispered.

"I've got quite the bull here," Val teased. "I hope you like it this way. Until your ankle's healed, this is how it'll have to be."

"No complaints. None at all."

He stretched onto his side and turned her to spoon against him. His hand splayed over her belly, spanning the ugly scars from the C-section she'd had at eighteen. Val couldn't look at those scars without remembering the baby boy she'd given up for adoption nine years ago. She'd been alone in Hollywood then, cast out by her father, with no resources to care for her child.

Casey's child.

Val nestled into his warmth and closed her eyes. Casey hadn't known about the baby until she'd told him a few months ago. Hurt and angry, he'd said some ugly things before finally coming to understand how desperate she'd been.

After some deep pain, they'd made peace and moved on. But the loss would always be there, like a dark layer between them—especially since the complications Val had suffered giving birth meant that she could have no more children.

Maybe that was why she could never bring herself to set a wedding date. What if, deep down, Casey still resented what she'd done? What if it turned out that he wanted a family more than he wanted her?

Val willed herself to take deep, slow breaths, a technique she'd learned from the yoga sessions in rehab. The breathing helped. She could feel her anxiety easing, feel herself sinking into sleep.

"Val?" The tension in Casey's voice yanked her back from the edge of slumber. Even before he spoke again, she sensed that the unspoken words would change their lives.

"What is it?" she murmured. "Is something wrong?"

He hesitated. "No, but there's something I need to tell you."

"This sounds serious." She sat up, her pulse racing as she turned to face him. What was it? Had he slept with another woman? Was he suffering from some fatal disease?

"Tell me," she said.

"I know I should have asked you first. But I was afraid you'd say no." He took a deep breath. "Val, I've hired a private investigator to find our son."

Val recoiled as if she'd been rammed with a two-by-four. She felt dizzy—almost ill. Struggling, she found her voice.

"You were right about two things, Casey. You should have asked me, and I would have said no. There's a reason for closed adoptions like this one was. If I'd known where my baby had gone, I wouldn't have been able to stay away. It would have been torture—for me and for the parents who adopted him. I had to let him go. It broke my heart, but I knew it was the best thing I could do for him."

"But you knew him, at least," Casey said. "You carried him, you gave birth to him, held him in your arms, and decided his future. He's my son, too. But I never had that chance."

Oh, Casey, please don't do this—to me, to yourself, and to our son!

Val clutched the sheet in front of her, feeling more vulnerable than she had ever felt with him. "What do you plan to do if you find him? Knock on the door, introduce yourself, and demand to be part of his life?"

Casey exhaled, shaking his head. "Give me some credit, Val. I'd never do anything like that. I only want to know what he looks like, where he lives, and what sort of life he has—maybe even see him from a distance."

"And if that isn't enough? Because I can guarantee that it won't be."

"It'll have to be." A chilling breeze had swept in through the open window. Val shivered. Casey draped the quilt over her bare shoulders. "I was hoping you'd want to find him, too."

She shook her head, a lock of hair tumbling over her face. "I can't handle wanting to find him. When I gave him up, I fell into a black hole. I crawled out once. But I'm not strong enough to do it over again."

"You were alone, Val. This time we'd be together."

"And what if we find out that something's gone wrong? As long as I don't know, I can imagine him in this happy, perfect world. But what if he's being mistreated? What if he's sick, or even dead because I gave him up—and there's nothing we can do?" The words felt as if they were being ripped from her throat.

"Don't punish yourself," he said. "It's long past time for that. Whatever we find, we'll deal with it together."

"You keep saying *we*. But I can't do this, Casey. I won't. If your investigator finds him, or learns anything about him, I don't want to hear it. This was your idea, and maybe I can't stop you. But count me out. You're in this alone."

"Blast it, Val—"

"No, I can't face the thought of finding our son and having to turn away again. I wish you'd give it up. But if you have to do this, promise you won't share it with me. *Promise*."

He exhaled, his muscular shoulders sagging. "All right. For now. But if you change your mind—"

"I won't." She lay down again, turning away and pulling the covers to her chin.

"Do you want me to leave?"

"No." Val blinked away tears. "I want you to stay. I need you to stay. But let's pretend we never had this conversation."

"All right." He stretched out on his back and lay still. She could hear him breathing in the darkness. "I love you, Val," he said.

She sighed and nestled against him. "And I love you. But why does love have to be so damn complicated?"

The next morning, before first light, Tess loaded Whirlwind into the small trailer for the drive. Ordinarily, Ruben or Pedro would have gone with her. But they were taking four bulls to a rodeo in Bisbee with the big trailer. It was never a bad idea to take an extra driver. But Tess didn't mind going alone. Cave Creek was barely three hours away. Arriving early would give Whirlwind eight hours to rest in his pen be-

fore the first night of the weekend event, when he was scheduled to buck.

By now the silver bull was accustomed to these outings.
He trotted up the ramp and into the trailer with no prodding.
Hand raised and pampered by Lexie, he was a model of perfect bull behavior. But with a cowboy on his back, he was
dynamite in the arena, racking up enough points to put him
in the top ten buckers in the PBR. Tess had lost track of the
offers she'd had to buy him. She knew she was taking a
gamble, turning down big money for an animal that could
become sick or injured, or even die, leaving the ranch with
nothing. But Whirlwind was family. And if luck held, after
he retired, his stud fees could keep the ranch solvent.

If I can keep the ranch out of Brock's hands that long.

She'd be seeing Brock at Cave Creek. Unless she
changed her mind before then, which wasn't likely, they'd
be sealing the deal for the black bull. After the delivery, she
hoped she'd be through with Brock for a while. When she
was with the man, it was always a battle for dominance.
Standing up to him tended to leave her quivering and exhausted. But she wouldn't let him win—or even think that
he could.

After latching the inside gate and raising the trailer ramp,
she climbed into the cab and started up the road to the pass.
Once they started moving, Whirlwind would probably lie
down for the duration of the drive. Reclining was more comfortable and easier on his legs than trying to keep his balance
in a bumping trailer. After they reached the asphalt, the bull
might even go to sleep.

By the time the laboring truck reached the top of the pass,
the sky was paling in the east. Shadows stole across the
desert, shrinking as the rim of the sun rose above the rocky
peaks.

Tess loved this time of day, when the night creatures
melted into hiding and the morning birds burst into song. As
she drove down the long, easy slope, she opened the side

window to hear their calls and to feel the cool air on her face.

Traffic was light on the narrow highway going out of Ajo. But once she cut onto the freeway, the morning commuter traffic through Phoenix was nerve jangling. It was a relief to find the exit and head for the Cave Creek Arena, a place Tess had come to know well.

Half an hour later, in the pens behind the arena, Whirlwind was safely unloaded and enjoying a breakfast of bull chow and fresh water.

Tess pulled the empty trailer into the back parking lot, leaving it hitched to the truck. She didn't plan to drive anywhere else until the event was over. There were security cameras above the maze of steel-railed pens, as well as an armed guard. But she wanted to stay close, keeping an eye on her precious bull.

Her gaze swept the lot as she walked back to the bull pens. In the row reserved for the larger rigs, she could see the silver trailer emblazoned with the Tolman Ranch logo— the silhouette of a bucking bull. It was longer than most because of the sleeping quarters in the front.

Brock had said he would be here. But had he traveled with the trailer? Or would he come cruising up in one of the pricy vehicles he owned? Looking for him would be a waste of time. He could be anywhere, probably meeting with business contacts. When he was ready to talk about the bull, he would know where to find her.

She was about to turn away when two men in cowboy gear climbed out of the truck cab. One of them was a man she'd glimpsed from a distance at Brock's ranch. The other was the young blond man she'd seen earlier. Two drivers. So Brock wouldn't have come with the truck. She made a mental note of that as she walked back to the bull pens.

Whirlwind had finished his chow and was prowling the confines of his pen, stretching, lowing, and shaking his horns. Tess leaned on a rail, studying his gait, his legs, and his body to make sure he was fit to buck. He appeared to be fine. But she found herself wishing for one of the electronic massage stimulators that many stock contractors used to warm up the bulls and treat sore muscles. The device wasn't cheap. But any improvement in Whirlwind's performance would be worth the money. Maybe now that Brock was her partner, she'd be justified in asking him for one. He undoubtedly used them on his own bulls. But the thought of owing him, even for such a small favor, rankled her. Somehow, she would find a way to manage it on her own.

Across the parking lot, the two ranch hands had opened the back of Brock's trailer and were shoveling manure and wet straw into a cart, cleaning up the space before the trip home. The job was one Tess would need to do as well, but for now, it could wait.

As she gazed across the maze of pens and chutes, she recognized some of the top bulls from the PBR. Chiseled, easily distinguished by his black coat and the tan stripe down his back, was penned nearby. And she glimpsed Woopaa, the current champion, being unloaded from a trailer into a chute. The competition for first-place bull was as keen as the contest for top rider. Rankings were based on points awarded over the season. All points counted toward the final score that would determine the world champion bull—and pay a handsome prize to his owner.

Whirlwind was too far behind the leaders to win this year. But he was still young, and his bucking scores were getting him noticed. Maybe next year, Tess mused. Maybe then, with a little more experience, he would have a real chance.

Her thoughts scattered as a heavy-duty black pickup with oversize tires rumbled into the lot and parked in the nearest row. She stood watching as the driver's side door opened. Trust Brock to make an entrance every time.

She waited outside the pens as he strode toward her, all broad shoulders, long legs, and confidence. If he were to trip and fall on his taut-muscled rear, it would give her no end of satisfaction.

"Good, I've caught you early." He glanced around. "Don't tell me you came alone."

"Ruben and Pedro had to take bulls to another event."

"Maybe you should hire more help."

"Maybe. I'll think about that later," Tess said. "For now, just so you won't have to ask, my answer is yes. I want that black bull."

A smile tightened his lips. "I think you're making a bad decision, but I know better than to try and talk you out of it. Let me know when you want him delivered."

"Early next week should be all right. I'll just need to make sure we have a place to keep him, away from our other bulls, until he gets used to his new home."

"That shouldn't be a problem. He gets along fine with other bulls. It's people that he doesn't like—oh, and coyotes."

"Thanks. I'll remember that. And he has a name now. I'm going to call him Quicksand."

"For that bull, it fits. So we have a deal then." He extended his hand.

"We have a deal." Tess's fingers were lost in his big, leathery palm.

"Have you eaten?" he asked. "I've got an early lunch scheduled with some business connections. As my partner in the Alamo Canyon Ranch, you're welcome to come. You might find it interesting."

Tess bit back a surge of annoyance. He was already talking as if he were the owner of her ranch and not just a shareholder. But some provocations were best ignored. "Thanks for the invitation," she said, "but I want to stay with Whirlwind and make sure he's settled. I brought sandwiches and drinks in a cooler."

"Well, then—"

An uproar of shouts and furious thumping came from the inside of the trailer where the two men were working.

"What the devil—?" Brock broke into a run, with Tess close behind him. They had almost reached the trailer when the younger man stumbled down the ramp carrying a shovel. The older man came behind him, carrying a pitchfork with something draped over the tines.

It was a dead rattlesnake.

CHAPTER 4

*B*ROCK FROZE AT THE SIGHT OF THE DEAD SNAKE—a four-footer, at least, its scaly body still twitching. Jim, the younger ranch hand, spoke. "It was in the straw." His voice quivered slightly. "Rusty, here, killed it with the pitchfork."

Brock cleared the tightness from his throat. "Did either of you get bitten?"

"Nope," Rusty said. "The critter struck at my boot, but it didn't bite through. It don't look like it'll be bitin' anybody else. But that skin should make a dandy hatband."

"Be my guest. It's all yours." Brock would need to inspect the bulls he'd brought. An animal with a 2,000-pound body mass could survive the venom with some swelling and discomfort, but a snake-bitten bull would be in no condition to buck.

"It must've been in the straw when we forked it out of the stack," Jim said. "But it's hard to believe that we could've missed anything that big and alive."

"Make sure there aren't any more in there." Brock felt

mildly nauseous. "Right now, I need to make sure none of my bulls got bitten."

"I'll go with you," Tess volunteered. "Two pairs of eyes are better than one."

"Thanks." He strode toward the pen complex, trusting Tess to keep up with him. Stretching her long legs, she matched his stride.

The four bulls were together in one of the larger pens. They were solid, PBR-worthy buckers, though not the championship contenders that Brock had always coveted. Getting into the pen with them would be too dangerous, but seen through the rails, the bulls appeared to be fine. None of them showed any sign of swelling, pain, or the two-fanged puncture wound of a rattlesnake bite.

"See anything?" he asked Tess, who stood next to him.

"No, but you might want to check back later. In an animal as big as a bull, a bite might not take effect right away."

"Good idea." Brock continued to study the bulls. "Damn, I wish I knew for sure how that snake got in the trailer."

"You heard your man. It must've crawled into the straw pile and been pitched into the trailer by accident. You're lucky it didn't bite one of the men—or one of the bulls, as far as we know."

"But why didn't the men see it, or hear it? Wouldn't it rattle a warning?"

"Maybe it crawled into the trailer before it was loaded, to get out of the sun. Even with the doors latched, there are ways a snake could get in." Tess frowned at him, her gray eyes narrowing. "Are you suggesting it might not've been an accident?"

Was he? For a wild moment, Brock was tempted to share his concerns about blackmail. After all, she was his partner. But he checked the impulse. Sharing anything about his past would be crazy. He could only be safe by keeping the secret to himself. No one, including Tess, would understand what had really happened all those years ago.

And partner or not, he and Tess had a history of bad blood. If Tess were to learn the truth, there'd be nothing to stop her from using it against him.

"Is there anyone who might have put that snake in your trailer—some enemy wanting to cause trouble?" she asked.

"A man like me makes more than his share of enemies," Brock said. "But I can't think of anyone who'd sneak onto my ranch and put a snake in my trailer—even if they could. I guess nobody will ever know except the snake, and it's dead." Brock made a show of shrugging off his concern. "You're sure you won't come to lunch with me? You might find it interesting."

"Maybe another time. But if you need to leave, I don't mind keeping an eye on your bulls. If I notice anything wrong, I'll call you on your cell."

He hesitated, then nodded. "Thanks. I'll owe you."

Defiance flickered in her eyes, like lightning through gray storm clouds. "You don't owe me a thing," she said.

Tess watched him walk away—his confident stride matching his John Wayne stature and top-of-the-line Stetson. Brock was all attitude. But today she'd sensed that something was off. He'd seemed troubled, especially after the discovery of the rattlesnake in his trailer.

Tess had noticed the subtle twitch of a muscle in his jaw and the way his eyes shifted when he spoke. Whatever was bothering him, Brock was making an effort to hide it. But by now she'd spent enough time with the man to read the signs. Something was wrong.

Not that she gave a damn about Brock's worries. His personal life was none of her business. But if the trouble had any bearing on her ranch, she was entitled to know.

Should she ask him? Tess weighed the question, then dismissed it. Prying would only put him on the defensive. If she needed to know something, for now, at least, she would have to trust him to tell her.

Leaning on the rails, she studied Brock's bulls—two of them reddish tan, one creamy white, and one spotted. They were sturdy, well-bred animals, all with good bucking records. But none of them possessed the fire she'd seen in Whirlwind and Whiplash. What would she discover in Quicksand—with his lineage a total mystery? Her pulse stirred at the prospect of bringing out the greatness she'd glimpsed in the black bull.

But what if Brock was right? What would she do if Quicksand were to prove uncontrollable?

After a few more minutes of watching Brock's bulls, and seeing no sign of trouble, she made her way back through the pens to Whirlwind. At the sight of her, the silver bull came to the rails, seeking attention. He snorted and closed his eyes with pleasure as Tess scratched behind his ears.

"I was hoping I'd find you here."

Recognizing the voice, she turned to find Clay Rafferty coming around the corner of the pen. Tess's pulse skipped. Rafferty, whom she'd met last fall in Las Vegas, was the livestock director for the PBR. As the man who chose the bulls to buck at PBR events, he held tremendous power over small stock contractors like the Champion family. It was Rafferty who'd picked Whirlwind out of a sea of contenders. It was also Rafferty who'd declared Whiplash too dangerous to compete. But then, with Whiplash's fate hanging in the balance, Rafferty had phoned Brock and offered him a chance to rescue the condemned bull.

"It's good to see you, Tess." A stocky, affable man dressed in jeans and a denim shirt, he wore his authority lightly. But it was there, tough and unmistakable. If he'd sought her out, it had to be for a reason.

"I've noticed that Whirlwind, here, is having a great season, racking up the numbers."

Of course, he'd noticed. Clay Rafferty, a former bull rider himself, noticed everything.

"He's a great bull," Tess said. "Of course, I hold my breath every time that gate swings open."

"Don't we all?" Rafferty smiled. "I hope he'll be ready for the finals in May."

Tess had been waiting for those words. She'd hoped that her bull would be chosen for the big event, but she'd learned that nothing was guaranteed.

However, there was one problem. "Whirlwind is in top form, and I would never deny him this chance," she said. "But my sister's baby is due early in May. With my luck, she'll deliver the week of finals, and I want to be there for her. I may need somebody else to bring Whirlwind to the competition."

"Of course. Family comes first," Rafferty said. But his tone suggested that Tess's choice might damage her standing, as well as Whirlwind's.

"Ruben, my foreman, should be able to bring him. He's been hauling rodeo bulls for years. If anything, he's more experienced than I am."

"I'm not doubting that. But the publicity people were hoping you'd be there for TV interviews. Women who raise bucking bulls are always good press. And I suppose that means Shane won't be available either. He did a great job with color commentary last time."

"I can't speak for Shane," Tess said. "Let's just hope the baby's timing works out for all of us."

"For now, I guess that's all we can do." Rafferty shrugged. "But that's not why I came to find you. I know Whirlwind is scheduled to buck tonight. But we've had a bull drop out of the final round tomorrow. I was hoping we could move Whirlwind to his place. It would mean you'd have to delay your departure." He paused, clearly waiting for an answer.

"Yes, that's fine." Tess pounced on the chance to show Whirlwind off to an even bigger crowd, and maybe even carry the winning rider. Staying overnight, even if it meant sleeping in the truck, would be worth the inconvenience.

"Well, then, it's settled. Get yourself a good night's rest, and I'll get back to you with the details tomorrow."

Tess watched him walk away, his bowlegs lending a distinctive sway to his gait. Her original plan had been to head home tonight after the event, but surviving on overpriced midway snacks, washing up in the public restroom, and catching a few hours of shut-eye on the truck's cramped back seat was nothing new. The Alamo Canyon Ranch couldn't afford fancy meals or hotel rooms. Besides, she preferred to stay where she could keep an eye on Whirlwind. Too bad she hadn't at least brought a toothbrush and a change of underwear. Maybe there was a Walmart within walking distance.

Looking back across the parking lot, she could see Brock's long silver trailer. It was a sure bet he wouldn't be sleeping in a truck tonight. His hired help bunked in a comfy compartment that was built into the trailer. They lived better on the road than she did. But what did it matter? At least she had the best bull. Wasn't that what counted?

She'd often wondered how someone got to be as wealthy as Brock Tolman. According to Shane, Brock had made some smart investments. But it took money to make money. Had Brock used family funds to get started? Had he sold some property, or even done something illegal, like dealing drugs or setting up a Ponzi scheme?

When it came to Brock Tolman, she only knew what he wanted her to know. And she didn't like it.

Maybe she should have accepted his invitation to lunch. Meeting some of his business contacts might have given her a clue about his activities.

But then she would have missed the chance to talk with Clay Rafferty.

Now she went back to check Brock's bulls. She found them relaxing in their pen, none of them showing any sign of a snakebite. To pass the time, she wound her way among the pens, admiring the bulls and chatting with people she'd met at other events. Despite its inherent rivalry, the stock contracting business was like family. People knew and cared about one another.

Several of them asked about Casey's injury. Tess assured them that he'd be back on his feet in a few weeks. She could only hope that was true. The arena was half of Casey's life. The other half was Val. The loss of either would destroy him.

A faint rumble below her ribs told Tess that she was getting hungry. She'd started her day before dawn, with only coffee for breakfast. Now it was past noon. The beef and lettuce sandwiches in the cooler would be filling, with enough left over to last her through supper tonight. Tomorrow it would be chili dogs and sodas until she could load Whirlwind into his trailer, fill her thermos with coffee, and head back to the ranch. If all went as planned, she'd be home in time to get a few hours of sleep before morning chores. After that, the first item on her list would be getting secure quarters ready for Quicksand's arrival.

She'd left the pens and was crossing the parking lot when Brock's shiny black truck pulled up in front of her, blocking her path.

The driver's side window opened. "I hope you haven't eaten lunch. I brought you some barbecue." He held out a Styrofoam takeout container. Her first impulse was to turn down his high-handed offer. But as the mouthwatering aroma reached her, Tess found her resistance crumbling like a mud wall in a storm. If Brock was trying to push her buttons, he'd chosen the right one.

"Thank you," she said. "As a matter of fact, I'm starved."

She reached up to take the container, but he laughed and pulled it back inside. "Not so fast, lady. Let me park, and I'll bring it to you. Meet me at those picnic tables next to the pens."

The tables had been set up for workers and contract people at the arena—one long one and a couple of small ones with umbrellas for shade. Only a few people were using them. With the sun getting warm, Tess took a seat under one of the umbrellas and waited.

She had no illusions about Brock's motives. This was a power play, making her sit here like a trained dog while he parked and brought her food. She reined back the urge to get up and leave. Only by staying might she learn what the man had in mind—if that was even possible.

A few minutes later, he appeared with two takeout containers. Sitting, he passed one across the table to her, along with a tall plastic cup of iced tea. Then he opened the other for himself. The meals were identical—barbecued brisket, baked beans, coleslaw, and a thick slice of Texas toast.

"I thought you were going to lunch," Tess said.

"I did. But I passed on the buffet because I'd decided I'd rather share some barbecue with my partner. This little place is the best."

Tess forked a bite of brisket into her mouth. It was fall-apart tender, the sauce rich and tangy. "It's good," she conceded. "But what I really want is for you to cut the crap and tell me what's on your mind."

"Tess, Tess." He chuckled and shook his head. "Why do I get the feeling that, as hard as I try to be nice, you still don't trust me?"

"Maybe because nice isn't part of your nature. When you show your horns, that's when I know I'm dealing with the real Brock Tolman. But when you bring me free barbecue, that's when I go on alert. So just tell me."

He took a sip of iced tea. "All right. I do have something in mind. You might even like it."

Tess sampled the beans, which were as tasty as the meat. "Go on," she said. "Pardon me if I eat while you talk. I'm famished."

"It's fine. Enjoy." His smile was unreadable. "Here's what's happening. Today I met with the people who manage some of my real estate holdings. They agreed with me that in order to protect what I have, I need to put some of the properties under names other than my own."

"Protect, you say? Protect from what?"

"It's complicated. I'll explain another time. But I assure you, what I'm proposing is perfectly legal."

"I'm listening."

"That property to the north of yours—with the hayfields and the vacant house. I take it you know what I mean."

"Yes, I figured it was you who'd bought it when you started charging us full price for the hay."

"Yes." Brock cleared his throat. "Anyway, what I want to do is put the entire parcel under the name of the Alamo Canyon Ranch. It would still be mine, of course. But if you'll agree to manage it—keep the hay watered and bill me for the harvesters to cut and bale it, you can have all the hay you want for free."

"I see." His proposal sounded almost too good to be true. "What's the catch?" she asked. "There's got to be one."

"No catch. I'll still retain the property and make money on the hay that's sold. If your family doesn't want to manage the hay, I'll hire somebody to live in the house and do the job, like the man who was there before."

Tess felt a chill. "The man who was there before murdered my stepmother. And that house isn't fit to be a pig wallow. It needs to be burned to the ground."

"Then I'd replace it and build something else—simple, but nice. Maybe some of your family—say, Val and Casey—could live there. I couldn't help noticing that your house is pretty crowded."

"What about property taxes?"

"I'd pay them, of course." He put down his fork. "So what do you think?"

Tess took time to weigh her answer. "I'd have to know more," she said. "And of course, this isn't just my decision. It would involve my entire family. Could you write up an offer with all the details?"

A smile tightened his lips. "I already have. It will be in your e-mail by the time you get home."

"Of course." How like Brock, to work out the plan ahead of time and spring it on her without warning. "One more thing," she said. "I can't make a decision unless I know why you're doing this. You said you'd explain later. I'd like to hear your explanation now."

Did he flinch? Tess couldn't be sure, but she sensed that she'd touched a nerve.

"All right, but for now, this is between you and me, understand?"

"All right." Tess had never seen him look so uncomfortable.

"I can't tell you the details," he said, "but someone is threatening legal action that could damage me. I'm hoping nothing will come of it, but in case I lose, I need to protect as many assets as possible—even small ones, like that land parcel. And I need to do it soon."

"What about a trust? Wouldn't that protect your assets?"

"I'm working on it, but I may have waited too long—and it may not cover everything. Does that answer your question?"

"I suppose so. For now."

"And you'll keep this from your family?"

"They're not fools, Brock. They're bound to figure it out."

"Then do the best you can. If they're interested, I can bring the paperwork and answer their questions when I deliver Quicksand."

"And if they say no?"

"Then I'll probably send the bull with one of my men, and that'll be the last you hear about the matter." He stood, gathering up his half-finished meal for the trash. "I've given you a lot to think about. But what do you say we forget about business and enjoy the event tonight? I've got two prime seats above the chutes. Clay mentioned that Whirlwind won't be bucking tonight, so you might as well use one. Otherwise, it'll just go to waste."

Tess hesitated, not wanting to owe him for the favor. But why not? With Whirlwind on hold, watching the competition from a choice seat would give her a chance to size up the bulls and riders.

"Here." Brock fished the ticket out of his hip pocket and thrust it toward her. "With three of my bulls bucking tonight, I'll be spending most of my time in the chutes. But you'll be seeing some great action."

"Thanks, I'll take it." Tess accepted the ticket and tucked it into her timeworn leather purse. "I'll be cheering for your bulls."

"You know how to find the seats. If I get a break, I'll join you." He glanced at his Rolex. "Sorry. I'm sitting in on a 1:30 directors' meeting. If you want to come—"

"No, I'd only be out of place. Go on. Thanks for the lunch and the ticket."

Puzzled, Tess watched him vanish into the arena. What was going on behind that handsome, arrogant face? She had never known Brock to do anything nice without a reason. The ticket, the lunch, and the offer to put the hayfield property under the name of the ranch all must have some dark motive behind them.

The more she pondered the story of the legal threat, the more skeptical she became. Brock was a multimillionaire. He could afford an army of lawyers. Why weren't they handling this issue? And compared to his other properties, the hayfields, with that junkpile of a house, were barely worth pocket change.

But if joined with the Alamo Canyon Ranch, in one parcel, under one name, the value of the combined properties could rise, even soar. That could be what Brock was thinking—register the ranch and the fields as one entity with him owning almost half of the acreage. From there, the next step would be to back her against the wall financially, remove her family, and take everything.

Clever, clever man!

Fury mounting, Tess rose, crumpled the Styrofoam container, the plastic cup, and the napkin, and flung them into the nearby trash barrel. She had to find a way to beat Brock at his own game. For now, that would mean pretending to be taken in. Get him to talk. Flatter him. Let him think he was charming her.

But most important of all, never, ever trust him.

Restless, Brock shifted in his chair and tried to focus on the discussion of plans for the coming Fort Worth finals and the tentative schedule for next season. He was flattered to be one of the stock contractors invited to the meeting. He knew what was being said was important. But his mind kept wandering to Tess.

He hated himself for lying to her about the legal problem—and about the trust. He'd had a trust drawn up years ago to protect his ranch and other major assets. But a trust couldn't protect him from blackmail. There was only one sure way to do that—find the threat and eliminate it.

At least his offer to transfer the hayfields to the Alamo Canyon Ranch had been made in good faith. Removing his name from the property records would shield Tess and her family from anyone seeking to damage him. But there were other advantages. Not only would the combined parcels go up in value, but should the ranch ever face default or have to be sold by the family, as part owner, he could prevent anyone but him from buying it.

Tess was a smart woman, honest to the bone, and fiercely proud. She'd be livid if she knew how he was playing her. But it couldn't be helped. She couldn't be allowed to know the secret that had reared its ugly head—the secret that could destroy him.

Tess leaned forward in her seat as Brock's bull, a red behemoth named Nitro, body-slammed the inside of the chute. The young Brazilian rider who was trying to mount shifted upward to keep his leg from being crushed.

From where she sat, Tess could see Brock in a black hat, working with the chute men. Tess knew he would not look up at her. He was totally absorbed in readying his bull. Moments like this were something they both understood. For all their differences, this was what they lived for.

A wooden wedge was lowered into the chute, forcing the bull away from the rails and allowing the rider to take his place. With the help of the chute crew, he pulled his rope tight behind the bull's massive shoulders, wrapped the gloved hand that gripped the rope handle, and moved forward. A nod signaled that he was ready.

The gate swung open. The bull burst out, starting the eight-second clock. Tess had seen Nitro buck before. He wasn't a high leaper, but he had a powerful kick. With two seconds left on the clock, the young rider lost his grip, flew off to one side, and landed rolling—out of the final round, but safe to learn and try again.

The three bullfighters moved in to distract Nitro while the rider scrambled to safety. Tess recognized Casey's teammates, working with a spare man. She couldn't help thinking how much Casey would want to be here—and how much Val wanted him to quit his dangerous job.

As Nitro trotted out through the exit gate, the scores

went up on the monitor: no score for the rider; forty-five points out of fifty for the bull. A great score. Brock would be pleased.

He shot her a quick glance, flashing a grin. Tess gave him a high-five sign before he turned away and headed for the exit chute to unfasten Nitro's flank strap and send the bull back to the pen.

It was as if she and Brock moved in two separate worlds, she mused as the next rider mounted the bull in the chute. There was the outside world where the two of them thrust and parried like dueling enemies, constantly testing, neither one trusting the other.

Then there was *this* world—a world of total understanding and shared passion for the sport they both loved—a familiar world, where they were equals, almost friends.

But that wasn't quite true. Two things were certain. The outside world was the real world, and Brock Tolman would always be her enemy.

As the event ended, Tess rose from her seat to join the crowds filing out of the arena. It was almost 10:30, a good time to find a restroom, check on Whirlwind, then crawl into her truck, lock the doors, and roll up in the old blanket she kept on the backseat. She would see Brock tomorrow. That would be a good enough time to thank him for the ticket and congratulate him on his third bull, Blastoff, who'd carried his rider, Cody Whitehorse, for a total of ninety-one points, putting them in the lead for the event.

But her plan was about to change. Hearing her name spoken, she looked back to find him striding to catch up with her. She paused long enough for him to close the distance between them.

"Did you see that ride?" A grin deepened the creases

around his tired eyes. "I've never seen Blastoff buck that well. And Cody's control made them both look good. I hope you're in the mood to celebrate with me. There's a place in the next block, close enough to walk. Good beer and nachos. My treat."

"I'm happy for you," Tess said. "But I'm ready to drop. I need my rest." She was about to excuse herself and disappear when she remembered her resolve to play along with him. This could be a useful opportunity. "Maybe a very short celebration," she said. "Can we check Whirlwind on the way out?"

"Sure. I'll have my boys keep an eye on him if you want."

"No need. I wouldn't bother, but I promised Lexie I wouldn't leave him alone too long. He's her baby, you know."

"Does that mean Whirlwind's going to have a little brother? How's that going to work?"

"We'll see. I'm sure Lexie will manage. I just hope her real baby doesn't show up the week of the World Finals."

They left the arena, pausing on the way out to greet people they knew. By the time they reached the pens, the lights had been turned low. Security cameras blinked their red eyes overhead. The armed guard who stood at the entrance recognized them and let them pass.

The bulls were settling in for the night. They snorted, lowed, and passed gas, the sounds blending in a murmur that was almost soothing. Whirlwind was snoring in his pen, fast asleep.

"We can check your bulls, too," Tess offered.

Brock had one remaining bull to buck in tomorrow's final round—a massive white beast named Cannonball. "Don't bother," he said. "They'll be fine. Let's go get some nachos."

Side by side, they walked through the parking lot. With

the sun gone, the spring night was chilly but not cold. The air smelled of exhaust fumes, tobacco smoke, and barbecue, but the coolness on Tess's face was refreshing.

The city lights obscured the stars, but the waning moon shone brightly, casting shadows across the broken sidewalk. Neither of them said much. It was as if they both sensed that talk would only heighten the tension between them.

Which world were they in now?

CHAPTER 5

"*T*HERE IT IS—LEFTY'S TAVERN." BROCK POINTED DOWN the block. Tess saw a sputtering orange neon sign, hanging above a nondescript door.

"It looks like a dive," she said.

"It is. That's half the charm of it. Great country music, dancing, beer, and nachos to die for."

"Sounds like I'm in for an adventure." Tess yawned. All she really wanted was to go back to the truck and sleep.

"Maybe you need more adventures in your life, Tess. Or at least more fun."

"This is enough adventure for tonight. Just don't expect me to dance."

"Relax. I'm not expecting anything." He opened the door and ushered her through.

Inside, Lefty's Tavern was dimly lit, with a half dozen round tables, a bar, and a dance floor with a bandstand, where two guitar players, a bass, and an ancient-looking

man with a deep, gravelly voice were performing an old
Hank Williams song.

"They're actually pretty good," Tess said, as Brock seated
her at a table.

"The old guy's here almost every time I come in. From
what I've overheard, he used to be a pretty big star, but don't
ask me to remember his name."

When the waiter, who walked with a limp and looked like
a former cowhand, approached their table, Brock asked for a
double order of nachos to split and a Corona. "And you,
miss?" the waiter asked.

"Just a Coke, thanks." Tess glanced at Brock. "I'm not
about to cheat on my sister."

"I never thought you would," Brock said. "I want you to
know I respect you for that."

"That just might be the nicest thing you've ever said to
me—unless it's something you say to all the ladies."

"Not that. Other things, maybe. But not that. Respect is for
you."

Tess fixed her gaze on the rodeo posters that covered the
walls, wishing she could take back her last words and what
they'd implied. Of course, Brock would have women in his
life. A man like him—handsome, virile, and powerful—
couldn't be expected to live like a monk. He could even
have a sexy, sophisticated mistress tucked away somewhere.

But why had she brought it up, even as a joke? And why
did his answer make her feel as if she'd been put in her
place, like a child who'd spoken out of turn?

"Respect is for you."

At least she wouldn't have to worry about him making
moves on her.

There were several couples on the dance floor in front of
the stage, moving to the easy throb of the music. Tess
watched them, too flustered to carry on the conversation.
This wasn't a date, or anything like it. They were barely

friends, if that. Still, she'd managed to make a fool of herself.

"How about a dance while we wait to eat?" Brock spoke without warning.

Tess's pulse skittered. "Don't even ask. I haven't danced since high school. I'd only embarrass you—and myself."

"If we embarrass ourselves, we can just sit down. Come on. I dare you. And I've never known the intrepid Tess Champion to turn down a dare."

"Then you don't know me at all. I'm just a quivering bundle of nerves."

"I know a remedy for that. Come on, just a turn around the floor. It's like riding a bicycle—you never forget how." Taking her hand, he drew her gently but insistently to her feet and led her away from the table. Tess could feel her heart pounding as he turned her toward him, his hand resting at the small of her back. She was vaguely aware that she smelled like a bull and hadn't combed her hair or put on makeup since leaving the ranch at dawn. But if Brock noticed, he didn't seem to care.

The music was slow and mellow, the song, "I Can't Help It if I'm Still in Love With You," had always tugged at Tess's emotions.

The song had nothing to do with tonight or with Brock, but Tess felt herself softening in his arms. Her body brushed against his, the light contact setting off sparks of awareness that tingled along her nerves, flowing downward to stir sensations that she hadn't allowed herself to feel since Mitch died.

Those tantalizing quivers went against everything she'd promised herself. But heaven help her, they felt good. He was solid and warm and dangerous, and as his hand tightened on her waist, she closed her eyes.

His chin, sandpapery with stubble, rested against her cheekbone. His breath whispered its way around the curves and contours of her ear. She was barely aware of her feet and the simple, shifting steps of the dance. It was like floating. But when her hips brushed the hard bulge beneath his jeans, it sent a shock wave through her body. She hadn't meant for this to happen. Time to break off, before he got the wrong idea.

But she needn't have worried. As the music ended, Brock released her and stepped back. "See, I told you it was like riding a bicycle. You did fine."

"Anybody can slow dance." She took a breath, willing her pulse to decelerate. "Look, our drinks are on the table, and here comes our waiter with the nachos. Let's eat."

Sitting, they dug into the platter of tortilla chips drenched in cheese sauce and dotted with bits of tomato, green onion, olives, and sliced jalapeños. The nachos were hot, messy, and delicious, meant to be eaten with the fingers. Tess tried to focus on the food, but she couldn't stop her thoughts from spinning backward.

What had happened on the dance floor wasn't worth remembering, she told herself. Brock was a man, his response fueled by the testosterone pumping through his veins. Like a breeding bull, almost any female would've had the same effect on him.

It was her own response that troubled her. She had never liked Brock. There had been times when she almost hated him. That he would rouse that long-buried surge of sensual heat had come as a shock.

But the dance had been no more than a diversion. Nothing had changed between them. They were still antagonists. And Brock Tolman was still a man whom no one should trust.

After they'd eaten, Brock walked her back to her truck. He didn't like the idea of leaving her there to spend the night—

in fact, he'd even offered to pay for a safe hotel room. But as expected, Tess had turned him down flat. "I've got a pistol, and I know how to use it," she'd said. "I'll be fine. Now go on back to your fancy hotel and let me get some sleep."

Cursing her stubborn pride, Brock had made sure she was safely locked inside the truck, then walked away and drove back to his hotel. At least he'd known better than to offer her one of the two beds in his suite. After their sizzling chemistry on the dance floor, Tess would have suspected the worst of his motives.

Brock had enough past experience to know when a woman was aroused. Tess had been smoldering, if not quite on fire, and his body had responded in kind. Under different circumstances, he would have enjoyed sweeping her up to his hotel room and ravishing her until she purred with satisfaction.

But this was Tess—as prickly and proper as she was fierce and proud. As his business partner, she was off-limits. Crossing the line could make it a problem for them to work together. And he needed their partnership even more than she did.

For years Brock had coveted the Alamo Canyon Ranch for its beauty and for its value as an investment. Adding it to the portfolio of choice properties he owned in other parts of the state would be a crowning achievement. But with the threats to his reputation and his own ranch, he had come to view it as a backup, a safe harbor, owned and controlled by him but protected by the Champion name.

As things stood, his best chance of getting control of the Alamo Canyon Ranch lay in a friendship with Tess and her family. So far, things seemed to be going all right. But one impulsive move could change that in an instant.

And now he had a different problem—an invisible enemy with the power to topple his world. Until he knew who they were and what they wanted, all he could do was wait for them to play the next card.

* * *

Casey woke to darkness and silence. The slight hollow where Val had slept beside him was cool and empty. There was no light showing beneath the closed door, no sound of footsteps or running water. She was simply gone.

With a weary sigh, he sat up and swung his legs to the floor. His sprained ankle hurt like the blazes. Maybe he'd twisted it when he and Val were making love. That had been fine, as it always was. Afterward, they had kissed and settled into sleep. He'd assumed everything was all right between them. But now Val was gone.

His flannel robe hung over the bedpost. Balancing on one leg, he shrugged into it, then reached for his crutch. Hobbling out of the room into the dark hall, he muttered a curse. This was the first time he'd ever been disabled, and he hated it. He thought of Shane who, barring a miracle, would never walk again. How did he stand it?

But Casey knew—or thought he knew—the answer to that question. Shane had a loving wife and a baby on the way, with the future hope that more children would be coming. Even without the use of his legs, he had a meaningful life.

The door to the master bedroom, where Shane and Lexie slept, was closed. Tess's door stood open. The room was empty, as was the living room. Val must have gone outside.

What if she'd left—the way she'd left him when she was seventeen, without a word?

But no—he found her in the rocker on the front porch, wrapped in the worn Navajo blanket that hung over the back of the couch. The dog leaned against her leg, tail thumping as she scratched its ears.

When she raised her head to look at him, the moonlight gleamed on her tear-streaked face.

He pulled another chair next to hers and lowered himself into it. "What is it?" he asked. "Is it me?"

Her breath made a sound like tearing silk. "Oh, Casey," she said.

His first impulse was to gather her close and hold her, but that would resolve nothing. What she needed, he sensed, was to talk.

"Tell me," he said.

For a time, she didn't speak. A wispy cloud crept across the moon, casting its shadow on the earth. A coyote called from the hillside below the pass. Val drew a sharp breath.

"Our baby," she said. "I can't stop thinking about him."

"Neither can I. But you know that."

"I asked you not to mention him to me again, and you haven't. But it's too late. It's as if you opened the floodgates. I never really cried for him, you know. I told myself I had to be strong. But I'm not strong."

Casey captured her hand and held it tight. "It's all right. We're both dealing with the loss."

"I told myself that it didn't matter, not being able to have more children. At least I wouldn't get my heart broken again. What I didn't know was that I'd be breaking yours."

He raised her hand to his lips and kissed it. "You don't have to say these things, Val. They'll only hurt."

"No, listen to me." She pulled her hand away. "I want you to leave me, Casey. Leave me and find a woman who can give you the children you want—*your* children."

Casey muttered a curse. He should have expected this. "Stop it. You should know better than to say that."

"I mean it. Maybe with luck, she'll even enjoy watching you get tossed in the air and pounded into the dirt."

"But she wouldn't be you. I love you, Val. And we're not having this discussion."

"Then where do we go from here?" She was on her feet, clutching the blanket around her. "I love you, but love isn't enough. It won't change my body. And it won't change the terror I feel every time you step into the arena. I can't become the woman you want."

"Damn it, you *are* the woman I want. Marry me, Val. We could drive to Vegas and get it done tomorrow."

She shook her head. "That wouldn't be a good idea—especially now that you're trying to find our son. It's brought home how much you'd miss having children of your own—and what a mistake it would be not to have them."

When Casey didn't—couldn't—answer, she pulled the blanket tighter around her body. "We're not good for each other right now. Maybe it's time you went back to Tucson."

Turning away from him, she stalked back into the house. As he followed, seconds behind her, Casey heard the door to Tess's vacant room close with a defiant click.

With a sigh, he passed the closed door and continued on down the hall. He would be sleeping alone for the rest of the night—and maybe for some time to come. But as much as he loved Val, there were two things he refused to abandon—his work as a bullfighter and the heartbreaking search for their son.

Brock roused himself at 5:30, already looking forward to the day. As he stepped into the hotel shower and lathered his body, his mind clicked down the mental list he'd made. First, a visit to the pens to make sure his hired hands had fed and watered the four bulls; then breakfast, maybe with Tess, if he could talk her into it. After that, he'd be spending more time with his best bull, Cannonball, who'd be bucking tonight in the championship round.

Cannonball, a hulking, white six-year-old, had an impressive record of buck-offs and high-scoring rides. He'd given a good performance in Vegas, and Clay Rafferty had already tapped him for the May finals in Fort Worth—so far, the only bull from the Tolman Ranch to make the cut.

Brock planned to move the bull to a separate pen and give him a going-over with the electronic muscle stimulator. Like Whirlwind, Cannonball was easily handled and would even come to the rails to be scratched. Working on him was an easy task. After that . . .

The jangle of his cell phone interrupted the rest of the thought. Brock shut off the water, grabbed a towel, and strode into the next room to answer the call.

"Mr. Tolman." It was Jim, the younger of his two ranch hands. "Get here as fast as you can. Something's happened."

Driven by the urgency in the young man's voice, Brock yanked on his clothes; collected his wallet, watch, and phone; and raced downstairs to his truck.

The night was barely fading as Brock pulled into the parking lot to see people gathering around the gate to the pens. As he climbed out of the truck, Jim, looking stricken, came running to meet him.

"It's Cannonball!" The young man was out of breath. "He's not moving! We think he might be dead!"

Sick with dread, Brock shouldered his way through the crowd and into the pen complex. He could see three of his bulls, milling and snorting on the far side of their pen. Cannonball lay on his side against the rails. A man Brock recognized as one of the PBR vets was reaching through, holding a stethoscope against the massive body.

The vet straightened as Brock approached. "I'm sorry, Brock, there's no pulse. He's gone."

"What the hell happened?" Brock reeled, struggling against denial. "He was fine last night. Did somebody do this?"

"I'd have to get into the pen and take a closer look. But I don't see a wound of any kind. And there's no discharge, which makes poison unlikely. My first guess would be a coronary attack or a brain embolism. It's rare, but we both know it happens."

"Yes." Brock had heard of bulls simply dropping dead. The great champion Pearl Harbor, ranked number one at the time of his death, had died suddenly of a blood clot near the brain. And more recently Air Support, a top-ranked young bull, had died of a brain embolism. There had to be others, less well-known. But Cannonball? This couldn't be happening.

"I could do a necropsy if you need to know everything," the vet said. "Or at least, for starters, I could analyze his blood." He took a large syringe out of his bag. "He's probably been dead for less than two hours. His blood's starting to congeal, but with luck I can get enough of a sample for testing."

"Yes, go ahead and do the blood work," Brock said. "This is a long shot, but there was a rattlesnake in the trailer. He seemed fine yesterday, but maybe if he was bitten in a vein . . ."

"That seems unlikely, but I'll check for venom," the vet said. "If nothing shows up, then we'll talk about the necropsy."

"Fine." The thought of his beautiful bull, laid out to be opened up and examined, was almost more than Brock could stand.

"Brock, I'm so sorry!" Tess had moved forward to stand beside him. "He was a great bull. What a loss. Do you have any idea what happened?"

"We're still working on that." Brock tried and failed to keep the emotion out of his voice.

"I can check the security cameras for you," Tess said.

"Thanks. At least they might give us some clue."

She hurried off. Someone was opening the gate to move the other three bulls down the chute to a different pen. Cannonball's carcass would be hauled away and put in cold storage like butchered beef until it could be examined. Brock stared down at his boots to hide a rush of emotion. He'd thought the world of that bull, a great bucker and a sweetheart to handle. Damned rotten luck.

But what if Cannonball's death wasn't just bad luck? What if someone had had a hand in it?

The walkway between the pens was covered in wood shavings, pressed by a multitude of feet. Looking for telltale footprints would be a waste of time. But what if there was a connection between the yellowed news clipping, the rattlesnake in the trailer, and the death of his prize bull? What if all three incidents were the work of the same person?

A chill crawled up Brock's spine.

A blackmailer would have nothing to gain by planting a snake or killing a bull. But what if the motive of the mysterious sender wasn't blackmail?

What if it was revenge?

But he was jumping to conclusions now, taking great leaps of logic that had no basis in evidence. True, the clipping was a worry. But the snake and the death of the bull were no more than coincidences. Even if they were connected, he'd be foolish to fly into a panic. If his enemy was smart and ruthless, Brock told himself, he would have to be smarter and even more ruthless. Somehow, he would beat the bastard at his own game—whatever that game might be.

He could see Tess, coming back, weaving her way through the crowd, a troubled expression on her face. As she came closer, she shook her head. "I checked with security. No luck. The camera that covers this pen had been reported out of order. They don't know why. They called a technician to come and look. They're still waiting for him to come." She looked up at him, her deep gray eyes overflowing with sympathy. "I'm so sorry, Brock. Losing a good bull like Cannonball is like losing family. What are you going to do now?"

"Talk to Clay, I guess, and then take the other bulls home. I was hoping to see Whirlwind buck tonight, but I don't have the heart to stick around. I'll see you in a few days when I deliver Quicksand to you." He forced a smile. "That bull's a handful. It's still not too late to change your mind."

"My mind is made up. I just have a feeling about him—

call it a hunch. At least he'll be a challenge." She turned to walk away, then paused. "Would you call me if you learn any more about Cannonball's death? You've got my cell."

"I'll do that," he said. "Good luck with Whirlwind tonight."

"Thanks." She hurried off in the direction of Whirlwind's pen. Brock watched her vanish. Then he went back to helping the arena crew move his bull to where it could be loaded onto a flatbed, covered with a tarp, and hauled away.

Whirlwind's performance that night was nothing short of spectacular. With seasoned rider Joao Reyes Santos on his back, the silver bull leaped, kicked, and spun his way to a 93.5 first place. As he was named Bull of the Event and she accepted the prize money, Tess's only regret was that there was no one here to share the moment. Not her family. Not Ruben or Pedro. Not even Brock, whose bull might have won instead. Only Clay Rafferty caught her eye and gave her a thumbs-up.

The untimely death of a bull was always heartbreaking. It meant the loss of income, the loss of future hopes, and the loss of a friend and family member. As Tess drove home through the night, with Whirlwind dozing in his trailer, she found herself imagining how it might feel to lose this precious animal. The tragedy would be unthinkable, but it could happen. Anything could happen.

She had never imagined losing her mother, or Mitch, or Jack, or Callie. Only her father had died predictably, of cancer. Wise people told you to hold on to those you loved, to keep them close. Treasure every moment.

It might be good advice; but God help her, it wasn't enough.

* * *

Tess arrived home in the murky hours before dawn. The headlights of her truck revealed Ruben, standing by the paddock gate to help her unload Whirlwind.

She backed the trailer up to the open gate and waited while her foreman released the bull, who trotted out to enjoy a roll in the grass and an early breakfast. Then she pulled forward and climbed out of the cab. The unhitching and cleaning of the trailer could wait for daylight.

When she told him about Whirlwind's victory and the extra prize money, Ruben's grin seemed to light the darkness. "He is an angel, that one. An angel in the body of a bull."

"Well, be prepared," Tess told him. "The new bull will be here in the next few days. But Quicksand is more devil than angel."

"We'll see." Ruben chuckled. "There's a place for devils in this business—if they can buck. Now get some sleep, *hija*. Everything here is taken care of."

With her purse looped over her shoulder, Tess made her way into the house. After the long day and the long drive, she was exhausted. Every joint and muscle ached as she crept down the hallway to her room. The bed she'd left neatly made up had been slept in and not remade. Typical Val. Tess could only guess that she and Casey had been at loggerheads again. But right now, she was too tired to care. After stripping down to her underwear, she flung herself onto the mattress, dragged the covers up to her chin, and tumbled into sleep.

Brock had watched Whirlwind's victory on TV last night. He was happy for Tess, knowing that no bull in the competition, not even Cannonball, could have beaten Whirlwind. But he was still reeling, not just from the loss of a prized animal, but from the implications surrounding Cannonball's death.

Yesterday, on arriving home, the first thing he'd done was check the voice messages on his landline phone and rummage through the mail that Cyrus had left on his desk. Nothing. No threats, no demands, and no more clippings. Maybe he was imagining things. But the envelope he had locked in his wall safe, with the clipping inside, was very real.

This morning, with no word from the vet who'd taken Cannonball's body, he'd saddled a horse and ridden out to view his kingdom. Seeing his ranch, the vast pastureland, watered by springs and broken by strips of natural desert, had always calmed his spirit. He started with the west pasture, where 1,600 head of red Angus beef, the financial backbone of the ranch, were fattening for market. Brock had little attachment to these animals, who were looked after by a separate crew of hands. But the income from this herd allowed him to pursue his real passion—the bucking bulls.

The adjoining pasture held the bucking cows and heifers. Most of the cows were pregnant, their calves to be born over the next few weeks. Although cows didn't compete, their lineage was as important as that of the bulls. In the breeding of great buckers, it had been shown that bulls got their size and athleticism from their sires. But the bucking gene, and the fighting spirit to drive it, came from the mothers.

Last year's calves had been sold or moved up to their own herd of adolescent bulls. Most of the new crop would likely be auctioned off next year, as well. But waiting in the wings for the next breeding was Whiplash, the only surviving full brother of Whirlwind. Brock could hardly wait to put the big brindle in with his best cows and see the calves that came from their mating.

Raising his binoculars, he spotted Whiplash beyond the fence in the next pasture. He was standing on a grassy hillock, apart from the other bulls, surveying the landscape as if it belonged to him—a magnificent bull who could have gone all the way if he hadn't been found guilty of killing an evil man.

Brock reminded himself to mention the sighting to Tess and Val when he delivered their black bull. The sisters would be happy to hear that Whiplash was doing well.

And the black bull . . . Brock used the remote to open the gate and close it behind him. As he rode into the pasture, he could see the bulls, clustered at the far end, like a smudge against the pale green earth. Riding closer, he passed the brushy patch where Tess had been thrown from her horse. He thought about stopping to hunt the snake down, but he didn't have anything to kill it with. And rattlers, nasty as they might be, were useful in controlling the prairie dogs, whose holes could break the leg of a cow or horse.

As he rode closer, the bulls turned to face him. Quicksand moved to stand in front of the others, snorting and tossing his horn as if to protect them from the human intruder.

Brock reined his horse to a halt. "It's all right, big boy. I'm not coming any closer. But be warned. Your life is about to change, big time."

He remained where he was, studying the small herd. These were young animals, with limited exposure to the arena. This summer, they would be taken out to minor events, bucked, and if they did well, moved up in the ranks. Quicksand was older, but because he'd already proven to be a problem, he remained in limbo—a talented bucker who refused to behave and had nowhere to go.

Tess, if she could manage him, just might have saved his life.

Brock had left the pasture and was riding back to the stable when his cell phone rang. He pulled it out of his pocket and answered.

"Brock, this is Tom Hammond, the vet who checked your bull. I ran a tox screen on the blood I took."

"Did you find anything?" Brock's pulse had kicked into overdrive.

"I did. No trace of snake venom, but plenty of ketamine and pentobarbital—in dosages high enough to knock out a rhinoceros. I could do the necropsy, but I'd say we already have our cause of death. If you want, I can call someone to dispose of the body. The bill will go to the PBR."

Cannonball deserved better, Brock thought. But he didn't have the mental energy to haul the 2,000-pound carcass back to the ranch and bury it here. "Do that. And thanks," he said.

Numb with shock, Brock ended the call. Ketamine was the drug used in tranquilizer guns to bring down an animal by inducing temporary nerve paralysis. Pentobarbital was the euthanasia drug that shut down the heart and brain. It was easy enough to picture what had happened, harder to block the awful image.

Lethal injection.

Some bastard had murdered his bull.

CHAPTER 6

Four days later

As TESS WATCHED BROCK'S RIG ROUND EACH SWITCH-back on the downward road, she felt as excited as a child at Christmastime. Quicksand was coming home at last. In the days ahead she would discover whether her choice of this bull had been a stroke of intuitive genius or a complete disaster.

The ranch family had gathered to see the arrival. Lexie and Maria watched with the dog from the porch. Shane had moved his wheelchair to be near the gate when Quicksand was released into the pen that had been set up. Behind him, Val and Casey stood side by side, Casey leaning on his crutch. Ruben and Pedro looked on from the opposite side of the gate.

All of them had placed their trust in Tess to choose the new bull. Had she let them down? She was about to find out.

Brock had phoned her two days ago with the chilling news about the vet's discovery. That someone would kill a fine animal so coldly and needlessly had left her shaken. But she'd been unable to offer anything more than sympathy. How the killer could get to the bull and do the job without being seen was still a mystery.

"You should call the police," she'd urged him. But he'd turned down her suggestion.

"The police won't care about a dead bull. And nothing they do will get Cannonball back. I can try to figure out who hated me enough to do such a thing, or I can forget it and move on. My choice."

He'd sounded calm and resigned. But knowing Brock as she did, Tess knew that he wouldn't rest until he'd caught the killer and found a way to make him pay. Involving the law would only create an impediment.

She hadn't forgotten about his proposal to add the hayfields to the ranch. She'd discussed it with her family. They were open to the idea but had issues and questions. "No promises," she told him. "But bring the paperwork, and we'll talk."

Now Brock was here, pulling into the yard with the trailer holding Quicksand behind him. She'd been so impressed with the black bull when she'd seen him at the Tolman Ranch. What if she saw him again and realized she'd made a mistake?

Stepping out into the yard, she raised her arms and began directing Brock to back the trailer up to the open gate of the pen. Anyone accustomed to hauling bulls could park a trailer on a dime, and Brock was no exception. He stopped with the back door of the trailer perfectly aligned with the gate.

After setting the brake, he climbed out of the truck. He was dressed in work clothes—a faded flannel shirt, well-worn jeans, dusty boots, and a Stetson molded to his head by rain and sun. Tess liked the look better than the dress-to-impress clothes he usually wore to bull riding events. Not that it mattered.

Today his usual cocksure attitude was missing. He looked

gaunt and weary, as if he hadn't slept well or eaten sensibly in the past few days. But he managed a smile as he walked around to the trailer door.

"Last chance to change your mind," he said. "Once this black bastard's in the pen, he's all yours."

From the inside of the trailer came the sound of thumping and banging. Brock unlatched the overhead door at the base and raised it upward. Then, stepping back to safety, he used a rope to pull open the gate inside.

For the space of a breath there was dead silence. Then, snorting like a steam locomotive, Quicksand barreled out into the fenced enclosure.

The pen, its walls six feet high and fashioned of steel rails, was not much bigger than an average-size bedroom. Quicksand galloped into it, then wheeled to face his captors, his dark eyes fiery with defiance.

Shane was first to speak. "Ugly big bugger, isn't he?" he drawled.

"He's no beauty." Tess sprang to the defense of her bull. "But just wait till you see him buck."

"That's assuming we can get him into the bucking chute and get the dummy on him," Casey said.

Ruben had studied the bull in silence. "Let's leave him alone for now," he said. "He's got food and water. He just needs time to settle down."

Brock pulled the trailer away while Pedro closed the gate and latched it securely. Quicksand eyed the strangers, snorting and raking the grass with his single horn.

"Go on inside," Ruben said. "I'll watch him and make sure he's all right."

"Come on," Tess said. "Maria's made us some tamales for lunch. The table's all set. After we eat, we can talk about that proposal for the hayfields."

They trooped up to the porch, leaving Ruben to watch the bull.

They were about to go into the house, with Shane maneu-

vering his chair up the ramp, when the dog left the porch and
trotted out for a closer look at the new bull. The young shepherd mix was an easygoing dog, accustomed to cattle. There
was nothing menacing in his approach. But at the sight—or
scent—of him, Quicksand flew into a bucking, snorting,
kicking frenzy, slamming against the steel rails in what appeared to be blind rage.

"Come on, boy." Shane whistled for the dog, called him
back, and let him into the house. As the bull calmed down,
to stand quivering and blowing in the pen, Casey shook his
head.

"Looks like we might have a problem."

"I should have warned you about that," Brock said. "I
don't know how much Tess has told you, but when we found
that bull as a youngster, he was alone in the desert fighting
off a pack of coyotes. That dog of yours must look like a
coyote to him."

"Well, we're not getting rid of the dog," Lexie said.
"We'll just have to keep them apart. I hope you know what
you're doing with that bull, Tess. He's not going to be an
easy one. And we don't have a lot of time to train him. We
need to get him into the arena."

Tess scooped a tamale onto her plate and slipped off the
corn husk wrapping. Usually tamales were her favorite, but
now her appetite had vanished. Nobody had anything good
to say about the bull she'd chosen.

After the meal, Maria took a plate outside to her father,
who was still watching the bull. Pedro went off to do some
chores. Casey, as if to make it clear that he wasn't a legal
family member, went down the hall to work out with the
weights. Val's gaze followed him as he left the room. Seeing
her sister's expression, Tess felt the tug of worry. Something
was wrong between those two people who loved each other.
And it wasn't just Val's fears about Casey's work.

Tess, Val, Lexie, and Shane sat down in the living room
with Brock to talk about the proposed transfer of the hay-

field property to the Alamo Canyon Ranch. Hanging over them all was the awareness that Brock was pressing Shane and Lexie to come and live with him. But for now, that issue was put on hold.

All of them had read the proposal. Tess allowed Shane to lead, knowing her sisters wouldn't hesitate to chime in with their own concerns.

"We know there'd be some advantages for us if we accept this," Shane began. "But if you were to take a piece of property that you own and make it part of the ranch, that would make you part owner of the ranch. It would give you a measure of control that makes us all uneasy."

"I understand," Brock said. "But the way this is written up wouldn't give me any ownership of the animals, the house, or the outbuildings and equipment—only the land."

"But if we do this, and we needed to sell, we couldn't do it without your approval," Lexie said.

"That's right. But you'd have the same control over the hay fields. I couldn't sell any part of that property without your say-so. But with my hayfields an actual part of the ranch, I'd have an interest in protecting the whole parcel. You'd never have to worry about back taxes, loans, or anything that could force you to sell. I have enough money to keep the ranch secure for all of us."

From where she sat, Tess studied Brock's ruggedly chiseled profile. The man was as smooth as a snake oil salesman, and she had yet to detect any lies or flaws in his argument. Still, her instincts told her not to trust him. Brock always had his own best interests at heart. And she had a ranch to protect.

Val cleared her throat. "Tess mentioned that you might be facing some legal action. If you get sued and lose or have to settle, how would that affect this arrangement?"

"Not at all. My name wouldn't be on the property except as an investor. Legally it would be yours."

"And what about that old house?" Lexie demanded. "The

man who lived there murdered our stepmother. It needs to be burned to the ground."

"Our agreement would give you the right to do just that," Brock said. "Then we could arrange to build a new house."

"One more thing," Shane said. "Our pastures could use a sprinkling system and a well, like the hayfields have. Would you be willing to pay for that?"

"I don't see why not. It could be added to the contract." Brock looked around the group. "Any more questions? If not, we could sign the papers now."

"Hold on." Tess rose to her feet. "It appears you've covered most of the bases, Brock. But before we make a decision, I'd like to run all this past a lawyer friend of mine. She helped us with dad's will, and she's close by, in Ajo. I could leave it with her tomorrow—unless, of course, you have some problem with that. In that case, you've wasted your time and ours."

Brock had done his best to give the Champions an honest proposal and to answer their questions truthfully. They were smart people. If he lied or even fudged the truth, they would be on alert. And his motives were honorable. He wanted to protect his property and theirs from the threat that was hanging over him. And he wanted to make sure that no strangers ever got their hands on this choice little ranch. Wasn't that honorable enough?

But Tess had surprised him—not with her caution but with her vehemence. Brock had known all along that she didn't trust him. But he'd underestimated her. In defense of her home, the woman was as fierce as a mountain lion.

Her defiance stirred his male urge to protect her—to use his resources and influence to make her life safe and easy. It was a pleasant fantasy—having her on his arm and in his bed, making her a rich man's plaything, without a care in the world. But he knew that Tess would never willingly accept a man's protection, especially if it might mean control. She was the most stubborn, independent woman he'd ever known.

She was more than that. She was damned magnificent.

"Of course, you can show your lawyer everything," he said. "Take your time. Give her my number in case she has any questions. We won't sign this agreement until—and unless—everyone is satisfied."

Standing, he laid the folder with the contract on the coffee table. "It's time I was leaving," he said. "Let me know when you've come to a decision. If it's a yes, I'll be back to put things in motion. Oh—and whatever you decide, you have my permission to burn that house down anytime you want." He turned to Tess. "Do you mind walking me out to my truck?"

"Of course not." Tess stepped ahead of him as he held the screen door for her. Outside, Quicksand was still tossing and snorting in his pen. Ruben stood outside, watching him.

"Good luck with that bull, Tess," Brock said as they neared the spot where his rig was parked. "You're going to need it."

"I know." She turned to face him. "Nobody seems happy about having him here. But I see something in him. Maybe in time, everybody will see it. I'm sorry about Cannonball. Have you learned any more about what happened?"

"Only what I told you about the drugs they found in his blood. I'm still trying to figure out how anybody, having those drugs and knowing how to inject them, made it into a guarded enclosure with other people around. Maybe I shouldn't have left. If I'd stayed, I might've learned something, or found some evidence. But right then, all I wanted to do was load my other bulls and go home."

"Of course. You were in shock," Tess said. "But the person who killed your bull is still out there. Has anything else happened?"

"Not that I'm aware of." He wouldn't tell her, or anyone else, about the clipping—although it could be connected to the death of his bull. "I need to get home now. Call me when you have a decision on the contract. And good luck with Quicksand."

"Thanks. I have hope." As she looked up at him, her eyes like sunlight shining through storm clouds, Brock was seized by the senseless impulse to bend down and kiss her soft, full lips. But he held himself back. This wasn't the right time or place—or even the right woman. His business partner was still off-limits.

"Keep me posted," he said, and climbed into the truck.

Pulling the empty, swaying trailer up the switchbacks left him white-knuckled. It was a relief to make it to the level road and then the straight asphalt highway.

The drive back would give him plenty of time to think. He'd kept himself busy the last few days, getting Quicksand ready to load and finishing the contract for the hayfields. Not wanting to involve his lawyers, he'd written it up himself, using a template. Now that the bull was delivered and the contract was on hold, it was time he got back to the most urgent problem—finding out who'd killed his bull, which might lead to whoever had sent the clipping.

The conversation with Tess had started his mental wheels turning. If the vet was right, Cannonball had been killed in the dark hour before dawn—a time when workers and stock contractors were already showing up at the pens. The bulls that had competed the night before were being loaded for the drive home. The security shift was changing. And the grounds people were already putting fresh wood chips on the walkways and cleaning out the empty pens. Cowhands were filling food tubs and water troughs. The bulls would be awake and stirring.

At that hour, the overhead security lights, still dimmed, would be casting shadows into the pens and walkways below. It would be easy enough for anyone to walk into the complex dressed as a worker or guard. But it would take planning and skill to find the bull, get him close to the rails, and deliver the injections without being noticed.

Had the killer targeted Cannonball, or had the white bull simply been the one within reach? Either way, knowing wouldn't change anything.

Brock had no way to explain the broken security camera. That could've been a coincidence—an unlucky one for him. A photo of the killer, even from above, could have gone a long way toward solving the mystery. As it was, he could only guess who was behind the crime.

It stood to reason that the killer was a specialist who'd been paid to do the job. Someone else had probably hired them. Someone out for vengeance, most likely.

But who? And why?

He was only guessing now, trying to make sense out of bits and pieces. For all he knew he could be way off track. He needed more evidence.

In Sells, the headquarters of the Tohono O'odham reservation, he stopped for gas and a chilled Red Bull. By now it was midafternoon. The sun glittered on the russet earth. A lizard skittered out of sight as Brock walked back to his truck.

Farther down the highway, ravens were flocking on a road-killed jackrabbit. Brock swerved around the spectacle. He felt raw inside, as if things in his life were slipping beyond control. He had to get that control back.

Tomorrow he would drive back to the Cave Creek Arena and find out everything he could. The PBR event had moved on, but a PRCA—Professional Rodeo Cowboys Association—competition was scheduled for the coming weekend. With luck the pens would still be set up, and the arena workers and security team would still be around. He would also call Clay Rafferty to see if the PBR had investigated his bull's death.

He was off to a late start, but he wouldn't stop until the people behind the crime were brought to justice—the law's justice, or his own.

Above the pass, the sun's day was ending. Its fading light streaked colors across the western sky—crimson, violet, tangerine, and blinding gold. Night-flying insects buzzed and fluttered among the cactus blossoms. Lights had come on in the windows of the house.

Tess and Ruben stood by the fence, studying the new bull. Quicksand was still snorting, trembling, and digging at the grass with his single horn.

"You've been watching him all day," Tess said. "What have you learned about him?"

"Not everything," Ruben said. "But there is one thing I know for certain. This bull is not mean or angry. He is afraid—more than afraid. He is terrified."

Tess stared at the bull. "How can you tell?"

"It shows in his eyes, the way he holds his ears, and the way he trembles. You told me how Brock's men found him in the desert, stolen from his mother, lost, alone, and in danger from coyotes. I think he has never gotten over that fear. In a new and strange place, like here, he still feels lost. He doesn't know he's safe."

"But with the other bulls on Brock's ranch—he was right out in front, as if he were protecting them."

"He probably felt safe with them. Or maybe he thought they were all in danger."

"So he's like a person with PTSD."

"My people have other names for it. But yes, I think maybe so."

"Can we do anything to help him?"

"Maybe. My people have an old song that is good for calming animals."

"Anything is worth a try." Tess remembered how Ruben's

mother, Juanita, had sung to Val to help with a bout of depression. Maybe it had been the power of suggestion, but the singing, which had taken all night, had made a difference.

"Can you sing your song for Quicksand?" she asked.

"It would be better with a shaman," Ruben said. "But I can try. It will take much of the night."

"Could I stay with you while you sing?" Tess asked. "Maybe if the song works, Quicksand will be less afraid of me."

"All right." Ruben stretched his tired limbs. "Meet me back here in an hour."

Tess took care of her needs and left the dog in the enclosed patio with food, water, and an old quilt to sleep on. By the time she returned to the place outside the pen, wearing a warm jacket, the stars were out. Ruben had made a fire from crackling sap wood. More kindling was piled nearby to feed the small blaze.

He had carried a lawn chair from the porch for Tess. A wool blanket, folded on the ground, marked the spot where he would sit. Next to the blanket was a skin drum with a stick and an unlit bundle of white sage.

"It will be your job to keep the fire burning," he said. "You can keep the sage burning, too. When I light it, you will see how."

"Thank you for doing this, Ruben," Tess said. "I only hope the change in Quicksand will be worth the effort."

"The best I can do is help him to be calm. The rest—the fierceness—must come from his heart."

"I understand. But the fierceness is there. I've seen it."

The pen was confining enough to keep Quicksand within a few feet of his captors. He stood against the rails on the far side, eyes rolling nervously. The lightning-shaped blaze down his face flashed reflected firelight.

Sitting cross-legged on the blanket, Ruben held the end of the sage bundle to the fire long enough to get it smoldering. As he waved it gently, pungent white smoke curled from the glowing leaves and stems. As the aroma reached him, Quicksand snorted and tossed his head.

Ruben laid the smoldering sage on a flat rock and reached for the drum. Tess added a stick of sapwood to the fire.

The mournful howl of a coyote echoed down from the ridge. She watched Quicksand, expecting a reaction, but he paid no attention. He would have heard coyote calls on Brock's ranch, she surmised. But he might not have connected the sound with the pack that had terrorized him.

Taking up the stick, Ruben began a low, throbbing beat on the drum—growing stronger with the first few repetitions but never changing its rhythm. As it became hypnotic, Tess found herself breathing in time. Even Quicksand had paused in his nervous shifting and head shaking.

Ruben began to sing in a reedy voice that was like the whisper of wind. It was nothing like his low, flat speaking voice. Tess was startled, then drawn into the sound and the way it shaped the words of the song. Ruben had implied that he wasn't a shaman, but the effect of his singing was as magical as anything she had ever experienced. She could only hope it would make a difference for her troubled bull.

As the time passed, her eyelids began to droop. She had to remind herself to feed the fire and perfume the air with sage smoke. But as she fought off sleep, the song went on and on. Through the steel rails, she could see Quicksand's hulking form against the darkness. He was standing still, his lowered head tilted with the weight of the single horn. Maybe he was falling asleep, too.

By the time Ruben's song ended, the waning moon had crossed the heavens to the western sky. The sapwood was gone, the fire burned down to glowing coals. The stub of the sage bundle remained, its smoke lingering in the air.

Quicksand was still on his feet, but his massive head hung low. His breathing was deep and even.

Ruben stood and stretched his limbs. Gathering up the blanket and the drum, he cleared the hoarseness from his throat. "I've done what I could. In the morning we will know if it was enough. No, leave the sage where it is, *hija*. The smoke will help keep him calm."

Tess folded the chair to carry back to the porch. "Thank you from the bottom of my heart, Ruben," she said. "Now let's get some rest."

Tess was skeptical by nature. She'd never been religious or believed in what she called New Age mumbo jumbo. The crystals, bells, incense, beads, and statuary that lured tourists to the shops of Sedona held no appeal for her. But tonight, she had experienced something old and real, something beyond ordinary belief. The sense of wonder clung to her as she fell into bed and lay sleepless, gazing up into the dark.

In the bedroom down the hall, Casey lay awake with Val curled lightly against his side. Their lovemaking had been strained tonight. Afterward, she'd been silent, her face turned away from him until, lulled by the muted cadence of Ruben's drumbeats outside, she'd eased into slumber.

But even as she slept, he'd sensed the silent resistance in her. It was as if she could tell that he was hiding something from her.

That morning he'd received a text from the detective he'd hired to track down his boy.

Found location of stored adoption record and person who will copy for $5,000. Send money or if not let me know.

Casey lay still, listening to the feathery sound of Val's breathing. He ached with love for her. Once he'd thought that being with her, close and intimate like this, was all he would ever want out of life. But that was before she'd told him about the baby that she'd given up for adoption.

Claiming his son was out of the question. Casey understood that. But the urge to see the boy just once, to know his name, how he looked, and where he lived, had lit a fire inside him—a fire that was burning him alive.

The asking price for a forbidden copy of the adoption records didn't surprise him. The person supplying the documents was taking a risk. Casey had the money, and he would pay it.

Then what? Would he take the next step and track down the boy's family? Would he share the information with Val, who was dead set against the venture?

Maybe it was time to go back to his bachelor condo in Tucson and handle the business from there. Val had asked him not to involve her in any way. And if he remained here, she was bound to guess what he was doing and to get emotional about it. But he couldn't help hoping that she would change her mind, and they would find their son together.

He would decide in the morning.

Val whimpered in her sleep and nestled against him. He pulled her close, breathing in the scent of her hair.

CHAPTER 7

AFTER A FEW SLEEPLESS HOURS, TESS WAS UP AT FIRST light. Yesterday's clothes lay heaped on the rug. She pulled them on, jammed her feet into her boots, and raced outside.

The morning air that struck her face was rich with sage smoke from the fresh bundle that lay on the rock. Ruben stood next to Quicksand's pen. As he saw her, his stoic face relaxed into a smile.

"Come and look," he said.

Quicksand, his head down, was munching on the hay that had been forked into his pen. As Tess approached, he raised his head, snorted, and pawed the earth in warning.

"It's all right, boy." A few more steps took Tess up to the rails. The massive bull lunged at her and stopped short—a warning. Tess jumped back. "Well, at least he doesn't seem scared anymore."

"The sage smoke seems to calm him. Maybe we can use it in handling and training him."

"Brock said he's been chute trained. But when they took him to a rodeo, he wouldn't buck."

"He was probably scared of the noise and the crowd," Ruben said. "After we've bucked him a few times with the dummy, we could take him to one of the small-town rodeos. If he does all right there, we can move him to a bigger audience. I know we need to get him making money, but we can't rush him."

"Yes, I agree."

But what if, in spite of all her hopes, Quicksand continued to freeze in front of a crowd?

They did have a little time. The PBR season would end after the May finals and start again in the fall. But the traditional rodeo season would continue all summer long and end with the National Finals Rodeo in December. There'd be plenty of rodeos left for Quicksand—if they could just get him bucking.

But right now, Quicksand was about to face another test. Someone, probably Maria, who was starting breakfast, had just let the dog out of the patio.

Hearing voices, the young shepherd mix came trotting around the house. Ears pricked and tail wagging, he pranced up to the pen where Quicksand was eating.

With a bellow, the bull lunged at the dog, crashing against the rails in an effort to get at the animal he saw as an enemy. The startled dog, tail between his legs, slunk back around the corner of the house.

"I'll be damned!" Tess swore. "Ruben, if your song did that for Quicksand, maybe you should sing it for me."

Ruben chuckled and shook his head. "I told you, the song and the sage were only to calm his fear. What you just saw was the real bull."

After morning chores, the ranch family gathered for a breakfast of tortillas, beans with bacon, and fried eggs. Tess was still in a celebratory mood, but that changed when Casey hobbled out of the hallway on his crutch. A protective brace was laced over his sneaker and around his ankle. Dressed for the road, he was carrying his duffel bag, which he tossed onto the couch. Val, her movie-star face an unreadable mask, followed a moment later.

"You can't be leaving us so soon, Casey." Tess pulled out the empty chair next to her, scrambling for some way to delay him. "Sit down. Have some breakfast."

"Sorry—I need to get this ankle checked by a doctor. I think I may have put too much weight on it."

That was a lame excuse if Tess had ever heard one. He and Val must've had words. But over what? Her problems with his work were old news. There had to be something else—something her sister wasn't telling her.

"Come on," she said. "Tucson's a long drive, and there's not much to eat along the way. Besides, we'll be bucking Quicksand with the dummy this morning. I'll need you here to tell me what you think of him and give me suggestions. You can go later if you need to."

"And you can't miss tonight, Casey!" Lexie rose out of her chair. "Val and I are planning a party—a house-burning party!"

Casey exhaled in defeat and took the seat next to Tess. "I've been to house-warming parties. I take it this is different," he said.

"You bet it is!" Lexie settled back onto her chair. "Brock told me we could burn down that old house where Aaron Frye used to live. Aaron murdered Callie and almost killed me. I still have nightmares about it. I'm hoping that when the house is gone, that awful memory will fade."

"That sounds like fun." Casey's voice carried an edge as he filled his plate with beans and eggs and poured himself some coffee. "Are you going to roast hot dogs and marshmallows over the flames?"

"We'll do no such thing," Shane said. "That house is toxic.

There could be anything in there, even explosives. Once the fire starts, nobody's going near it, especially you, Lexie. You don't want to inhale any fumes."

Until now, no one had mentioned the party to Tess. But she'd be as relieved as anyone to see that horror of a house gone. "We'll need to clear the ground on all sides of the place and wet it down," she said. "And we'll need a hose with a sprayer in case the fire starts to spread."

"Trust you to take the fun out of it." Val had taken a seat at the foot of the table. She was sipping her coffee, her plate empty and a sour expression on her face. "I was thinking we could paint our bodies and dance naked around the flames, but I suppose that's out, too, isn't it, boss?"

Tess raised an eyebrow but decided not to respond. Something was definitely eating at Val this morning.

"I need to go into Ajo this afternoon to leave Brock's offer with my lawyer friend," Tess said, changing the subject. "I could pick up some cider and donuts, or whatever sounds good, for the party tonight. Let me know if there's anything else I can bring home—you too, Maria."

"I'll get you a list," Maria said.

"Meanwhile," Tess said, moving on, "I want you all to see Quicksand buck. Ruben and Pedro, I'll need you on horseback to guide him into the chute. Casey, maybe you can help me get the flank strap and the dummy on him—if you're staying, of course."

"Sure. I know when I'm outgunned." He glanced toward Val, but she pretended not to notice.

There was a definite strain between those two, Tess mused. The question was, should she try to get to the bottom of it, or should she leave them to sort it out for themselves?

Getting Quicksand into the bucking chute was easier than Tess had expected. The bull was accustomed to being moved by men on horseback. He barely resisted when Ruben and

Pedro herded him into the narrow metal chute and closed the gate behind him.

Tess was beginning to understand how Quicksand thought. Things that were familiar—horses and riders, the bucking chute, and hopefully other bulls—were all right. But new situations—different people, dogs, and noisy arenas, tended to throw him into a panic. At least, understanding Quicksand's behavior should help her correct it.

Getting the 24-pound metal box strapped onto the bull where a rider would normally sit was never easy. But Tess had enough experience to do the job efficiently. With Casey working the opposite side of the chute to hook and lift the buckle, Quicksand was soon readied for bucking.

Shane, Lexie, and Val watched from outside the bucking pen. Ruben, on his well-trained horse, waited in the pen to lasso the bull in case of trouble. Pedro had dismounted to pull the gate rope.

Tess climbed the rails, gripping the remote. "Ready," she called to signal Pedro.

"Ready," Pedro called back. Quicksand was slamming the chute, his horn clattering against the metal.

"Go!"

The gate swung open. Quicksand shot out, flying like a winged devil, kicking, spinning, and twisting, making up in sheer fury what he lacked in finesse.

At eight seconds, Tess released the dummy. The box popped into the air, trailing the strap. Quicksand jumped a few times, then lowered his head and made a beeline for Pedro, who'd taken shelter behind the gate. Pedro scrambled up the rails in time to escape a crushing blow.

Ruben's lasso circled the bull's neck. Whiplash pulled and bucked, then settled enough to be herded into the chute, where the rope and flank strap were removed. Then he was released to the freedom of the paddock.

"Well, what do you think?" Tess was out of breath from racing around the pen.

"The bastard can buck, that's for sure," Shane said. "Let's hope he'll do it in the arena, with a real rider on his back."

"But you say he has no pedigree and no registration?" Lexie was the breeding specialist of the ranch family.

"That's right," Tess said. "According to Brock, he was a stray—no identifying marks and no ear tags, although the holes in his ears were there. The best guess was that he was stolen and turned loose by the thieves when the police got too close. Look at him. He's got all the lines of a quality bull."

"But without the papers, he'll be worthless as a stud," Lexie said.

"What about DNA testing?"

"That might give us some idea where he came from. But the level of detail we'd need to get him registered for breeding wouldn't come cheap. I say we wait, at least until we know what kind of bucking career he's going to have."

"You never know," Tess said. "A really great bull could start his own bloodline."

Val shook her head. "Dream on, sister. Right now, our job is just to get that bull making money."

Brock had spent the morning at the Cave Creek Arena, talking to anybody who might have been nearby when his bull was killed. He'd checked with security first. The man on duty had confirmed that the camera covering Cannonball's pen hadn't been working for several days—which meant it had been out of order well before his bulls had been herded into the pen—a lucky coincidence for the criminal. The arena workers had been busy that morning. None of them had noticed anything unusual. The stock contractors and cowhands taking care of their bulls were no longer here. This whole damned trip had been a waste.

By now it was noon. The midway was opening up before the early events—mutton busting for little kids, mini-bull riding, and the junior rodeo competitions. The speakers were blaring old cowboy songs, and the air smelled of popcorn, fried pastries, and barbecue.

Brock treated himself to a beer and a hot dog dripping mustard. Sitting at an outdoor table, he watched families and clutches of wholesome-looking teens parade past on their way to the arena. All the while, his mind was mulling over one vital question.

Of all the people he knew—and all the people who might have access to the stock pens—who would hate him enough to murder an innocent animal?

Jim and Rusty, his two hired hands, had been here to drive the truck and take care of the bulls. But they had no reason to hate him. And they weren't educated men. It was unlikely that either of them would have the knowledge and skill to administer the deadly shots.

There was a friendly rivalry, of course, among the stock contractors who raised the bulls and brought them to events. They and their workers had access to the bulls. But if Brock had enemies among them, he wasn't aware of it. And it wouldn't be like any of them to kill a bull in such a manner. They loved and respected the animals too much for that.

His original idea that the person who'd sent the clipping had hired someone to inject the drugs still made the most sense—in which case, the guilty party could be anyone.

He was gathering the remains of his lunch for the trash when one more possibility struck him. Brock's breath jerked. His hands clenched into tight fists.

There was someone else who knew his bulls, someone with the intelligence and skill to deliver the shots, someone who had been at the arena the whole time—and who had reason to resent him for past wrongs.

Tess.

* * *

Tess had talked Val into riding to Ajo with her to pick up party supplies and deliver the hayfield documents to the lawyer. She'd hoped her sister might open up about her problems with Casey. But Val, true to her nature, was hard to crack. Tuning the car radio to an '80s rock station, she cranked the volume up loud.

Tess let it play until the gravel road joined the asphalt highway. Then she reached over and turned the music down. "It's all right, Val," she said. "You don't have to talk to me if you don't feel like it."

"Thanks. I don't." Val folded her arms and turned away to gaze out the window. A few miles later, Tess glanced over to see a tear trickling from under the frame of her sister's sunglasses.

"What is it?" she ventured. "Is it Casey? Is he being a jerk?"

Val shook her head, her mouth pressed into a tight line. Tess waited, giving her time.

"I could handle Casey's being a jerk," Val said. "But he's not a jerk. He's just being Casey, following his stubborn heart like he always does. If anybody's being a jerk, it's me. But I can't help it." Her voice broke. "I can't do what he wants."

Tess kept her eyes on the road ahead, knowing better than to interrupt. There'd been some tension between them when Val had first come home, but now that Lexie was married and living a separate life, the two older sisters had grown closer.

"It's our baby—the little boy I gave up." Val struggled to keep from breaking down. "Casey's hired a private detective to get the adoption records and find him."

"But it was a closed adoption." Tess was familiar with Val's story. "Isn't that illegal?"

"Probably. But Casey doesn't care. He swears that he won't have any contact with the boy or his family. He just wants to know where his son is and that he's all right. But you know that won't be enough. He'll want to see the boy. And then what? Where will that lead? I'm scared, Tess. He could go too far and end up getting arrested, or ruining lives."

"Let me guess. He wants you to get involved."

"That's right. I told him that I didn't want any part of it. My heart broke when I gave up my baby. I can't stand the thought of finding him and then giving him up again."

"So that's why he decided to leave." Tess slowed the car to let a family of quail cross the road, the babies like tiny balls of thistledown.

"This morning, when I pressed him, he admitted that he had a chance to get the adoption records. I gave him an ultimatum—either give up on the whole idea or go back to Tucson and pursue it without me. He didn't even hesitate, just got up and packed his duffel."

Val took off her sunglasses and wiped them clean on the hem of her shirt. "I know you want him to stay, Tess. I know you want us to work things out. But letting him go right now is our only chance. Please don't try to stop him."

"All right, I understand." Tess slowed to the reduced speed limit as the long white line of tailings, left from Ajo's copper mining days, came into view. She did understand, but she was worried about Val. Her sister had been emotionally fragile since her return from rehab in California last summer. Casey's actions, or even the happy arrival of Lexie's baby, could be enough to push her into the danger zone.

By the time they reached Ajo's warehouse-style grocery store, they'd agreed that it would save time for Val to take the list and do the shopping while Tess visited her lawyer and checked the mail. Tess left her sister at the store's entrance and drove to the post office, where she picked up a handful of bills and junk mail, then continued on to her lawyer's place.

Andrea Simonelli, a widow, lived in a former company house that was small but tastefully remodeled with a charming yard landscaped with native plants. Tess had tried to phone her from the ranch but had to settle for leaving a voice mail, explaining what she needed. If the woman wasn't home, she reasoned, she could always drop the packet through the mail slot in the door.

She was about to ring the bell when the door opened. A petite woman with a youthful face and silver hair stood in the doorway, dressed for travel and wheeling a large suitcase. "I was hoping you'd get here before I had to leave, Tess," she said. "My son is getting married in Salt Lake City this Tuesday, and I've got a plane to catch. I won't have time to look at your documents until I get back next week, but you're welcome to leave them. I'll call you when I've finished my review."

Tess thanked her, left the packet of papers, and went back to her car. She didn't have a problem with waiting to sign the contract. Brock might. He was not known to be a patient man. But that was his problem. Meanwhile, she'd have time to help Val finish the shopping. Then it would be back to the ranch to set up for the house-burning party.

Brock hadn't planned on driving home by way of the Alamo Canyon Ranch—especially since he'd just been there to deliver Quicksand. But the idea that his mysterious enemy could be Tess had struck him like a thunderbolt.

For the rest of the day, he hadn't been able to think of anything else. His mind warred with the notion that a woman as gentle as Tess would kill an animal just for spite. Such a cruel act didn't seem like her at all. But then again, how well did he know her? Maybe she had a dark side—a side he'd never seen.

Maybe spending more time with her would either harden his suspicions or put them to rest.

He needed an excuse to return to the Alamo Canyon Ranch. A gift might ease his welcome. Browsing in a high-end specialty store for rodeo supplies, he'd found just the thing. It was something she'd mentioned the day she'd come to his ranch to choose a bull—a bucking dummy in the shape of an actual rider.

Known as a Sticky Ricky, the dummy came with a detachable head and torso and two detachable legs that could grip the sides of a bull. Its plain black body could even be dressed in clothes and a hat. With pads and a stout strap underneath to hold the device in place, it could also be stripped down and used as a regular box dummy.

It was an expensive toy, but worth the money if it served its purpose. He would give it to Tess as a present. If that didn't buy him some time with her, nothing would.

If she accepted the gift and didn't send him packing, he would play it from there. He would watch her, listen to her, question her—hell, maybe even put a few moves on her. She might be his partner, but if she was secretly sabotaging him, all the rules were out the window.

By late in the day, the area around the old house had been cleared of dry grass and weeds, the ground wetted down with a hose attached to the irrigation system. The job had taken a couple of hours, with Tess, Val, Pedro, and Ruben pitching in and Casey helping where he could. He and Val were clearly avoiding each other. Knowing what was at stake, Tess had made no effort to interfere.

The horses and cattle, including the bulls, had been herded to a safe distance. Lexie had volunteered to make sure the dog was safely indoors. The fire wasn't to be lit until after dark, when the blaze would be at its most spectacular. In the meantime, there'd be time to wash up, rest, and have a light supper. Then the fun would begin, with music, chilled cider, donuts, and the grand spectacle of the burning house. Val had even suggested they throw a few fireworks into the blaze. To Tess's relief, no fireworks could be found.

Tess stood in the yard, surveying the dilapidated, prefab house from a distance. Taking off her hat, she raked her hair back from her hot face. She was sweaty from pulling weeds and spattered with mud from plying the hose. Val had already gone inside to shower and change. It was time she did the same.

Just then her ears caught the sound of an engine. A black pickup, which she recognized as Brock's, was coming down the road from the pass. What was he doing back here so soon? Had something gone wrong? Or was he just showing up to complicate her life?

She was a mess, and there'd be no time to freshen up before he arrived. But what did it matter? This was just Brock. It wasn't as if she was trying to impress him.

By the time the pickup pulled into the yard, Val had come outside, looking fresh and pretty in a mint-green blouse that set off her eyes. Shane and Casey were on the porch, Shane in his wheelchair.

Brock pulled into line with the other parked vehicles, stopped, and climbed out of the cab.

"Weren't you just here? Did you leave something behind?" Tess hadn't meant for her greeting to sound sarcastic, but it did.

If Brock had noticed the sharpness, he chose to ignore it. "I drove back to Cave Creek to learn what I could about Cannonball's death," he said. "It might have been a wasted trip, but I happened on something that made me think of you, Tess. It might not be your birthday, but I couldn't resist bringing you a present."

He opened the shell on the back of the vehicle and lowered the tailgate to reveal a cardboard box about three feet square. Straining under the weight, he lifted it in his arms and set it down at Tess's feet, within view of the porch.

"Here," he said, opening his pocketknife and handing it to her. "You do the honors."

Tess accepted the knife. That Brock Tolman would bring her a gift was the last thing she'd expected. She wasn't happy with the idea, especially if it meant she might owe him a return favor.

"I don't know what's in here," she said, "but you certainly didn't need to bring me a present, Brock."

"I know. Go ahead and open it."

The box was sealed with tape. Tess took her time working the blade under the cardboard flaps. Val was dancing with anticipation.

"For heaven's sake, Tess, just rip the blasted thing open! Here, let me help you!" She strode off the porch and began tearing into the box, which was filled with packing peanuts. Val reached deeper. "What on earth . . . ?" She pulled out a black vinyl object in the shape of a human head and torso. Tess stared at it, puzzled.

"If I didn't know any better, I'd say it was some kind of voodoo doll," she said.

"Holy shit!" Shane whooped. "I know what that is! Brock just brought you a state-of-the-art bucking dummy. It's a Sticky Ricky!"

Tess's hand worked down through the packing material. She pulled out two long, curved pieces that appeared to serve as legs, along with some assorted hardware, an instruction manual, and a remote control wrapped in plastic. In the bottom was the strap and the weighted box that made the dummy work.

"Wow." Stunned, she found her voice. "This will come in handy for training, especially with Quicksand. Thank you, Brock. I'm overwhelmed."

And she was—that he would remember a passing remark of hers and get her this lavish but useful gift had her head spinning—until she remembered that Brock never did anything without a purpose. He was a master of manipulation. What was he going to ask for next?

"So you like it, do you?" he asked.

"I think everyone here will like it." One thing was certain. Any notion of rejecting his gift was out the window. Her family would never allow it.

"You must stay for supper, Brock." Val gave him a dazzling, cinematic smile. "It won't be anything fancy, just soup and grilled cheese sandwiches. But afterward, when it gets dark, we're going to have that house-burning party we talked about. If you want a hot time, stick around, mister." She spoke the last words in the voice of an old west saloon girl she'd played in a single TV series episode.

Brock chuckled. "With an invitation like that, how could I say no?"

"I know that Tess would love to keep you around." Val was having fun now, stirring up a bit of mischief. "Wouldn't you, Tess?"

Tess battled the urge to throttle her sister. "You know what?" she said. "While we've got some daylight left, I'd like to put that dummy together and try it out on a bull—one that hasn't been bucked in a few days, maybe Rocket Man. What do you say?"

"Great idea!" Shane was already skimming through the instructions. "Come on, Brock. Give us a hand!"

The first tryout of the bucking dummy was a rousing success. Brock watched with the Alamo Canyon family as Rocket Man, a husky, tan bull, bucked and kicked his way across the pen with the dummy, dressed in old clothes, flopping back and forth like a real rider.

When Tess pressed the remote and the whole device flew into the air, everybody cheered. Brock was pleased that his gift had been so well received. But building good will with the Champions was secondary to his real purpose.

The whole time while the dummy was being assembled, the bull prepped and bucked, Brock's eyes had remained on Tess, watching for any sign of guilt or evasion, any suspicious looks. But he'd noticed nothing except the way her cheek dimpled when she smiled and her habit of brushing her hair back from her face. All he had noticed was how beautiful she was, even in her mud-stained clothes, with her face bare of makeup. He'd even entertained a moment of fantasy—Tess in a clinging black silk nightgown, the dark cloud of her hair spilling over his pillow, her stormy eyes gazing up at him . . .

But damn it, how could she not be the one who was tormenting him? Everything fit, even the Tucson postmark on the envelope that had held the clipping. Only one piece didn't fit the puzzle—the clipping itself. But that didn't mean she hadn't killed his bull. That clipping could've been sent by someone else who wanted to ruin him.

The journey from lot boy at a Missouri car dealership to one of the most powerful ranchers in Arizona hadn't been easy. He'd made his share of enemies along the way. Tess was one of them. But was she out to get him? Was she working with a partner, or was she entirely innocent? He was still searching for answers.

By the time the bucking demonstration was over and the gear put away, the light was fading fast. The sun hung blood red above the horizon, silhouetting the giant saguaros that rose like sentinels along the ridgelines. Birds and animals, in hiding through the day, awakened to hunt and forage.

Supper was eaten hastily, with everyone eager to get to the business of burning the hated house—not everyone for the same reason. Lexie had nearly died in that house when Aaron Frye had caught her searching for evidence. Val looked on the burning as an excuse to have a good time. For Tess, the house was the last remaining vestige of the man who'd tried to destroy her family. She wanted it gone. But she was also aware that the fire could be dangerous. For that reason, she'd volunteered to stay on the far side of the house, away from the celebration, to make sure the fire didn't spread in that direction. Brock had offered to go with her, but she'd turned him down, perhaps not trusting her own vulnerability. "You won't want to miss the fun," she'd told him. "Stay with the others."

Earlier, Pedro had splashed an outside wall of the house with gasoline so the fire could be started from a distance by lighting a trail of oil-soaked straw litter. Lexie, who had the worst memories of the place, had been given the honor of lighting the straw.

How like excited teenagers they seemed, Tess mused as she took the Kubota four-wheeler up the road that joined the two properties, circled behind the house, and left the vehicle at a safe distance. The hose lay where she'd last left it, hooked up to the sprinkling system that watered the growing hay.

She could feel a light breeze on her face, blowing from the southwest, away from the ranch. So far, so good, as long as it didn't change.

Taking a safe vantage point, she waited. From where she stood, she could hear the group counting down. "Ten . . . nine . . . eight . . ."

CHAPTER 8

BROCK COULD IMAGINE WHAT THE BURNING OF THE house meant to the people of the Alamo Canyon Ranch. The building was a worthless eyesore, to be sure. But it was also a constant reminder of the betrayal and murder that had violated their trust. If they needed a celebration to purge it from their lives, so be it.

But that didn't mean he wasn't worried.

The moon had come up, flooding the landscape with light. Standing where the dirt road began, he measured the line of straw with his eyes. He estimated the distance to the house to be about thirty yards. Setting fire to the place should be safe enough if everybody stayed back, and if the house held no surprises.

But something could still go wrong.

The people around him were in a festive mood, drinking cider and feasting on glazed donuts carried from a table set up in the yard. No one was drinking alcohol, out of consideration for Val. But they could still miscalculate the danger—and two of the men, Casey and Shane, were in no condition to fight a spreading fire.

The wind was tricky as well, shifting one way, then another. A stiff gust could send sparks over the sprouting hay fields or, far worse, blow them in the direction of the ranch.

The only other person who seemed concerned was Tess. He was uneasy about her, as well. He shouldn't have let her go beyond the house alone, with nothing but a garden hose to control the fire. But when he'd offered, she'd made it clear enough that she didn't want him along.

The countdown had begun. Lexie touched the flame of a cigarette lighter to a rolled-up length of newspaper and used it to reach down and ignite the straw. The flame flickered, then blazed. Within seconds the fire was racing along the straw path toward the house.

Brock swore silently. He wouldn't relax until the house was gone and the fire was out.

Tess heard the cheers. The breeze carried the stench of burning oil. Somebody, probably Val, had turned on some music. Johnny Cash's "Ring of Fire" blasted through the darkness.

This was crazy. Why hadn't she put her foot down and stopped it? At least, she might have talked sense into a couple of the men. Now it was too late.

From where she stood, on a grassy slope that rose behind the waiting house, she couldn't see the flaming straw. But the flickering light against the darkness and the raw burn of smoky air in her throat told her that the fire was getting close. She backed uphill a few more yards and waited, gripping the hose and holding her breath until her lungs ached. The bare area around the house looked too small now. They should have cleared away more of the dry grass and weeds.

With a whoosh of air and a roar of igniting flame, the gasoline-splashed outer wall caught fire. From there the cheap wooden structure went up like a torch.

A pack rat darted out of a hole under the foundation and scurried into the night. An owl, nesting in the attic, shot out ahead of the flames, barely escaping a fiery death. Tess looked for more fleeing animals, saving themselves from the fire. She saw none.

As she watched the flames consume the house that had held so much hate and evil, a memory of Aaron Frye surfaced in her mind.

Over the years, the man had become like family, freely dropping by the ranch house to share a meal or sit on the porch and visit. Aaron and Bert Champion, Tess's father, had both been gun fanciers. More than once, she recalled hearing them talk about reloading ammunition by filling used casings with gunpowder and replacing the lead tips. Reloading saved money and also allowed the bullets to be customized.

Aaron had mentioned setting up a reloading bench in his house. If it was still there—and he'd never been known to get rid of anything—there would almost certainly be gunpowder.

Her pulse lurched. If there was gunpowder stored anywhere inside that house, when the fire reached it, the gunpowder would explode. The force of the blast would depend on the amount of powder and what it contained, but it was bound to be dangerous, even deadly. She reached for the walkie-talkie she carried to warn the others to get back.

But there was no more time. With an ear-shattering boom, the house became a giant fireball. The roof rose and disintegrated in flame. Fragments of burning shingles shot in all directions, sending out showers of sparks. They fell around her, singeing her skin and igniting tufts of dry grass that blossomed like glowing flowers as the fire touched them.

The breeze had freshened, driving flames and smoke to-

ward the hayfields. Tess still had the hose, but the faucet to
turn it on was too close to the burning house to be of any
use. She dropped it and began to run uphill away from the
fire, which was spreading fast, climbing the slope behind
her.

The Kubota was where she'd left it. Tess was headed that
way when she realized that if the fire reached it, the vehicle's gas tank would explode. She couldn't take the risk of
riding it. As the flames climbed higher, she did the only
thing she could do. She kept running, across the slope, into
the shifting wind, with the flames moving behind her.

As soon as the roof blew off, Brock knew that Tess was
in trouble. The fire was spreading fast. In the direction she'd
gone, there was nothing but smoke.

Running wouldn't get him there fast enough. He would
take his truck and do his best to stay clear of the fire. As he
sprinted to the vehicle, the rest of the ranch family was moving back, readying the hoses in case the wind changed.

As he vaulted into the driver's seat and switched on the
headlights, he heard someone shouting to get Tess. Then
he was gunning the engine, shooting up the dirt road toward
the burning house.

The explosion had blown the house apart and scattered
debris in all directions. With little left to burn, the fire was
ebbing there, but the flaming pieces had ignited grass fires
that were spreading fast. With luck, if the wind held, they'd
burn themselves out where the rocks crowned the ridge or
scour the sprouting hayfields and die on the edge of the
gully at the far end. Worse, if the wind strengthened and
changed direction, the people behind him could be fighting
to save their ranch and their animals, or even their lives.

But meanwhile, there was Tess. He had to find her.

As he strained to see through the billowing smoke, a
stray thought flickered in his mind. If Tess was the one

who'd killed his bull and made his life a hell of uncertainty, the fire could be doing him a favor. But what was he thinking? This was Tess, she was in danger, and he had to get to her. He could figure out her guilt or innocence after she was safe.

Before reaching the fire, he swung the wheel to the left and took a diagonal course up along the grassy slope. The engine roared; the oversize tires dug into the earth. Peering through the smoke, he could see the Kubota engulfed in flames. His pulse jerked. If Tess had been driving it—

But no—his headlights found her now, not far above him. She was coughing and stumbling through the smoke, barely keeping ahead of the flames. Unable to get the truck any closer, Brock pulled the handbrake, flung himself out of the door, and pounded up the slope toward her.

When he shouted her name, she turned to look at him, her hair blowing in the wind, her eyes bloodshot. In the next instant he'd scooped her into his arms and was striding back toward the vehicle.

She pressed her face into his shirt. Her body was trembling. Brock had never seen her act scared, not even after she'd fallen off her horse, landed face-to-face with a rattlesnake, and been stalked by a herd of bulls. But she was scared now.

He stopped on the protected side of the truck and opened the passenger door with one hand, sheltering them from the wind and smoke. Her feet slid to the ground, but she continued to cling to him, shaking and pressing against his shoulder. Her breath came in gasps. Through his shirt, he felt the dampness of tears.

Holding her released a wellspring of desire inside him. His arms tightened around her. "It's all right, Tess," he murmured against her hair. "I've got you. You're safe."

His thumb tilted her chin upward. Her face was streaked with tears and soot, her eyes laced with red. Her damp, swollen lips parted. When Brock bent and kissed them, they tasted of smoke and salt. She resisted for an instant, then responded with the hunger of a woman who'd been too long alone, whimpering softly as she stretched on tiptoe to deepen the kiss. Brock's body stirred and began to harden. But with the fire moving close, this wasn't the time or place. Right now, he had to get both of them to safety.

He ended the kiss and boosted her into the passenger seat. "We can take that up later. For now, let's get out of here," he said, closing the door.

By the time he'd walked around the truck and climbed into the driver's seat, Tess had regained her composure. She sat rigidly erect, her seat belt fastened. "What happened outside—that wasn't real," she said. "I want you to forget it."

"It felt real enough to me, but whatever you say." He put the vehicle in gear and stomped on the gas pedal. The tires spat dirt as Brock swung the wheel around and headed back toward the ranch.

"Is everybody all right at the house?" she asked.

"As far as I know. When I left, they were getting ready to fight the fire in case the wind changed direction. But now it seems to be blowing the fire back toward the hayfields. Hay is a lot easier to replace than people and livestock and buildings."

"I'm sorry about the hay," she said.

"It'll grow again. But whose damned cockeyed idea was it to have a party and burn that house without checking inside first? You're lucky there wasn't a propane tank in there."

"Since I wasn't involved in the planning, I can't answer your question. But the house was filthy inside—rats, cockroaches, spoiled food, and heaven knows what else. Nobody wanted to go in. As for the propane tank, there was one on the back of the house. But the propane company took it when nobody paid the bill."

Brock parked at the edge of the front yard. Tess opened the passenger door and stumbled out into the arms of her sisters.

The worst of the fire danger appeared to be over. The wind was blowing the fire away from the ranch, sending smoke and burning fragments over the hayfields. The stubble would burn, but the green blades should sprout again.

Tess's sisters, flanking her on either side, rushed her into the house, leaving Brock by the truck with his lips still tingling from their kiss. Something told him Tess would not want to face him anytime soon. And the rest of the ranch family was busy making sure the fire didn't change its path. It wasn't his job to lecture them about how the house burning should have been handled. It was time to get the hell out of Dodge.

After making his excuses and promising to clean up what little remained of the burned house, he climbed back into his vehicle and drove up the switchback road to the pass. Stopping, he climbed out and looked back over the ranch.

By now the fire was burning itself out. Seen by moonlight, the blackened hayfields stretched to the rocky gulch. But aside from burning an old wooden fence, the blaze had not touched the ranch. Brock had never been a praying man, but he murmured a word of thanks in case anybody was listening.

It was time to get back to the rest of his life—the mysterious clipping and the unknown stranger who seemed intent on ruining everything he'd worked for.

Was it Tess? The memory of that brief but torrid kiss still burned on his lips—even though, afterward, she'd turned cold again.

Did that flash of heat between them mean anything? Maybe he'd never know. But he'd be foolish to rule her out as a suspect. She'd had motive, means, and opportunity to kill that bull. But how would she have learned about his past, and where would she have found the clipping?

As he swung the truck onto the asphalt, he switched on the radio, tuned it to a classic '80s rock station, and punched the volume to the max to keep him awake. He wouldn't be home until after midnight. He was bone-tired. His throat burned from breathing smoke. His head ached from thinking in circles. And he couldn't recall that kiss and the feel of Tess in his arms without wanting more.

He'd been away from his ranch for one very long day. The worst of it was, he'd learned nothing. And for all he knew, another crisis could be waiting for him when he arrived home.

Tess sat on the edge of her bed, dressed in her softest flannel pajamas. Her hair had been washed in the shower, the spark burns on her arms, hands, and cheeks dotted with pain-numbing salve.

Now that the fire was out, the house was quiet. Ruben and Pedro had volunteered to keep watch for any flare-ups. Everyone else was settling down for the night. Thank heaven the danger was over and that the damage, which could have been devastating, wasn't worse. Now Tess's only challenge was to relax enough to get some sleep.

Mitch's photo, the one he'd had taken before he was deployed, sat on the nightstand in its silver frame—a handsome man with dark blond hair and sky-blue eyes that would never open again. As she had almost every night since she'd last seen him, she whispered a barely spoken *good night* and reached for the switch to turn off the lamp, then paused.

Tonight she had kissed another man—willingly and passionately. And not just any man. Driven by fear and relief, she had melted into the arms of her sworn enemy.

She had sensed that Brock was going to kiss her. She could have stopped him with a word or even a look. But she hadn't. She had just let it happen. And that kiss had reawakened desires she'd buried so deeply, and for so long, that she'd almost forgotten them.

Afterward, sitting in the vehicle, shame had washed over her like cold, muddy water. She'd made a fool of herself. Whatever had happened between her and Brock, she had to stop it at once. So she had.

But now, gazing at the image of Mitch's innocent face, she couldn't deny what had happened. That would be lying. All she could do was make sure her dealings with Brock were strictly business and that she never lost her self-control again.

Still, the guilt that tightened a knot in her stomach made her want to lay the photograph facedown so she wouldn't have to look at it. Instead, she switched off the light, crawled under the covers, and closed her eyes. But try as she might to forget Brock's kiss, it lingered in her memory as she drifted into fitful dreams.

As the night deepened, Lexie lay on her side with Shane spooned against her back. In the final weeks of her pregnancy, a good night's sleep was hard to come by. The days drained so much energy that she went to bed exhausted. But there was no such thing as a comfortable position. And even when she could settle, the baby's shifting and kicking kept her awake.

They had chosen a name for him—Jackson, the given name of Lexie's late brother, and Shane after his father. Jackson Shane Tully. It had a nice ring to it. But right now, Lexie just wanted him to settle down and let her rest.

Shane's hand lay on her belly, his palm cradling his unborn son. "Hey, I can feel him," he said, chuckling. "The little rascal's kicking up a storm."

Lexie sighed. "I wish it was you he was kicking. Maybe then I could get some sleep—not that I'd sleep anyway. I've been lying awake, stewing. What are we going to do about Brock?"

"Do we have to decide that now? We were going to wait till after the baby arrived."

"I know, but at least we need to talk about it. Between my family and your work, we don't get much chance for private conversation in the daytime. And at night, we're so tired that we just fall asleep."

"So let's talk." He kissed the back of her neck. "Tell me what you're thinking."

"I was just wondering why he came by today, with that bucking dummy to ensure his welcome. Did he talk to you?"

"Only to say hello. I had the impression that he was focused on Tess."

Lexie giggled. "Val keeps saying he's got a thing for her. Maybe she's right."

"Why not? Tess is an attractive woman. And a ten-year age difference isn't too much. Hey, if he were to marry her, we'd be off the hook. He could father his own heirs."

"I wish him luck. Tess hasn't looked at another man since Mitch was killed. This ranch has been her whole life." Lexie sighed. "That's one of the reasons against our going with Brock. Val's never been much of a cowgirl. Sooner or later, she'll leave with Casey. If we go, too, Tess will be alone here except for the hired help."

"She could sell the place, divide the money with you and Val, then travel, or live anywhere she wanted. Brock would buy it in a heartbeat. And knowing Brock, he'd give her a decent price. The man can be bossy and controlling, but at least he's up front about it."

"Is he? You know that letting us annex those hayfields, with him as owner, will give him the right of first refusal should Tess decide to sell the ranch."

"I know," Shane said. "That's why she took the contract to her lawyer. Brock's a complicated man. He can be unbelievably kind and generous. But you already know why I left him. I was tired of being owned."

"We'd all be owned if we moved to his ranch."

"I know." Shane's arm tightened around the curve of her belly. "But when I think of young Jackson here, and maybe his future brothers and sisters, how they'd be able to do anything they wanted—go to the best colleges, travel, choose any career, without the limitations of being poor . . . Lexie, we're barely surviving here. Tess pays me a fair wage for what I do, but we're not paying for rent or food. That comes out of the ranch budget. On what I earn here, we couldn't survive living anywhere else. And how could we raise children in this house? There's no room. Sooner or later, we're going to need a place of our own. The guest bungalows on the Tolman Ranch are big enough for a family. We'd have plenty of privacy. And with me working for Brock, we'd never have to worry about money again. I could even start that rodeo school I've been talking about. Students could fly into Tucson from all over the country and stay at the ranch."

Lexie lay still. Seconds crawled past before she spoke. "We don't have to talk about this anymore, do we? I can tell you've already made up your mind."

As the darkness paled above the eastern skyline, Casey sat up, rolled his legs off the side of the bed, and reached for the underwear and jeans he'd laid out the night before.

Val was already awake. Neither of them had slept much. "So it's time," she said as he maneuvered into his clothes.

Casey stood, easing his weight onto his right leg. The left ankle injury was already healing, but he couldn't take a chance if he wanted to be fit for the PBR finals in May. "You could come with me," he said. "It's not too late. We could still find our son together."

"You already know how I feel about that," she said. "There's a reason most adoptions are closed, Casey. If you find him, you'll understand why. Seeing him, knowing he belongs to somebody else, and that you won't get to watch him grow up, won't even know your own grandchildren—it will rip your heart out. Please, for the last time, don't do this."

He stood by the bed and looked down at her lying propped on one elbow, her fiery hair spilling around her face. He loved this woman to the depths of his soul. But the urge to find his son was a raw hunger inside him, too powerful to deny.

Lord help him if she forced him to choose.

"Come with me," he said.

She shook her head.

"I'll call you then."

"Don't call unless it's to tell me this is over."

"I love you, Val."

When she didn't answer, he picked up his duffel and walked out to his truck.

Before breakfast, with the help of Ruben and Pedro, Tess bucked Quicksand with the new dummy. The bull did well enough that she decided to try him this coming weekend at a town rodeo in nearby Gila Bend. The arena was outdoors, and the crowd would be small. Hopefully the situation would be less fearful for Quicksand than the big indoor arena where he'd frozen in the chute.

The Alamo Canyon Ranch would be bringing four bulls to the event. Quicksand seemed to get along with other bulls, but Brock had warned her about loading him in the trailer. Ruben and Pedro would work on that problem between now and the weekend.

Meanwhile, Tess had other concerns. The fire had left a mess. Brock had promised a crew to clean up the remains of the house, but ashes and debris were scattered over the pastures and ranch yard. The trash would need to be picked up and the ash hosed into the ground before it could harm grazing cattle. The Kubota was torched, so they would have to use the older pickup and throw trash into the back. The dirty job would start after breakfast.

Casey's truck was gone, Tess noticed. She could only hope that Val had left with him. But no—almost as if the thought had summoned her, Val ambled onto the porch sipping coffee. She looked frayed. Something must've happened between her and Casey. But never mind, it would take all able hands to clean up the mess. Val would be helping. Only Shane, Lexie, and Maria would be excused.

There was silence around the breakfast table. Val gazed morosely into her coffee cup. Shane and Lexie kept glancing at each other as if they were keeping a secret—a secret that was as plain as if they'd written it on matching T-shirts.

They'd decided to throw in their lot with Brock.

Tess couldn't blame them. Why be poor when you could be rich? Why worry about your family's future when they could be heirs to a ranch worth millions?

They had made the only sensible choice. Now it was just a question of timing.

Tess lowered her gaze and focused on finishing her eggs and beans. A day of grubby, backbreaking work lay ahead. For now, she would concentrate on cleaning up the fire mess and getting her new bull ready for competition. And she would try to forget that her family was breaking up, and that the person responsible was the man she had kissed.

CHAPTER 9

BROCK HAD ARRIVED HOME WELL AFTER MIDNIGHT. TIRED as he was, he'd taken time to check the mail that Cyrus had left on his desk. There was nothing from the mystery sender—just some junk, a ranching magazine, and a couple of bills. He didn't know whether to be frustrated or relieved. Maybe there wouldn't be another clipping or mailed message. Maybe one had been enough.

The next morning, he was up early, determined to get to the bottom of what was happening. In addition to Cyrus, there were five cowhands and a cook on his payroll. They lived in a modern bunkhouse on the far side of the stable. All of them, except young Jim, who'd signed on nine months ago, were longtime employees. Each of them had earned his trust—or so Brock told himself. He couldn't imagine any of them would have the knowledge, the skill, or the resources to find and send the clipping or kill the bull. But he had to start somewhere. Maybe one of them had seen something out of place at the ranch.

Without revealing his real concerns, he planned to make up an excuse to question each one. He would start with Mack, the cook, who'd be alone in the bunkhouse making breakfast at this hour.

Mack, short and burly with a dark beard, had been a cook in the army. He'd mastered the art of making cost- and time-efficient meals to satisfy hungry men. When he wasn't cooking, he did a good job of keeping the bunkhouse presentable. Brock found him in the kitchen, frying bacon in a big, cast-iron skillet. "Hungry for some real food, Boss?" He grinned as he turned over the sizzling slabs of meat.

"Another time," Brock said. "I'm just putting folks on alert. When I was in Cave Creek, I heard rumors of some wingnut protestors vandalizing ranches that raise rodeo stock. They may have even killed that good bull we lost. I don't suppose you've seen any sign of them around here, have you? Like maybe tracks you don't recognize or supplies missing, or somebody sneaking around at night?"

"Can't say as I have. But I'll keep my eyes open and make sure the alarms are set at night."

Brock thanked him and moved on. The next three cowhands, Williams, Curtis, and Morton, gave similar answers. They hadn't noticed anything unusual, but they'd stay alert.

Brock was most interested in talking with Jim and Rusty because they'd been with him at Cave Creek when Cannonball had died. They'd also been the ones who'd found the live rattlesnake in the trailer.

Jim Carson was barely twenty, a young man who'd shown up wanting to work hard and learn to cowboy. Brock had taken him in partly because he remembered another youngster who'd grown into manhood on the ranch—Shane Tully. Jim was milder in his manner, without Shane's drive. But he'd proven responsible, quick to learn, and cheerfully did whatever he was asked.

"I got up and checked on your bulls twice that night," he said. "I never saw a thing until I came out in the morning and found Cannonball dead. I'm sorry. If I'd seen anybody sneaking around, I'd have raised a ruckus."

"How about the snake in the trailer. Do you know anybody on the ranch who might've done it? Somebody with an ax to grind or just wanting to make a little mischief?"

Jim shook his head.

"No talk around the table? No complaints or bragging?"

"No, sir. Only thing I can figure is the snake was hiding in the straw and got forked in, or he crawled into that trailer by himself. But if you think there might be trouble afoot, sir, believe me, I'll keep my eyes and ears open."

Silver-haired Rusty McGill, Brock's senior cowhand, gave much the same answer. "I can vouch for the men," he said. "If any one of them was up to deviltry, I'd know it. But yes, I'll keep an eye out all the same."

"So did you see any sign of trouble the night Cannonball was killed?"

Rusty shook his head. "You know me, Boss. I sleep like a log and snore fit to wake the dead. I gave Jim the job of checking on the bulls. If he says he did, you can believe him. He's a good kid. I've never known him to lie."

Brock walked back to the house and sat down to coffee at the kitchen table. At least he'd gone through the motions of talking to the men. If he'd been hoping for a clue, he hadn't found it. But then, he hadn't expected to. He was just covering his bases.

"I don't suppose you've noticed anything suspicious around here, have you?" he asked as Cyrus set a plate of bacon, sausage, and fluffy scrambled eggs in front of him.

The old cowboy chuckled. "I wouldn't notice unless it happened right in front of me. I mind my own business. That's how I've managed to live this long."

Brock finished his breakfast and walked out onto the porch. Usually the sweeping view gave him satisfaction. This morning all he felt was frustrated rage. How could he fight back against an enemy that refused to show their hand?

Unless that hand was a kiss.

Was it really Tess who was working against him? Was she playing on his lust, luring him into her web like a female spider?

She had plenty of reasons to resent him—including his past treatment of her father, the partnership he'd forced her to accept, and what she would see as his threat to take in Shane and his family. So far, no other theory made sense. But he needed evidence, and he had yet to find any proof that she was involved in a scheme to ruin him.

Cursing under his breath, he paced the length of the porch. What he needed was a break to clear his head. Maybe he could take the Cessna and fly up to his lodge for a few days of trout fishing. Standing in a swirling creek with a fly rod had always calmed his nerves. But this time he knew it wouldn't help. There could be no escaping the worry that gnawed at his gut.

Stepping off the porch, he strode around the house to the stable. Jim was cleaning out the stalls, forking the soiled straw into a wheelbarrow. He glanced up as Brock walked in. "Anything I can do for you, sir?"

Brock hesitated, then shook his head. "I'll be taking the sorrel out. But go on with your work. I'll saddle him myself."

He led the rangy gelding out of its stall and cross-tied it while he buckled on the saddle and bridle. As was his practice, he slid a loaded rifle into the scabbard. Mounting, he rode across the yard and out into the pastures.

The morning was cool and clear, the grass damp with dew. The air rang with bird calls. Brock opened the horse up and let him run at a full gallop along the fence line and up to the east pasture, where the beef cattle grazed. These were steers, bought as calves and put out to be fattened until they reached market weight. Much as Brock loved his bulls, it was these beeves that kept the ranch solvent. Prime, grass-fed Angus beef from the Tolman Ranch always commanded top prices.

He paused at the top of a knoll, gazing out over the pasture and the desert that lay beyond the fence. Sunlight glistened on dew-beaded clumps of cholla. A jackrabbit, its mulish ears twitching, regarded him with curious eyes before it bounded away. As Brock inhaled the fresh morning air, he felt some of the tension leaving his body. This new threat would not crush him, he vowed. He was ready to go back and fight with all the resources at his command.

He was turning the horse to head back to the house when he happened to look up. Two thin, black Vs, etched like calligraphy against the sky, circled overhead.

Vultures.

Now there were three of them, then more, spiraling downward toward something beyond the next hill. Brock felt a cold tightening in the pit of his stomach. He urged the horse to a lope, flying over the uneven ground.

As he crested the top of the hill, he saw them—two steers, hopelessly tangled in the barbed wire of a downed fence. The hideous black birds were already flocking around them.

As he rode close, Brock could see that one animal was dead. The other one was beyond saving. Drawing the rifle, he fired a shot to end its suffering. At the sound, the vultures rose in a black cloud, circled, and settled at a short distance, waiting.

How long had the two steers been here? Twenty-four hours at least, Brock calculated. Long enough for them to die in misery. Just as vital was another question—how long had the wires been down?

Anger boiled in him as he turned away and studied the fence. The metal posts lay at a slant, leaving the loose wire, with its cruel barbs, high enough to trap a steer's legs. The animal's struggle would have made the tangle worse. The stakes had been planted deep in solid ground. A steer bumping against the fence wouldn't have budged them. To tilt them that far, they would have to be pulled at an upward angle—something that could best be done with a rope and a horse.

Brock scanned the ground but found nothing definitive. Steers, mounted cowboys, and wildlife had passed along this fence, leaving prints that vanished with time and wind. But he didn't need tracks to tell him that what he'd found was no accident. Someone was sending him a message.

Tess couldn't have done this herself. The time frame was wrong. But she could have had someone in her pay do it—maybe even one of his own cowhands. Or she could be entirely innocent. Brock's curses purpled the air. He'd fought his share of battles and won most of them. But this invisible adversary was driving him crazy.

He was going to need help cleaning up this mess and fixing the fence. Bringing his rage under control, he reached for his walkie-talkie and made the call.

Quicksand was the last of four bulls to be loaded for the rodeo in Gila Bend. At first he balked at the trailer and refused to go up the ramp. Tess feared she might have to give him a touch with the Hot Shot—a risky step that could add to the bull's stress. But then Ruben had an idea.

Lighting the bundle of sage, he wafted the smoke around and inside the entrance to the trailer. Calmed by the familiar scent, Quicksand allowed himself to be herded up the ramp.

"Make sure you take that sage with us. We might need it." Tess closed the inside gate, raised the ramp, and locked the back door of the trailer. Ordinarily, Ruben and Pedro would be hauling the bulls to this small-town rodeo. But Tess was anxious to see how Quicksand would perform— more than anxious. A better word would be *petrified*.

She climbed into the driver's seat and started the engine. "What will we do if he doesn't buck?"

"Why worry about something that might not happen?" Ruben responded. "Maybe he'll buck just fine."

They arrived at the Gila Bend arena in time to unload the bulls and give them a few hours of rest before the rodeo; bull riding would be the last event. Quicksand, first out of the trailer, bolted into the holding pen, snorting, tossing his head, and pawing at the bed of wood shavings. But the other three bulls, accustomed to the routine, seemed to have a calming effect on him. Once they were all in the pen, he settled down and nibbled the chow set out in one of the rubber tubs.

"Since we didn't have breakfast, I could use an early lunch," Ruben said. "There's a pretty good café in town. Want to come with me for a bite?"

Tess shook her head. "I don't want to leave Quicksand. You go on. Unhitch the truck and take it if you don't want to walk that far."

"You need to eat, *hija*. I'll bring you something."

"Please don't bother. I'm too nervous to swallow a bite."

She watched him walk back to the truck, unfasten the trailer hitch, and drive out of the lot. Despite what she'd told him, Tess knew that he would bring her something from the restaurant and watch to make sure she ate it. Ruben had always looked after her and her sisters as if they were his own daughters. In some ways he was more like a father to her than the distant, driven Bert Champion had ever been.

"So you're giving him a chance." The deep voice startled her. She spun around to find Brock standing almost at her shoulder.

"Sorry if I made you jump," he said. "I didn't mean to sneak up on you."

Tess found her tongue. "What are you doing here? Did you bring some bulls, too? I don't see them."

"No, I'm just here as a spectator." He put a boot on the bottom fence rail and studied the bulls with a practiced eye. "I was hoping to see Quicksand buck—assuming you can make him perform."

"He's doing better. Ruben and I agreed that a small arena like this one might be the best place to try him. But how did you know we'd be here?"

"I have my sources—Shane, in this case. When I called and asked, he told me you were planning to take Quicksand to this rodeo."

So he was communicating with Shane behind her back. Tess bit back a sharp comment. To react would only make her sound petty.

"It's a long drive from Tucson, just to spend eight seconds watching a bull buck," she said.

"Maybe that's not the only reason I came. I'd enjoy treating you to lunch. Have you eaten?"

Tess's pulse surged. He couldn't be asking her out, could he? But that was a joke. If he took her to lunch, it would only be because he wanted something.

"I haven't eaten," she said, "but I want to stay close to Quicksand. Anyway, I'm sure Ruben will bring me some food."

"Fine. But I want to make you aware of another attraction here this weekend. Maybe you've already heard of the McKennas."

"The name sounds familiar. But I don't remember where I've heard it."

"You'll remember after today. Ranchers from southern Colorado. Big extended family—aunts, uncles, and lots of cousins. Anyway, the three oldest ones, two boys and a girl, are taking the PRCA rodeo circuit by storm—saddle bronc and bareback riding mostly. And the girl's a devil of a barrel racer. But they can do other things, as well. They've taken home money in almost every event they've entered."

"Interesting." Tess was relieved that the subject had shifted to one they both understood. "Are any of them bull riders?"

"Not that I've heard. But you never know." He reached into his vest pocket. "I've got this extra ticket, front row, over the chutes. You can watch the events with me until it's time for your bulls. Here." He slipped the ticket into her shirt pocket, taking care not to let his hand brush her breast. "I'll be leaving you now. But if you get time, come up in the stand and join me. Give it some thought, okay?"

"We'll see." She glanced down at the stub end of the ticket protruding from her pocket. "But I've got to hand it to you, Brock Tolman. You know what it takes to tempt a rodeo girl."

By the time the rodeo started with the flag display, the national anthem, and a prayer, Tess was still wavering. Brock never offered anything without wanting something in return. But she was curious about the young rodeo stars. As the events started, she found herself straining to see past the fence and the bleachers into the arena. Finally, Ruben, who knew about the ticket, spoke up.

"Go on. If I need help with the bulls, I'll ask the chute men. That's what they're paid for."

"Don't worry. I'll be back in plenty of time."

He gave her a dismissive wave. "Go, *hija*. Enjoy yourself."

Tess made her way up front to the gate and presented her ticket. She'd always liked going to small-town rodeos. The people here tended to be down-home folks, friends, families, neighbors, genuine fans who went for the sport, not the big names or the glamour. And the cowboys and women who competed were in it with all their pounding hearts. It was at events like these that tomorrow's rodeo superstars got their start.

The women's barrel racing had just begun. Tess waited for the break between rides before she walked down the front row and took the empty seat next to Brock. He gave her a grin.

"I was wondering when you were going to show up."

"Like I say, you waved temptation in my face, and this rodeo girl couldn't resist."

It was always like this with Brock. Most of the time, she wanted to claw his mocking eyes out. But their passion for rodeo was like a bridge between them—or maybe a flag of truce. "Catch me up on what's happening," she said, gazing out at the arena, where three orange and white barrels had been set up in a wide triangle formation. Horse and rider had to gallop out of the gate, circle each barrel, and ride back. The winner would have the fastest time with no mistakes.

"You've missed the first two rides," Brock said. "The first out was a local high school girl. She did the course in a little over seventeen seconds."

"That's not too bad," Tess said.

"No, the second rider knocked over a barrel—that's a five-second penalty—so the first girl's in the lead, but that won't last. Look down there behind the gate. That's Miss Cheyenne McKenna waiting for the clock. And she's got a great horse."

Looking over the rail, Tess caught sight of a slim girl with black hair streaming below her straw hat. She was mounted on a small bay mare with sturdy quarter horse lines. An instant later, she was out of the gate like a shot, headed around the first barrel. The mare made up for its size in speed and sure-footedness. They rounded the next two barrels, cutting close, and rocketed back through the gate. The crowd cheered. The clock, which measured to a thousandth of a second, had stopped at 14.899.

"Now that's damn fast riding," Tess muttered.

"Nobody's going to beat that time," Brock agreed. And he was right. None of the next six women who raced came close to Cheyenne McKenna's time. Of course, the competition wasn't over. The women would race multiple times. The times for each race would be added up for a final score. But Tess had little doubt who the event winner would be.

There was a break in the action while the grounds people

carted away the barrels and groomed the surface of the arena for the next event. Brock turned toward Tess and cleared his throat. Tess braced herself for whatever was coming next.

"I hope you won't mind my asking you a few questions," he said. "I'm trying to get to the bottom of a mystery."

"That sounds interesting, but I don't know how I can help."

"You might be the only one who can. In Cave Creek, the night my bull was killed, you were asleep in your truck, in the parking lot, right?"

"Of course. You already know that."

"And did you see or hear anything—anybody coming into the lot or the pens?"

She shook her head. "I was exhausted. I slept through the night. But you already know that, too. I'm sorry I can't be more help. It was a terrible thing for somebody to do."

"But somebody did—somebody who hated me enough to kill a valued animal. I've made my share of enemies, but how many of them would know where I was going to be with my bulls? How many would know how to inject a bull with euthanasia drugs, and how many would have access to the pens without alerting security?"

In spite of the warm sun, Tess felt an icy chill. "What are you asking me, Brock? And why? Just come out and say it."

"I've tried to be a friend to you, Tess. But I know you have reason to resent me. Is your family still holding a grudge over that land I bought out from under your father? Do you still believe I'm trying to get my hands on your ranch?"

"You think it was *me*?" She was on her feet, outrage surging through her body. "Listen, Brock Tolman. If I were capable of killing, it wouldn't be a beautiful, innocent animal. It would be *you*!"

She turned to stalk away, but his hand caught her wrist in a firm grip. "Damn it, Tess, sit down. I had to ask. And you need to know where I'm coming from. If you go, I won't get a chance to tell you." He tugged at her hand. "Come on. If you go storming off, people will think we've had a lover's quarrel."

Still fuming, Tess sank back onto the bench. She'd enjoyed their brief camaraderie as they watched the barrel racing, but that was over, maybe for good. "I can't believe you'd suspect me of doing such an awful thing," she muttered.

"I don't know who to suspect anymore," he said. "It isn't just the bull—I've been threatened in the mail and in other ways. In Cave Creek, when the boys were shoveling out the trailer, they found a live rattlesnake. And just the other day, I lost two steers to barbed wire where a fence had been pulled down. No clue who's responsible."

"Well, it certainly wasn't me. If I were out to get you, you'd know it up front."

His mouth tightened in a grim smile. "I can imagine. You'd be a charging tigress and I wouldn't stand a chance. Sorry, but you can understand why I'm on edge. Can you think of anyone who might be out to damage me?"

"Aside from the usual suspects—like me?" She paraphrased the old movie line. "No. But then, I don't know many of your high-rolling associates. Besides, the snake and the steers could've been just plain bad luck. Call it karma."

"Karma? I've never believed in that mumbo jumbo," he said, "especially not this time. Will you at least let me know if you see or hear anything suspicious?"

"Maybe. Unless I'm better off keeping it to myself."

He made a grumbling sound and turned his attention back to the arena.

They made it through several more events, exchanging no more than a few comments. Tess enjoyed watching the two young McKenna men win their events—Reese in bareback and Randall in saddle bronc. But it was as if a cloud had drifted over the sun. She could feel the tension simmering in the silence between her and Brock. She had been totally honest with him. But his behavior told her that he didn't trust her any more than she trusted him.

She was relieved when the time came to ready her bulls for the final event of the day. Excusing herself with a murmur, she left Brock and made her way back to the pens, where Ruben waited with the bulls.

He frowned as she joined him. "I told you to stay and have a good time."

"And I said I'd be back here to help. Come on, let's do this."

They'd brought four bulls. Another contractor had brought two. They would alternate, with Quicksand bucking fifth. The sixth bull would be held in reserve in case a reride was needed. Tess could only cross her fingers and hope that wouldn't be necessary.

The first two Alamo Canyon bulls were rodeo veterans. They could be counted on to put on a good show, buck their eight seconds, and trot out the gate without a fuss. As Tess helped Ruben attach their flank straps, she could hear the cheers of the crowd as the team roping contest ended. An expectant silence followed as they waited for the most dangerous and exciting event of the rodeo.

The safety barrels were rolled out. By the time the bullfighters, dressed and made up as clowns, had taken their places, along with the mounted roper, the first bulls were in the bucking chutes, ready for their riders.

This was small-town rodeo. The prize money was lower, the bulls less spectacular than in big-time competition. But the riders were every bit as hungry—younger ones after their first taste of glory, older men with families to feed, some just needing survival cash till the next rodeo. Some were local boys who'd rodeoed in high school. Others followed the circuit, driving their old cars and pickups through the night from one gig to the next. It was a known fact that the single greatest cause of death among rodeo cowboys was highway accidents.

Tess took the end of the flank strap Ruben handed her
and fastened it on Quicksand's back. The bull was agitated,
snorting and slamming against the rails of the narrow pen.
Was he scared or just eager?

Tess patted his side. "It'll be all right, big boy," she murmured. "You're going to get out there and knock their socks
off!"

Herded into the bucking chute, he slammed and reared
while the young rider, a recent state high school champion,
tried to mount him. Tess caught the name—Rowdy
McKenna—from the announcer.

Only when a wedge was thrust against Quicksand's side
was the rider able to get a solid seat. Rowdy McKenna
rubbed the rosin on his bull rope as the chute men pulled it
tight. After wrapping the rope tail around the handle, he
moved forward, just behind his gloved hand, and gave the
nod.

As the gate swung open, Quicksand exploded into the
arena, leaping high, kicking straight back and up with a
twist of his hindquarters, then rising in front like a giant
wave of power and coming down into a spin. Young McKenna
was a promising rider, but at the six-second count, when
Quicksand made a sudden direction change, he lost his grip,
flew off to one side, and landed rolling in the dirt.

The scores were posted in seconds—no score for the
rider, 44.5 points for the bull. Tess was beside herself, jumping and cheering. But meanwhile, Quicksand wasn't finished. Lowering his head, he charged the downed cowboy,
who was scrambling to get away. One of the clowns, doing
his job, flung himself in front of the bull. After butting him
aside, Quicksand went for another clown, who escaped into
the barrel as the rider climbed the fence to safety.

By the time the roper's lasso settled around his neck,
Quicksand's reputation as a rank bull was assured. He trotted out the gate, head high, into the narrow pen where his
flank strap would be removed.

Tess fought tears as she unfastened the strap and sent her bull back to the pens. Her hunch had been right. Quicksand had the makings of a great bull.

Bursting with pride, she wove her way back through the chute complex to the bleachers. Right now, there was just one person she wanted to share Quicksand's triumph with— one person who would truly understand.

The fans were leaving now, gathering up their gear, their snacks, and their children as they made their way toward the exits. Struggling against the flow of the crowd, she climbed the steps to the front row of seats, eyes searching for Brock's tall form, broad shoulders, and black Stetson. Surely, he would be waiting for her.

Breathless with excitement, she reached the top of the steps and stopped as if she'd hit a wall.

Brock's seat was empty.

CHAPTER 10

BROCK SWUNG HIS SUV ONTO THE FREEWAY RAMP, gunned the engine, and headed back toward Tucson. He'd been surprised and impressed by Quicksand's performance and happy for Tess. But showing up to share her victory would only sour her celebration. There was too much conflict between them now. Too much anger and suspicion.

Had she told him the truth, when she'd denied having anything to do with killing his bull? Brock wanted to trust her. But right now, he'd be a fool to trust anybody—especially a woman he wanted as much as he wanted Tess. If he let desire cloud his judgment, he might as well be flying blind.

He'd told himself to forget that impulsive kiss. It had meant nothing—no more to her than it had to him. But even the memory sent a jolt of lust through his system. Proud, stubborn, passionate, impossible Tess. He wanted her in his arms and in his bed, her lithe, lovely body quivering as he pleasured her again and again. Just the thought made him ache.

But even if he could have her—which would be damned near impossible—he knew better than to let it happen. He already had enough trouble on his hands.

By the time he drove through the ranch gate and pulled up to the house, it was getting dark. He could see light through the windows of the bunkhouse, where the men were probably having supper. Brock hadn't thought much about food today, but as he opened the front door and the aroma of Cyrus's pot roast wafted out of the kitchen, his appetite came roaring back.

"That smells delicious, Cyrus." He tossed his hat onto the rack by the door. "Go ahead and set it out. I'll be along as soon as I check the mail in my office."

"Comin' right up, Boss." The old man's voice rose above the muted clatter of dishes and utensils.

Brock strode down the hall to the open door of his office and turned on the light. The mail was delivered to a box outside the ranch gate, where Cyrus, or sometimes Brock himself, would pick it up. Today, as usual, Cyrus had left the mail in a neat stack on the desk. There were a couple of catalogs, a utility bill, and a plain white envelope lying facedown. When Brock turned it over, his heart lurched. It was a perfect match to the envelope that had held the clipping— same blue ballpoint pen, same grade-school printing. Except for one thing. This envelope had no postmark. It had been put directly into the box.

Willing his hands not to shake, Brock used a letter opener to ease open the flap with a minimum of tearing. Inside was a single newspaper clipping—this one smaller than the first, as if it might have been a brief item from the inside page of a newspaper. It was fragile and yellowed with age. Brock picked it up carefully.

Ben Talbot receives three-year sentence.

Yesterday in Ridgewood County Court, Ben Talbot, the driver in the rollover crash that killed 15-year-old Mia Carpenter, was sentenced to three years in the Missouri State Prison at Jefferson. Talbot, who pleaded guilty to charges of drunk driving and negligent homicide, was led away to serve his sentence. Chase Carpenter, prominent Ridgewood businessman and father of the deceased girl, told the press, "Justice may have been served, but no amount of punishment will bring my daughter back to life."

Brock's appetite had fled, to be replaced by rage and a cold, sick dread. The worst of it, he knew, was that this harassment was far from over. Whoever was behind it—and he could no longer imagine that it was Tess—they wanted to crack him by degrees, little by little, until he was utterly broken.

Sitting at the table in his Tucson condo, Casey opened the manila envelope that Val had sent him last fall—the one he'd received after he'd learned about the son she'd given up. There were three things inside—the damning letter from Val's father, threatening to jail the man who'd gotten the seventeen-year-old pregnant; a photocopy of the birth certificate; and the Polaroid photo of an exhausted Val, cradling the baby she was about to surrender.

Casey pushed the letter aside. He already knew that Bert Champion had refused to let Val come home with her child. It was the other two objects that tore at his heart—the birth certificate, naming him as the baby's father, and the photo, barely showing a tiny rosebud face with a thatch of fiery hair.

It was surprising that Val would have been given these souvenirs. Maybe hospital regulations had allowed it, or maybe some kind soul had taken pity on the young girl who would never see her baby again—and due to complications, would never have another child.

All Casey knew of his son was in this evidence Val had given him. He had tried to be satisfied with that, but it had never been enough. After months of agonizing, he had contacted the detective who specialized in such matters for an exorbitant fee. The money didn't matter. Casey had been saving to buy a house, but finding his boy was more important.

He stared down at his phone where it lay on the table. Should he call Val and tell her his news—that the detective had received a copy of the adoption record, and that he now knew the names of the adoptive parents and where they'd been living at the time?

He reached for the phone, then forced his hand to stop. He had promised not to tell Val what he'd found. She wanted no part of it. As she said, she'd already suffered enough. That was why he'd left her at the ranch and returned to the condo.

Casey understood why she felt as she did. But even though his search had driven a wedge between them, he couldn't give up, not when he was so close.

He reached for the phone again, picking it up this time. Maybe if he could hear her voice—just talk about everyday things, like how her day had gone and how her family was doing, the awful sense of separation would ease. Maybe if he didn't mention his quest to find their son, things would be all right between them.

He scrolled to her number. The phone rang once on the

other end. Then he ended the call. He couldn't trust himself
not to give her the news. And that, he knew, would only
make things worse between them.

Val pulled the jangling phone out of her purse. Her
pulse quickened as she saw Casey's name on the caller ID
screen. But before she could answer, the call was gone. Had
he lost the connection? The cell phone service at the ranch
had improved since last year, though it still wasn't the best.

But she knew better. Casey had started to call her, then
had second thoughts. And she wasn't about to put him on the
spot by calling him back and asking what he wanted.

Laying the phone on the coffee table, she opened the
screen door and walked out onto the porch. The night was
warm, the smoke smell from the house fire still lingering in
the air. The rising moon cast shadows across the yard.

Lexie was stretched out on the chaise, her belly as round
as a bread loaf ready for the oven. The dog raised his head
and wagged his tail as Val pulled up one of the lawn chairs
and sat down next to her. The two women were alone. From
the house, she could hear the sound of Shane working out in
his weight room. Tess was doing some research on the office
computer.

"Did I just hear your phone ring?" Lexie asked.

"Wrong number," Val lied. But something told her Lexie
wasn't fooled.

"I don't even know what you're doing here, Val. You've
been wandering around looking lost while your man's in
Tucson with a sprained ankle. If I were you, I'd be on the
road to him, or at least on the phone. What's wrong between
you two anyway? If you need to talk, you know I'm a good
listener."

Val scrambled for a clever reply but came up empty.
Maybe it would help to talk. She'd already confided in Tess.

But Lexie, so close to becoming a mother, would understand as no one else in the family would.

She shifted the chair closer to her sister. Painfully at first, then spilling out of her, the story emerged.

Lexie reached out and squeezed Val's hand. "I want to cry every time I think of how hard it must've been for you. Dad should've let you come home. If he had, everything would be different now."

"I know. And I understand what Casey must be going through. But what will he do if he finds the boy? The adoption was legal. If he tries to contact his son, he could be arrested. And if he sees the boy and can't go near him or have any kind of relationship with him—Lexie, it will break his heart. And me—I gave up my baby to give him a happy life. And then I had to walk away because it was my only hope of finding peace. But it wasn't enough. I turned to drugs and alcohol and men to kill the pain."

Val's cheeks were wet. She tasted the salt of her own tears. "Casey wants me with him in this. But I can't walk away a second time. I can't go through that hell again."

"Oh, Val." Lexie's clasp tightened on Val's hand. "When I think about how awful it would be to give birth to my baby and then have him taken—I can't even imagine how that must have been for you. But think about Casey. You're both hurting. He needs you. And you need him. What good will it do if you stay apart and won't even speak to each other?"

Val stood, pulling her hand away. "I know you mean well, Lexie. But if Casey insists on going ahead with this madness, he'll have to do it alone. Maybe when it's over, and he's been burned and wounded by what he found, we'll be able to put the pieces back together. Or maybe we never will."

Half-blinded by tears, Val opened the screen door and walked back into the house. Her phone lay on the coffee table, where she'd left it. She picked it up. Maybe Lexie was right. If ever there was a time when Casey needed her, it was now. It wouldn't take much. All she'd have to do was scroll to his number, call him, and say the right words.

Could she do it? Could she support Casey in his search and risk bringing back her old demons?

For the space of a long breath Val stared down at the phone. Then she shook her head, switched it off, and thrust it back into her purse.

Quicksand's triumph was followed a week later by another high-scoring buck-off in Wickenburg. Tess was over the moon. The only thing she missed was sharing the victory with Brock, who'd told her that the one-horned bull was nothing but trouble. She'd have relished facing him and saying, *"See, I told you so."*

In the excitement, she'd almost forgotten the contract papers she'd left with her friend and lawyer, Andrea Simonelli. But the matter had been in the back of her mind, and she knew that the business with Brock and the hayfields needed to be settled.

While she'd been busy with the bulls, Brock, true to his word, had sent in a backhoe and a trailer to clean up the remains of the burned house. The scorched hayfields, given extra sprinkling, were already sending up new green sprouts. The fact that Brock had kept his promise improved the chances of her family accepting the contract and him—but surely Brock would know that. She'd never known him to do anything without a good reason.

Was that why he'd kissed her?

Tess forced herself to dismiss the thought.

The Monday after Quicksand's second rodeo, Tess phoned Andrea, who'd planned to read the contract after returning from her son's wedding in Utah.

Andrea answered the phone on the first ring. "Tess, I was hoping you'd call," she said. "Yes, the wedding was divine.

They're so much in love. I can hardly wait for them to make me a grandma. But now, about the contract . . . Yes, I've read it through. No problems there. I could mail it, but why don't you come by and pick it up? There's something I need to tell you, and I'd rather do it in person."

Intrigued, Tess took Maria's shopping list and left for Ajo. An hour later she was pulling up in front of Andrea's small company house with its garden of artfully arranged desert plants.

Andrea opened the door before she could ring the bell. "Come on in," she said. "I've made us some cold lemonade. We can enjoy it on the patio before the heat moves in."

"Before I forget, here, with my thanks." Tess handed her the check she'd written.

Andrea glanced at the amount. "But this is too much! You know I have a special rate for friends."

"You need to live, like everybody else. And I'll still be your friend."

"Well, thank you. I appreciate it." Andrea put the check aside and led Tess out to the patio, which was even more inviting than the front yard. The manila packet containing the contract lay on a round table next to a pitcher of lemonade and two glasses. Tess took a seat opposite her friend in one of the matching rattan chairs.

"I made a few comments on the contract." Andrea filled the glasses with lemonade and added a mint sprig to each one. "Mostly suggestions on the wording and a couple of questions you should ask before you sign. We can go over them if you like. But for the most part, it's pretty much a standard contract. I couldn't find anything in it that might have been added to trap you or take unfair advantage. It does give Mr. Tolman the right of first refusal if you ever want to sell the ranch, but you already know that."

"Yes, I do, although I don't much like that part." Tess sipped her lemonade. "Don't worry about going over the pages. I can read your comments later and call you if there's a question. What I'm curious about is what you wanted to tell me in person."

"Oh, yes. That." Andrea took a deep breath. "How well do you know Mr. Brock Tolman?"

Tess's pulse skipped like a needle on a scratched vinyl record. "I've known him since he conspired to buy a piece of land that my father needed for grazing. I've talked with him at rodeos, and he's visited the ranch a few times." Any mention of the kiss was definitely out. "And as you probably know, last fall, he forced a partnership with the ranch by buying my father's loan."

"Yes, you mentioned that earlier. So tell me, what do you think of him?"

"Arrogant, controlling, scheming . . . But he can also be generous, and I've never known him to break his word." Tess felt a shadow of foreboding. "Why are you asking?"

"Because I believe in practicing due diligence, I took time to investigate Mr. Tolman's background—insofar as I was able. He is every bit as rich as he claims to be, much of his wealth in stocks and in his ranch. And he has no arrest record—not so much as a speeding ticket."

"You sound as if something's wrong," Tess said. "What is it?"

Andrea finished her lemonade and set the glass down. "Just this. Until twenty-one years ago, the man named Brock Tolman didn't exist."

The mail usually arrived at the Tolman Ranch between 10:00 and 11:00. The box, a deep one with a locked door that opened from the back, was mounted next to the gate. Deliveries were made by a postal driver who deposited the mail in the box, then turned around and went back to the highway.

The distance from the gate to the house was about a quarter mile. When a sensor on the box sent an automatic signal to the house, someone, usually Cyrus, would take the four-wheeler ATV to collect the mail. At least, that had been the routine before the arrival of the envelope without a post-mark.

Now it was Brock, armed with a pistol, who picked up the mail. Every day, before going to the box, he checked the footage from the security camera mounted above the gate. So far he'd seen nothing except the mail truck and a few ranch employees going in and out. Even the twenty-four hours before the envelope had appeared showed nothing suspicious.

As the days passed and nothing else happened, the strain on Brock's nerves was beginning to show. Somebody was out there, somebody who knew about his past and hated him because of it. Whoever it was, they were taking their time and they knew what they were doing. It was slow torture, not knowing what to expect or how this was supposed to end.

He hadn't told Cyrus, or anyone else, about the contents of the envelope, only that it had contained a threat. He had locked the clipping away, with the earlier one, in his safe. But he couldn't lock away his nightmares—the pitching car, the crash that ended in blackness, then nothing until he woke in the hospital and learned that Mia had died.

However, he couldn't let worry keep him from running his ranch. He had bulls to send to spring rodeos. He had accounts and payroll due, which he preferred to handle himself, and he needed to protect his assets from this unseen threat to his reputation and the wealth he had built.

By now, Tess's lawyer friend should have reviewed the contract for the hayfields. But Tess hadn't contacted him. It was time he took the matter into his own hands.

When he phoned her at the ranch, she picked up on the second ring. "Hello, Brock." Her voice had an edgy quality. "I've been meaning to get in touch with you."

"Well, since you haven't, I hope you don't mind my reaching out," he said. "Did your lawyer finish her review?"

"She did. No red flags, evidently—just a few comments. We can go over them with my family before their final vote. But there's no rush. Maybe we can get together after the PBR finals."

She was definitely putting him off. He recalled their conversation in Gila Bend, when he'd implied she might be connected to his bull's death and the downed fence. He couldn't blame her for being angry. He should have held his tongue.

"I was hoping we could wrap this business up sooner," he said.

"I understand. But I need more time." She paused. "To be perfectly honest, I'm not sure I want to do it at all."

"What's wrong, Tess? Is it something I've done?"

She didn't answer. In the silence, he could hear the electronic buzzer that told him the mail had been delivered early today. But the trip to the mailbox could wait.

"I owe you an apology, Tess," he said. "I was out of line when I suggested that you might be trying to damage me. I should've known that you wouldn't harm my animals."

Her laugh was strained. "As I said, if I'd been out to kill something, it would've been you."

"So am I forgiven?" he asked.

Again, she paused. In the silence, he heard the sound of the ATV starting and heading out toward the gate. Had Cyrus forgotten that he wasn't supposed to go for the mail anymore? It wasn't worth stopping him, but the old man would need to be reminded when he got back to the house.

"You're forgiven," Tess said. "But I still need time to think about the contract. Signing would give you a lot of power over the ranch—maybe too much power."

Brock weighed his words before he spoke. He could hear the sound of the ATV fading with distance. "I'm already a partner," he said. "The contract won't change that either way.

But if—no, when—you sign, you'll have control over the hayfields. You'll have all the hay you need, for free. Besides that, I've promised a watering system for your pastures and a replacement for that old house. What have you—?"

A violent explosion from the direction of the gate, so loud that it rattled the windows, cut off his words. Brock sprang to his feet, the phone crashing to the tile floor.

As he charged outside and took off running, he could see a column of ugly black smoke rising above the paloverde trees that framed the gate. Sick dread congealed in his stomach as he braced himself for what he would find. Only a bomb would explode like that—a bomb most likely placed in the mailbox. A bomb almost certainly meant for him.

He could only pray that Cyrus had somehow been spared the force of the blast.

But that was not to be. As he neared the gate, he could see that the ATV was little more than twisted metal and melting rubber, probably from the exploding gas tank. Cyrus lay nearby on the ground, burned beyond recognition. Mercifully, he was dead.

Brock clenched his teeth to keep from howling like a bereaved dog. The old man had worked in his house for years. He'd been kind, gentle, and always discreet. The last thing he deserved was to die in such a miserable, meaningless way.

Fighting bitter tears, Brock cursed.

Men were coming from the yard, running toward him. Brock stood in the road and put up his hands as a signal to stop. "Go on back. There's no need for you to see this or to leave your footprints on a murder scene." He fumbled for his phone, then realized he'd left it in the house. "Somebody call nine-one-one. We've got to get the police out here."

Tess had heard the explosion, followed by the sound of the crashing phone. Her heart dropped. Brock had mentioned threats and mysterious sabotage. Was this more of the same? Could he be hurt, even dead?

"Brock, are you all right?" she demanded into the phone. There was no response. She ended the call and tried again. The phone rang several times, then went to voice mail. Worry growing, she left a message. "Brock, what happened? I need to know you're all right. Call me."

By the time she ended the call, Tess's imagination was running wild. She pictured him lying on the floor, bloodied and lifeless. The man had been a thorn in her side for as long as she'd known him. But what would her life be without him? Could it be that she cared more for him than she'd realized?

If Brock was gone, she would miss his ironic charm, his determination, and his raw, masculine energy. The world would be a less exciting place without him.

She remembered Andrea's revelation—that at some point Brock had assumed a new identity. She'd planned on confronting him with what she'd learned but wanted to wait for the right time. If Brock was dead, she would never know the truth. But never mind that, it was Brock himself that mattered. The thought of losing him tore strangely at her heart.

But for now, she was helpless. There was nothing she could do except worry and wait.

CHAPTER 11

ANXIOUS HOURS CRAWLED PAST. IT WAS MIDAFTERNOON, on a day of clouds, wind, and dust, when Tess's phone rang. Brock's name was on the caller ID, but that meant little. Someone else could be calling on his phone.

Heart in her throat, Tess answered.

At the sound of Brock's deep voice speaking her name, her knees went limp with relief. "It's really you." She struggled unsuccessfully to keep her voice from quivering. "I was so worried."

"I'm sorry, Tess." The mocking tone she'd grown accustomed to was gone from his voice. "It's been a bad day. A terrible day."

"The explosion? I heard it and thought—"

"Somebody left a bomb in the mailbox. It exploded when Cyrus opened it. He was killed—instantly, it appears."

"Oh, no . . ." Tess had met Cyrus only a couple of times, but now she remembered his kind manner. "How could anybody hurt that old man?"

"This wasn't about Cyrus. Lately I'd been going to the mailbox myself. That bomb was meant for me."

Tess stifled a gasp. "So you think someone's been watching your ranch—the same person who killed your stock?"

"I'd bet my life on it. The police have been here, along with the CSI team. They took Cyrus's body—it's a murder investigation now. The old man didn't have a family. I'm making plans for his remains here on the ranch. Would you tell Shane what happened? He'll take it hard. Cyrus was like a grandfather to him."

"Of course. I'll tell him right away."

"He can call me if he wants to know more." Brock paused. "You know I've invited him and Lexie to move to the ranch. But until this mess is resolved, I don't want them anywhere near the place."

"I understand. Neither do I." This was no time to discuss her issues with the move. Lexie and Shane would have to make that decision for themselves.

"That goes for you, too, Tess. I can't risk you or anyone in your family getting hurt because of their association with me. Stay clear of my ranch. And you mustn't be seen with me in public until this is over."

"I understand that, too. But what are you going to do? Did you tell the police about the bull and the fence?"

"No. I had to call the police about the bomb, but I'll handle the rest by myself. They'd only be poking all over the ranch, ruining what little peace I have left."

And they might be poking into your past, as well. Tess knew better than to voice the thought, but she had her own suspicions about why Brock wouldn't want the police getting too close.

"If you want to wait on the hayfields contract, it's fine," he said. "But if anything were to happen to me, you'd be out of luck. You'd be better off with the deal in place. If your family approves the contract, we could meet privately at that big rodeo in Las Vegas next weekend. You do plan on being there, don't you?"

"Yes, two of our bulls will be bucking on Saturday. Ruben and I will be driving Friday night to give them plenty of rest before the event."

"Providing things have calmed down at my ranch, I'll be staying at the Plaza. We could meet there, in my suite, and sign the papers. How does that sound?"

"Fine, so far. I'll have to let you know my family's decision."

"No problem. Call me when you have an answer. I've got to go now. Things are still pretty crazy here."

Tess heard voices in the background as he ended the call. She slipped the phone into her pocket, her head spinning as she tried to take in what he'd told her and what she needed to do.

Shane would have to be told about Cyrus. And sometime in the next few days, a family meeting would have to be held for a decision on the hayfields contract. The looming question was, how much should she tell them about Brock?

Once they learned about the bomb, there'd be no point in holding back about the other threats he'd received. But she would keep his name change to herself until she knew more about the reason. Before signing the contract—assuming her family was in favor—she would tell Brock what she knew and demand answers. Once she had them, she would make the final decision herself.

Brock's phone call, after the explosion, had shown her a more vulnerable side of the man. He had been shocked and grieving. And he'd shown genuine concern for Shane, for her, and for her family.

Before that call, Tess had assumed she knew all there was to know about his hard-driving personality. But she could no longer be sure of anything—not even her own emotions.

* * *

Three days after the explosion, the medical examiner released Cyrus's body. Two days later, in a brief ceremony, the old man's cremated remains were scattered from a grassy hilltop overlooking the ranch that had been his home.

To Brock's surprise—and worry—Shane had shown up alone in his custom van and allowed himself to be transferred to a new four-wheeler for the uphill ride. Brock drove the vehicle, with Cyrus's ashes, in a metal canister, on the bench seat between them.

On the way up the hill, there was no way to talk over the noisy engine. But on top, waiting for the ranch hands to arrive, they had a few minutes for private conversation.

"You shouldn't have come," Brock said. "You might not be safe here. After all that's been going on, I'm jumping at every shadow, never knowing what to expect."

"I wanted to come," Shane said. "Cyrus was family. You know how I loved that old man. I wouldn't miss the chance to pay my respects."

"You would've been paying your respects to me if I hadn't been on the phone when that bomb went off. Otherwise, I'd have gone for the mail myself. I can't help feeling guilty for that. Cyrus was one of the kindest, most honest men I've ever known. He didn't deserve to end his life that way." Brock gazed out over the pastures where his cattle grazed on well-watered native grass. "I know I invited you to bring Lexie here to see the ranch and the bungalows. But for now, until the person who planted that bomb is behind bars or dead, I don't want your family anywhere near this place. You shouldn't even be here now."

"So you said. Anyway, with the baby almost due, Lexie doesn't feel like going anywhere."

"Do you think she'll like this place?" Brock asked.

"Anybody would. But with a new baby, she'll miss having other women around, especially her sisters. Except for when she was in college, she and Tess have never been apart."

"Not that this is the time, but I'll be hiring a new cook and housekeeper. A woman or a couple might not be a bad idea." Brock gazed back down the slope. He could see the hired men coming up the trail on their horses. They were only a few minutes away. "How much have you told Tess about your plans to move here?" he asked.

"Not much. We're waiting until after the baby comes to make the big announcement. But something tells me she's already guessed—and that she's none too happy about it. If Val leaves, too, Tess will be left to run the ranch alone."

"I suppose we can cross that bridge when we come to it," Brock said, although he couldn't help wondering how Tess was going to manage and how he could involve himself.

As the riders reached the hilltop and dismounted, Brock climbed out of the ATV holding the canister. Since he wasn't much for speeches, he settled for going around the circle of men, including Shane, and inviting each one to say a few words if they wished. Most of them were willing. They mentioned Cyrus's friendliness, his wisdom, and his folksy sense of humor. Brock was fighting tears by the time the last turn—Jim's—came.

"If you wouldn't mind, I'd like to offer a prayer that my grandma taught me," the young man said.

The men nodded and bowed their heads. Some closed their eyes as Jim began to speak, intoning the words like an old-time preacher.

"Dear Lord, we give the soul of this good man into thy keeping. Welcome his innocent spirit as a lamb unto thy fold." There was more. He droned on for several minutes before ending with a theatrical "Ah . . . men!"

Brock removed the lid of the canister and shook it off the brow of the hill, letting the breeze carry his old friend's ashes out over the pastures. The men stood for a moment, then turned away and climbed onto their horses. Rusty was the first to break the silence.

"Say, Jim, where'd you learn to pray like that? You sounded like an honest-to-goodness preacher. You say your grandma taught you?"

"That's right. Grandma pretty much raised me after my dad died. She always wanted me to be a preacher. But I had my heart set on the cowboy life. I guess if I get tired of mucking stables and roping steers, I can always change my mind. Grandma would like that. She's in a nursing home now, but she's still pretty sharp."

The conversation faded as the men rode off. Brock climbed back into the ATV with Shane. "I'm taking you straight to your van," he said. "Then you're to leave and not come back here until I tell you it's safe. Losing Cyrus was bad enough. I don't want to lose you, too. If anything were to happen to you, I'd never forgive myself."

"Does that mean you blame yourself for what happened to Cyrus?" Shane asked.

Brock nodded. "Somebody's out to get me for something that happened in the past. If I'd gone for the mail that day, it would've been me, not Cyrus, who caught that blast. Whoever did this won't give up until they kill me—or until I stop them. So you're to steer clear until I do. You've got a wife and baby to think about."

Brock started the ATV and, with the engine roaring, headed downhill. Now that Cyrus had been honored, it was time he declared all-out war on the unseen enemy who could be watching the ranch even now.

With the bulls loaded in the trailer and Ruben ready to go, Tess took a moment to say goodbye to her sisters. As they did most evenings, Val and Lexie were sitting on the front porch, watching the blazing hues of sunset pale and fade.

"I take it you'll be seeing Brock," Val teased. "If he

makes a move on you, go for it. Something tells me that man could give you just what you need."

"If I see Brock, it'll be strictly business." Tess was grateful for the fading light that hid a rush of heat to her face. "I know the family gave me the go-ahead to sign that contract, but I still have a few questions for him. And if I don't hear the right answers, I won't be signing anything."

"And *you*, little sister." She turned to Lexie. "You hang on to that baby until I get home. There's no way I want to miss the chance to welcome little Jackson into the world."

Lexie shifted her position on the chaise. She looked swollen and miserable. "Don't worry," she said. "I'm not due for another couple of weeks. I'm sure I'll be here when you get home, still looking as big as a pregnant cow. But I do want you here, Tess. I want both my sisters here. Promise you'll be with me when the baby comes."

"Of course, I promise. I wouldn't miss it for the world." Tess turned to go. "I'll see you on Sunday. Wish us luck in Las Vegas."

"Bring us home some cash," Val said. "And remember what I said about Brock. Go for it."

Ignoring her sister's teasing, Tess strode to the truck and climbed into the passenger side. Ruben would be driving the first part of the night. Then Tess would take over. They'd both be tired by Saturday morning, when they reached the Core Arena where the event would be held. But they'd have most of the day to relax and doze before evening when the bulls would be bucking.

Brock had taken a suite at the Plaza Hotel adjacent to the arena. They could meet there to finalize the hayfields contract. As Tess thought about him, Val's teasing words came back to her.

"Go for it!"

Even the thought made Tess shake her head. The only man who'd ever made love to her was Mitch. So many years had passed since then, she'd almost forgotten what it was like. And with Brock? That could turn out to be the biggest mistake of her life.

They pulled into the parking lot at the rear of the rodeo grounds and unloaded the bulls into their pens. Across the lot she could see the long silver Tolman Ranch trailer with its sleeping quarters up front. So Brock's bulls were already here. Brock should be here, too. But he preferred a fancy hotel to roughing it, and he didn't usually come with the truck. Maybe he'd driven one of his vehicles or even flown his plane.

After seeing Ruben off to get some breakfast, she took a moment to splash her face with a water bottle and finger-comb her wind-tangled hair before she fished out her cell phone and called Brock's number.

"Tess. Are you here in Vegas?" His deep, velvety voice set off a sensation that was like being stroked. Tess willed herself to ignore it.

"We just got in and unloaded. Ruben's having breakfast. I'll be staying here with the bulls until he gets back."

"Have you eaten?"

"I'll just grab a power bar out of a vending machine."

"No, you won't. You need to take better care of yourself. Let me know when you're coming up and I'll order room service for both of us."

She hesitated, then sighed. She really was hungry. "All right. I'd be a fool to turn down a nice meal. I'll call you."

A few minutes later, Ruben was back. Tess explained where she was going, found her briefcase, made a quick call to Brock, and strode the distance between the parking lot and the towering hotel.

Brock had told her how to find his suite. Her stomach fluttered as the elevator took her higher and higher. Maybe this whole adventure was a mistake. She could have signed the contract and left it at the desk.

She found the numbered door near the end of a lushly

carpeted hallway. Brock answered and ushered her inside. The suite was modern in style, decorated in earth colors. Through the open door to the bedroom, she glimpsed a king-size bed, rumpled from the night. Val's teasing words came back to her. *"Go for it."*

Don't be an idiot, she scolded herself. *This is nothing but business.*

Turning, she gazed out through the floor-to-ceiling windows with their dizzying view of the city—a forest of lavish hotels and casinos with ant-size people bustling along the sidewalks.

"I'm surprised you don't get vertigo up here," she said, making conversation.

He smiled. Dressed in jeans and a soft, blue linen shirt, open at the collar, he looked as powerful as a sheikh. Blast it, why did she always feel so overwhelmed by him? "I don't mind heights," he said. "Maybe that's why I enjoy flying my plane."

"Is that how you got here from your ranch?"

"It is. With what's going on, I didn't want to be away from there any longer than I needed to. My Cessna's at a private airport just outside of town. If you're interested, I could take you for a spin after breakfast."

Tess shook her head. "No way. I've only flown a couple of times, on big airliners. I was terrified then. If I were to go up in your little plane, my breakfast would soon be in a paper bag."

"That surprises me. I've never known you to be afraid of anything, including rattlesnakes, bulls, and fire—well, maybe fire. Have a seat." He indicated a buttery leather sofa. "Breakfast will be arriving any minute. But I just made coffee and it's still hot. Want a cup?"

"Sure." Tess sank into the sofa. Maybe coffee would at least make her more alert after the long drive. "I brought the contract," she said, setting her briefcase on the low table. "There are a few things we need to go over."

"The contract can wait until we've eaten." He poured steaming coffee from a carafe into a white stoneware cup. His fingers brushed hers as he handed it to her, the brief contact like an electric spark. She lowered her gaze, adding a packet of creamer from the tray on the coffee table. "Did you bring Quicksand?" he asked.

"No. We talked about it, but he isn't ready. He needs more experience before he goes to a big rodeo like this one."

"Too bad. When he bucks, he's dynamite. He could be a real crowd-pleaser."

Tess sipped her coffee, which was very hot and very strong.

"I know. But if he freezes here, nobody will want to have him at their rodeos. Even as a stud, he'll be worthless."

"That's probably a good decision. Give him time to grow up. When he's ready for the big leagues, I'll be cheering the big bastard right along with you."

Their conversation was interrupted by the arrival of room service. The breakfast of French toast, crisp bacon, and fluffy scrambled eggs was delicious. "I hate to bring it up, but have you learned any more about that bomber?" she asked him.

"No. I'm cooperating with the police. They've analyzed the residue, but the materials were common. The bomb was a type so simple that a kid could make it. It was rigged to detonate when the box was opened. No fingerprints. The box was wiped clean. The bomber was likely a professional."

"So you've got nothing."

"Not yet. I've hired security guards, dressed as cowhands, to guard the gates. If anybody suspicious shows up, they'll grab him."

Tess had been wondering how to approach the issue of Brock's identity change. He had just given her an opening.

"Speaking of suspicious . . ." She hesitated, clearing her

throat. "Before we get to the contract, I need to ask you about something I learned from my attorney."

Did he stiffen slightly? Did a muscle twitch in his cheek? The difference in his expression was slight, but she could sense his unease. "Go ahead and ask," he said.

Tess shifted on the sofa to face him more directly. "As part of her service, Andrea, my lawyer, did a background check on you. She told me that—"

The ringing of Tess's phone interrupted her words. What bad timing. She was about to ignore the call. Then she saw that it was from Shane. "Excuse me, I've got to take this," she said.

"What is it, Shane? Is Lexie all right?"

"I don't know." He sounded shaken. "We're in Ajo, at the hospital. The baby's coming early, and there might be a problem. Her doctor's in Tucson, but we couldn't make it that far."

"How is she?" Tess could feel her heart pounding.

"Scared. Crying. The doctor's talking about a C-section to save the baby. Val's here. Lord, Tess, this isn't the way we planned it. We could lose our boy—or even lose both of them."

"Give her my love. Keep me posted. Oh, Shane, I promised to be there for her. I'm so sorry. I'll be praying."

Brock's face showed his concern. "Lexie?" he asked as the call ended.

"I don't know how much you could hear. It looks like the baby's coming early. She's in Ajo. I promised I'd be with her. And now—"

"I could take you in my plane, Tess. There's an airstrip outside Ajo. I could drop you there, and you could call for a ride to pick you up."

"You'd do that?" She stared at him.

"You're damn right I would. If Ruben needs help with the bulls, I'll see that he gets it. Just say the word."

Tess weighed her terror of flying against the need to be with her sister. There was no question of what her answer would be. "Yes, and thank you," she said. "Let me call Ruben. Then I'm all yours."

Tess made the call. "Go, *hija*, and don't worry about me or the bulls," Ruben said. "Just be with your sister. And give Brock my thanks."

Taking only her purse, she let Brock usher her to the elevator for the seemingly endless plunge to the lobby. In the entrance, Brock hailed a taxi and gave directions to the private airport where he'd left his plane. As the cab wove through traffic, Tess's fingers crept across the seat—and stopped. She could use some hand-holding, but if she wanted to deal with Brock as an equal, she couldn't let herself come across as weak and dependent. Not even now.

She thought of Lexie, in pain and terrified for the life of her precious baby—and Shane, as scared as his wife was. She needed to be there. She needed to be strong with them.

Please, Tess prayed silently. *Please let them be all right.*

The cab pulled up to the security gate of the private airport. Brock paid with his credit card, presented his ID, and escorted Tess inside.

The airport was small—a control tower, a fuel depot, a row of hangars, and a single long runway. Parked in front of the hangars were several planes, including two Learjets. They were of varying sizes, but all of them looked luxurious.

Brock pointed out one of the smaller single-engine planes, silver and black with a pointed nose, a streamlined body, and long, graceful wings. "That's my Cessna TTx. It should get us there in about two hours—less if we have a tailwind. Come on, I'll help you inside. The preflight check will take a few minutes. Then we'll be off."

Two hours. Anything could happen to Lexie and the baby in two hours. But there was no way to get there any faster.

While she waited in the cockpit for Brock to finish the pre-flight check, she put in a quick call to Val at the hospital.

"How's Lexie?" she asked when her sister picked up.

"She's stable for now. The doctor's consulting with her regular OB in Tucson. Until something happens, all we can do is wait."

"I'm on my way," Tess said. "Brock's bringing me to Ajo in his plane. He says we should be there in a couple of hours. Can you pick me up at the airstrip?"

"Sure. Call me when you get close. And tell Brock we owe him."

"I will. Tell Lexie I'm coming." Tess ended the call as Brock climbed into the plane.

"Fasten your seat belt." He glanced at her. "Are you all right?"

"Don't ask." Tess clicked her buckle as the plane's engine purred to life and began to warm up. On the inside, the cockpit reminded her of a luxury car, upholstered in leather with two more seats tucked in back. The control panel was like nothing she'd ever seen before. A screen, much like a large computer monitor, dominated the space in front of her. Brock controlled the images that appeared with a touch of his fingertip.

"Wow," Tess said. "It looks like something out of *Star Trek*."

"This system is a Garmin 2000," he explained, pressing in some data on a keypad below the screen. "I've entered our flight plan, and this screen is giving me all the information I need to get there. This computer could almost fly the plane by itself. It's even got autopilot."

"I hope you're not going to demonstrate," Tess joked in an effort to calm her screaming nerves. "By the way, I hope you have a paper bag in here."

"Pocket in the door panel. Relax, you'll be fine. Here we go."

The plane, its engine surprisingly quiet, taxied onto the runway. Tess had expected it to have a steering wheel, like a car, but Brock used a lever to steer. He was so calm and competent that he put her fear to shame. This was a man she could count on to keep her safe.

The runway appeared on the screen, with the front wheel aligned in the center. As the plane revved up to takeoff speed and began to climb, Tess's stomach started to flutter. No, she swore, she wasn't going to disgrace herself by getting sick in Brock's beautiful airplane. She would be fine if it killed her.

Brock leveled the plane off at 8,000 feet. The flight would be relatively short. No need to go higher. Cruising at 220 mph, he should get Tess to Ajo in less than the two-hour target. He'd fueled up at the ranch. There'd been no time to refuel before leaving Vegas, but with the plane's 1,200-mile range, that shouldn't be a problem.

He glanced at Tess. She sat rigidly in her seat, staring down at her clasped hands. He knew she was worried about Lexie and anxious for the trip to be over. But what a shame she couldn't relax and enjoy the flight, which would take them past the tip of Lake Mead and over the Grand Canyon, then follow the path of Route 93 as far as Phoenix before cutting west, over the Tohono reservation, to Ajo.

"We've got a beautiful view out there," he said. "You should take a look."

Making the effort, at least, she turned toward the window and gazed out for a moment before turning back. "It is beautiful," she said. "But all I can think of is how far we would fall if we were to crash."

"We'll be fine, Tess." Brock checked the gauges. The plane seemed to be using more fuel than usual. But there was plenty left to get to Ajo and back to Las Vegas, or at least to Phoenix, where he could refuel. A shadow crossed his mind—a vague sense that something wasn't right. Maybe after dropping Tess off, he'd be smart to continue on to the ranch. It wasn't that far. He could check in with Rusty, whom he'd left in charge. If everything was fine, he could refuel from his own tank and head back to Vegas from there.

For now, he would turn his attention to a more troubling matter.

"I have a question that needs an answer," he said. "Before that phone call from Shane, you mentioned something you'd learned from your lawyer—something about me. I need you to tell me what it was."

He heard the slight catch of her breath, but no answer came.

"Go on," he said. "Whatever it is you heard, I need to know."

"All right," she said. "My lawyer did a background check. Due diligence, she called it. She could find no record of any kind for you until twenty-one years ago. You didn't exist. I'm assuming you changed your name. Would you care to explain?"

Brock made a course change to avoid the air traffic over Phoenix, which would be coming up in a few minutes.

"Did you change your name?" she demanded. "I can't sign that document until I know who you really are."

"Who I really am is the man you see," he said. "My name change was legal, and I did it for a good reason."

"I need more than that," Tess said.

"I know you do. But it's a long story, and this isn't the time or the place. It'll have to wait."

"Fine. But I'm not signing that contract until I hear it all, and maybe not even then."

"Understood. You'll hear it." It was a story Brock had never told anyone. But if he wanted a future partnership—or anything else—with Tess, she needed to know. "Right now, I've got to fly this plane and get you to your sister."

He turned his full attention back to the controls. That was when he noticed the fuel gauge. It was dropping rapidly.

The plane had two fuel tanks, one inside each wing. As usual, he'd been pumping from both tanks at the same time to keep the wings evenly balanced. Now he switched the fuel selector to the left tank, then the right tank. Both tanks were almost empty.

Something—a tank, a line, a pump, or the engine itself, was leaking—so fast that, minutes from now, the fuel would be gone. The engine would stop, and the plane would crash.

There was no time to wonder what had gone wrong. He had to land the plane now, any way he could.

CHAPTER 12

FROZEN WITH TERROR, TESS WATCHED THE DESERT LAND-
scape rush closer, as if the plane were standing still and the
ground rising up to meet it. Her brain was still trying to
process what Brock had told her. The plane was out of fuel.
They would have to glide to the ground.

Glide was the word Brock had used to calm her. But she
knew what was really going to happen. They were going to
crash-land in the middle of nowhere. There was no guarantee they would even survive.

Brock was icy calm. He had radioed their position to anyone within range. Now he sat intent on the controls, using
the plane's technology to hold steady and adjust the angle of
the glide. On the screen, Tess could see the flight path,
marked by the plane's small front wheel. The ground, rough,
rocky, and scattered with thorny cactus, looked about as
hospitable as the surface of Mars.

"We're going in. Bend over. Protect your face and hang

on." Brock's voice was calm but terse. If he was scared, he hid it well.

The ground became a blur as the plane sailed forward at a downward angle that was almost flat. Tess felt a bump as the front wheel touched and bounced. Then, with a sickening crunch, the plane slammed down and slid forward, accompanied by the screech of more tearing metal. As the motion stopped, Tess lowered her hands from her face. Incredibly, she and Brock were alive.

He turned toward her, clearing his throat. "Are you all right?"

Tess was shaking. She swallowed, fighting tears. "I . . . think so. That was quite a landing. Thanks for getting us down in one piece."

"You can thank the plane—or the people who designed it," he said. "It was built to hold up in a situation like this—although I'm pretty sure we lost the wheels." His gaze narrowed. "Are you sure you're all right?"

Tess nodded yes, but that was a lie. She pressed her hands to her face as emotions welled inside her. Fear and relief burst to the surface as violent sobs.

"It's all right, Tess." Turning in the seat, he reached across and pulled her awkwardly close. His hands massaged her back. "It's okay to be scared. Anybody would be," he murmured. "But everything's going to be fine. I radioed a Mayday signal before we crashed. People will be looking for us—and they'll find us."

For a moment she let herself be comforted, leaning into his strength as her tears soaked his shirt. Then she remembered.

"Oh, no!" Her body went rigid. "Lexie—I promised to be there. Val will be waiting for me. I've got to call her!"

She whipped her phone out of her purse, then groaned at what she saw. *No service.*

The plane's control panel had gone dark, as well. Brock tried different buttons and switches and attempted to start the engine. Nothing worked. He swore, muttering curses that would make a streetwalker blush. Then he glanced at Tess. "Sorry," he said. "I forgot there was a lady present."

"Don't apologize. If I thought it would do any good, I'd swear right along with you. I don't suppose you can fix any of this."

"Not on this plane. I'd only make things harder for the genius that actually knows how it works. But don't worry. I figure we're somewhere between Phoenix and Ajo, either on the military range or the res. Either way, there'll be planes out there. We shouldn't be hard to spot."

"So what do we do now?" Tess asked. "Can we walk to a road and catch a ride?"

"We don't know which way the road is, and the sun's getting hot," Brock said. "We're better off staying here. There's a survival bag behind the back seats with a few water bottles, some energy bars, a first-aid kit, a flare gun, and a space blanket in case we need them. But I'm guessing we'll be found in the next few hours."

"And what about my sister and her baby?" Tess felt a surge of anger, even though she knew the crash wasn't Brock's fault. "At least if I'd stayed in Las Vegas, I'd be able to phone her."

His mouth tightened. "I know. And I'm sorry, but there's not much I can do. Until we're rescued, all we can do is wait and hope."

Standing next to the airstrip, Val glanced at the time on her phone. When Tess's call hadn't come, she'd decided to drive here and wait for the plane. But more than half an hour had passed, and there was no sign of it. Worry was gnawing at her, chewing on her nerves.

She found Tess's number. The phone rang several times before the call went to voice mail. "Where are you, Tess?" she demanded. "This is getting scary. Call me."

She gazed up at the sky, empty except for a dark-winged bird and the contrail of a passing jet. Maybe Tess had been delayed in Las Vegas or changed her mind about climbing into a small plane. Val knew she was terrified of flying. But if she wasn't coming, why didn't she answer her phone? Why didn't she call?

There was just one obvious answer.

Val felt fear rising like nausea. With one sister missing and the other undergoing a high-risk birth, she could lose them both.

On the verge of panic, she called Shane at the hospital. "There's no sign of the plane, and I can't reach Tess," she said. "How's Lexie doing?"

"The baby's in distress." Shane's voice was flat, his steadiness forced. "They're taking her in for the C-section now. Come on back, Val. One way or another, Lexie's going to need you. Tess will get here when she gets here."

After scanning the sky one more time, Val climbed into her car and started back to the hospital. She had never been the strongest sister. That job had always fallen to Tess. But it was her turn now. And somehow, she would have to find a way to be there for her family. If only Casey were here to lend her his strength. But Casey was gone, maybe for good. Any strength she needed, she would have to find within herself.

The Cessna lay belly-down in the long, shallow trench it had dug on landing. The front wheel had snapped off like a matchstick. The two taller wheels behind it had crumpled and bent under the fuselage. Aside from some scratches and dents, the rest of the plane was intact. But whether from the shock of impact or the lack of fuel to run the engine, nothing else on the craft worked.

The midday sun blazed overhead. Without air conditioning, the inside of the plane had become an oven. Brock had brought the emergency bag outside, passed Tess one of the water bottles, and laid the space blanket on the ground below the wing, which was tilted high enough on one side to provide a meager spot of shade.

The desert around them was adobe-colored sand, interspersed with clumps of sharp-edged brown rock. Teddy bear cholla, with barbed needles that could pierce flesh at the lightest touch, grew in abundance, along with prickly pear and a few lanky saguaros crowned with knobs of budding flowers. There was no sign of water, no shelter, and no shade closer than the distant hills. At least, in this open country, the plane wouldn't be hard to spot. But it would take a helicopter to land in this rough country and rescue them.

Tess, wearing sunglasses, sat on the silvery blanket sipping water, her back against the side of the plane. Damp tendrils of hair clung to her face. Her denim shirt was dark with splotches of perspiration. She knew this country. She knew what to expect and how to survive. Brock could only hope they wouldn't be stranded out here for long.

As he came around the plane, she shifted to make a place in the shade beside her. Brock ducked under the low wing and sat down. "Did you discover anything new?" she asked.

"I'd have to open up the wing and expose the fuel system to see the leak. That would do more harm than good. But one thing's for sure. This was no accident. Somebody's out to get me. I'm just sorry you were involved."

She shrugged. "How would they create the leak? Puncture the fuel line, maybe?"

"Most likely. Not everyone would know how, especially on a plane like this one. For that matter not everyone would know how to euthanize a bull or make a bomb. I don't know of a single person who has all of those skills."

"Maybe you don't know them. Maybe they're like some kind of hit man, being paid by somebody else—somebody who hates you and wants to scare you before they kill you. So the next logical question is, who could that be?"

Brock sipped from his water bottle and gazed out across the desert, where the sunlight cast mirages that looked like shimmering pools of water. Tess was making sense. Maybe too much sense. He didn't know who was after him. But he knew—or at least suspected—why.

"Come on, Brock, work with me," she said. "I know you've done some ruthless business in your time. You did it to my family when you outbid my father for that land."

"You're right," he said. "I have made some ruthless deals. It's called outsmarting the competition. But this isn't about business. This is personal."

Tess took off her glasses, wiped them on the hem of her shirt, and tucked them into her shirt pocket. Her serious gray eyes seemed to penetrate the depths of his black soul. "You promised me a story," she said. "I can't think of a better time or place than now."

Brock nodded, still hesitant. If he told her everything, he would be at her mercy.

"If you're worried about my sharing your secrets, don't," she said. "You have my word—I won't tell a soul."

"All right then." After a long, painful exhalation, he began.

"My name was Ben Talbot. My parents died when I was so young that I can barely remember them now. I grew up in the foster system. At eighteen, I was kicked out to survive on my own.

"I didn't have much going for me, but I was ambitious and wanted to make something of myself. I found a job as a lot boy at a car dealership—slept over the garage to keep an eye on the place.

"The owner, Chase Carpenter, was the richest man in town. He had two children. Jeff was a little younger than I was. Mia was about fifteen. His wife, Johanna, was a pretty woman, and nice enough, but I only met her a few times."

Telling the story now was like awakening ghosts. Brock

could see the sympathy in Tess's eyes. But that would be gone by the time he finished.

"I worked hard, and my boss seemed to like me. Over time I became close friends with his son, Jeff. You might say we were both a little wild, but the fun we had was mostly harmless. Jeff had this beautiful car—a black '95 Porsche 928. His father had gotten it on repo and gave it to Jeff on condition that nobody else was to drive it. Jeff promised, and he kept his word. I know because I begged him to let me drive that car, and he always said no."

Brock closed his eyes as the memories came rushing back—memories he'd almost managed to bury—until that clipping had arrived in the mail and turned his days and nights into a living purgatory.

"The night that changed everything was a Saturday," he said. "Chase and his wife had gone to the theater in another town. Mia was sleeping over at a friend's house. Jeff and I were out on the town. We ended up drinking at our favorite bar.

"We'd been there a while when the bartender told Jeff he had a phone call from his sister. Mia was in tears. Some boys had shown up at her friend's house with beer, and things were getting out of hand. There were only a couple of bars in town, so she'd tracked down her brother and begged him to pick her up and take her home.

"I left the bar with Jeff. We were both pretty drunk. Jeff had had even more to drink than I had, so I offered to drive. But there was no way he would let me, so I got into the passenger seat.

"Mia's friend lived on the far side of town, on a country road with a dry canal running along one side. We made it to the house. Mia was waiting on the porch. She got into the back seat and we started home."

Brock glanced down at Tess, who was sitting close to him to share their narrow strip of shade. He already felt drained, but the story had a long way to go. "It gets worse from here," he said. "I can stop now if you want."

She shook her head, the breeze fluttering a tendril of her hair against his cheek. "I need to hear this," she said. "Please go on."

Brock cleared the tightness from his throat. "Jeff was weaving all over the road. I heard Mia scream as a wheel caught the edge and we rolled off the bank into the canal bed. My head hit something. Then everything went black. I woke up a few hours later in the hospital. That was when I learned that Mia had been killed."

"Oh, I'm sorry, Brock. That must've been awful." Tess laid a hand on his arm. Her fingers were warm and lightly calloused.

"The first person who walked into my room was Chase. He shooed the nurse out, said he wanted to talk to me alone. He looked devastated—I could understand that. He'd just lost his daughter, and his son was at fault.

"I told him how sorry I was about Mia. Then, since I hadn't heard, I asked how Jeff was. 'Fine except for a few bruises,' he said. 'That's what I want to talk to you about. You were found lying on the driver's side of the car. Jeff told the police you were driving.'

"'That's a lie!' I almost jumped off the bed. 'Jeff wouldn't let me drive!'

"'I know,' he said. 'And I know it's a lie. Jeff had a bruise where the inside door handle on the driver's side hit his left hip, a perfect match. He was the only one conscious after the accident. I'm guessing he got scared about being blamed and moved you around to the other side of the car. I made sure he had a cover story for that bruise. But I've got a proposition for you. Don't stop me till you've heard it.'

"So I sat back and listened," Brock said. "And what he offered me was so unreal that I thought I might be hallucinating.

"'My wife just lost her child,' he said. 'It would kill her

to know that Jeff was responsible—especially if he had to go to prison, which he likely would. And Jeff is my only son—he's got a great life all mapped out. He's been accepted by two Ivy League colleges, wants to be a lawyer. None of this would be possible for an ex-convict.'

"I was beginning to get his drift," Brock said. "But even when I heard the words, I could scarcely believe them. 'I'm offering you a hundred thousand dollars to take the blame for the accident and Mia's death,' he said. 'Plead guilty to the charges, serve your sentence, and the money will be waiting for you when you get out.'

"The answer came to me in a flash. 'I'll do it on one condition,' I told him. 'I want the money now—in cash.'"

Tess was staring at him. "So you took it."

"I took it. It was my only chance to get ahead. Before my trial I put the money in a safe deposit box. Then I pled guilty and served my sentence. Prison was no picnic, as you can imagine. But I kept to myself and learned to be tough with bullies. In my spare time, I studied investing. I devoured every book and magazine I could get my hands on. I lived in the library, even took an online business course. The prison encouraged that sort of thing—I was lucky. When my sentence was up, I changed my name, took that money, and started investing. Between what I'd learned and a natural talent that surprised even me, I started making good money. It took time, and frugal living, but after about ten years, I finally had what I needed to retire and buy the ranch."

Tess had drawn away from him. "That's incredible. But I can't believe that what you did was legal."

Brock took a deep breath before answering.

"I won't try to whitewash what I did, Tess. Lying to the court was the worst of it, even though the statute of limitations is up now. But I thought I was helping Jeff's family—at least that's what I told myself at the time. And, of course, I was helping myself, too."

She'd gone cold. He could tell by her stony expression.

Honor and integrity were woven into the fabric of Tess's being. She would never understand how a young man, desperate for the chance to better himself, could have done what he did.

"I need to stretch my legs." She pushed to her feet and jammed her sunglasses back into place. "Don't worry, I won't be long."

"Be careful," Brock called as she vanished around the plane. It was a needless warning. Tess had grown up in this country. She knew all about cholla spines, fire ants, and rattlesnakes. But maybe not enough about men like him, who were accustomed to taking what they wanted.

With a muttered curse, he gazed at the brutal sky. He couldn't change his past or the kind of man he'd become—not even for Tess. If she couldn't accept him, he was out of luck. And that was too bad, because of all the women he'd known, Tess Champion was the one he wanted to keep.

Tess stood still, gazing up at the sky, wishing for a miracle—a plane that would see the wreck, or better yet, a helicopter that would pick her up and take her to the hospital. For all she knew, Lexie could have had the baby by now. Everything could be fine. Or something could have gone wrong, and her family might be facing a tragedy. She had never felt more helpless in her life.

A collared lizard scampered across her boot. She watched it dart into a clump of brittlebush, out of the hot sun. It was time she returned to Brock—to hear the rest of his story and fight the urge to sympathize. He didn't deserve her sympathy for what he'd done. But what she couldn't help wanting to give him was deeper than sympathy.

She recalled sitting next to him, the emotion in his voice as he ripped open his past. She'd fought the impulse to take his hand and lay her head on his shoulder. Brock Tolman wasn't a very good man. But the way he'd revealed himself to her—raw and real—had touched her in a surprising way.

For years, she'd kept Mitch's photo on her nightstand, telling herself that no one could compare to him. He'd been her only love, and she would never find anyone to take his place. Then Brock had stormed into her life—brash, forceful, and infuriating, yet surprisingly tender. He had touched buried responses that were more than just physical, making her feel alive in ways she'd all but forgotten.

Heaven help her, was she falling in love with him?

But that wasn't going to happen. She was a sensible woman. And falling for a man like Brock would be the most foolish mistake of her life.

She would hear the rest of his story and take it as a cautionary tale—a reminder of what kind of man she was dealing with and what he was capable of. Then she would act in the best interests of her family and her ranch.

She walked back around the plane, sat down beside Brock, and took a few careful sips from the water bottle he handed her. They both knew better than to drink too much. They could be stranded here for longer than they'd hoped.

"See anything?" He stretched his legs to the edge of the blanket.

"Not in the sky. At least the buzzards aren't circling us yet. But to take up where we left off, I have one question. Do the attacks on your property and your life have anything to do with the story you just told me?"

"I believe they have everything to do with it."

She stared at him. "But how do you know that?"

He told her then about the mysterious clippings that had arrived in the mail. "At first I thought it was just a matter of someone wanting money—that was when I started taking steps to protect my assets. But when no demand came, and things started happening, I realized it wasn't cash they wanted. It was revenge."

"But you did the family a favor by keeping your friend Jeff out of prison," she said.

"I thought so at the time—not that Jeff was my friend after that. We never spoke to each other again."

"Could it be Jeff who wants you out of the picture, to protect himself? How many people knew the truth about the accident?"

"Besides me, only Chase and Jeff. And it doesn't make sense that either one would share the story. They both had too much to lose."

"So where are they now?"

"Both dead. Chase died of cancer while I was in prison.

Jeff got his law degree, married, and had a son. Then things fell apart. He started drinking heavily, lost his family, and finally committed suicide—shot himself on a boat and fell into the water. His body was never found, but he left plenty of evidence behind. I read about it after it happened."

"What about Jeff's wife? Maybe he told her."

"Evidently she left him. I was told by an old acquaintance that she was dead, but that's all I know."

"And the son?"

"He went to live with a relative. Again, that's all I know. But why would anybody who knew the truth want to track me down and harm me? I took the blame for Jeff's mistake. I made it possible for him to get on with his life. What happened to him afterward was his doing, not mine."

"Maybe Jeff faked his death. Maybe he wants to silence the last person who knows that he was guilty."

"You've been watching too many TV crime shows, lady." Brock stirred, suddenly restless. Telling Tess his story had forced him to relive everything that had happened on that awful night and afterward. Worse, the story had lent her a degree of power that he'd never given to anyone else— power over his very life.

What had made him believe he could trust her with that power? What if he had just made a very foolish mistake?

He pushed to his feet. "I'm going back into the plane to take another look at the radio," he said. "Who knows, maybe I can get something to work. If you see or hear a search plane, fire the flare gun."

"I'll do that," she said. "But before you go, I have one last question for you. We talked about people who might have known the truth about you. What about the people who *didn't* know the truth—the ones who believed the lie, and still believe it to this day?"

The question struck Brock like a kick in the ribs. Tess had raised a valid point—something he should have thought of himself. But it cast a net of suspicion over the whole community of Ridgewood—all the people who had known, and might have loved, Mia Carpenter.

Mia had been a beautiful young girl, just coming into the full bloom of womanhood. Brock—as Ben—had been aware that Jeff's sister had a schoolgirl crush on him. He'd been flattered, but he'd known enough to keep his distance. Maybe some other boy—or man—had loved her and carried his grief all these years—and even saved the clippings related to the accident. Maybe, not long ago, they'd recognized Brock from a newspaper or magazine photo and decided to act.

The idea made sense. But if it was correct, he was back to square one. He had no idea who was trying to destroy his life. He only knew that somehow they had to be stopped.

Val walked out of the hospital room, her knees shaking with relief. Lexie was awake and smiling. And young Jackson, after a harrowing birth by C-section, was wailing at the top of his lungs. He was small—barely six pounds—but healthy and beautiful, sporting an unruly thatch of dark hair.

Too emotional to walk steadily, Val leaned against a wall. Her eyes stung with bitter tears. She'd been frightened and worried during the procedure, and relieved when it was over. But what tore at her heart was the moment when the nurse had placed the baby in Lexie's arms. The memory had come crashing in on her—holding the tiny, red-haired boy for the few moments she was allowed, then sobbing into her pillow after he was taken away forever.

She thought of Casey, searching for the son he'd never known. How could she blame him for yearning to find that missing part of himself? How could she judge him when, right now, all she wanted to do was call and tell him that she'd been wrong—that she understood and supported him.

Impulsively, she found her phone and scrolled to his number, then paused. This was no time for a rash decision. She was too emotional about the baby and too worried about Tess. Calling Casey would have to wait until she knew her own mind.

Shane was in the room with his new family. He and Val had agreed not to tell Lexie that Tess's plane was overdue. That could wait until she was stronger. Maybe by then there'd be good news.

But when it came to good news, Val was skeptical. She'd had too much bad news in her life to be a bubbling optimist. She would hope for the best but brace for the worst. It was all she could do.

CHAPTER 13

*T*HE SUNSET HAD DEEPENED INTO TWILIGHT. STILL THERE was no sign of rescue. Tess and Brock had spent much of the afternoon gathering dry wood to make a fire. Bending over in the hot sun, picking up prickly cactus and dead brush with their bare hands, had left them both sore and tired, but they'd kept at it until the light faded and the air turned chill. By then they had a three-foot stack of kindling piled at a safe distance from the airplane.

The plan was to build a small fire in a shallow pit and feed it through the night. If they heard or saw what might be a search plane, they would pile on more wood and shoot off the flare gun. Meanwhile, the fire would lend some warmth and discourage coyotes, javelinas, and other nighttime visitors.

Even with the fire crackling, the night was chilly. They moved the blanket closer, opened two more water bottles, and divided a chocolate peanut energy bar between them.

"This isn't bad," Brock said, unwrapping his half of the

bar. "But when we get back to civilization, I'm taking you out for the juiciest, tenderest prime steak in the whole damned country."

"Right now, I'd settle for a platter of nachos at Lefty's."

Tess studied the way the firelight enhanced his chiseled face and brought out the shadow of beard that had darkened during the day. His free hand rested on his knee, the rolled-up sleeve exposing a tanned forearm sprinkled with black hair. She recalled the night when he'd danced with her, his strong arms around her, his body brushing hers, setting off forbidden tingles all the way down to her thighs.

That night had awakened responses she'd buried when Mitch died.

She checked the impulse to reach for his hand. She'd only end up making a fool of herself. Brock was a compellingly attractive man, and he wouldn't be above seeing the gesture as an invitation. But he wasn't a keeper. Domesticating him would be like trying to keep a wild leopard in the house.

And right now, Brock was the least of her worries.

"What are you thinking, Tess?" His voice, close to her ear, was like rough velvet.

She gave him a faint smile. "Just the usual questions. Is Lexie all right? Is my family worried about me? Will we ever be rescued, or will some traveler find our bones next to what's left of a rusted plane?"

"Let me try to answer your questions," he said. "First, we know that Lexie and her baby are in skilled hands. All we can do is hope for the best. Second, of course your family is worried about you. They love you. And third, this isn't the Sahara Desert. People will be looking for us—I can promise you they'll find us. And just so you'll know, the plane won't rust. It's made of a high-tech composite that will probably last forever. Did that help?"

Tess gazed into the flames. "Not really. But thank you for trying."

"Tess, Tess!" He slipped a companionable arm around her shoulders. "I love your honesty—among other things. You're an amazing woman."

Tess willed herself to ignore the words. They were only Brock's way of joking.

"You're shivering," he said.

"I know. It's getting cold, and we mustn't waste wood on a bigger fire. Too bad neither of us brought a coat."

"Too bad? I wouldn't say that." He wrapped his arms around her and pulled her close, cradling her like a child. His body was warm through the light linen shirt he wore. Turning in his arms, she rested her head against his chest. The sound of his heart, beating close to her ear, was strong and steady.

"How's that? Better?"

"Better."

"Not shivering anymore?"

She shook her head. His shirt smelled of sweat and sagebrush. She closed her eyes, letting the rich, masculine scent flow through her. Slowly she began to relax.

"Sleep if you feel like it," he said. "I'll keep watch and wake you if anything happens."

"I'll be fine. I just want to be warm." As the minutes passed, Tess became aware that she was anything but sleepy. With his closeness seeping into her senses, her heart had quickened to a gallop. Desire pulsed in the depths of her body, growing warmer and more urgent. Could he tell?

They had both fallen silent. She could hear his deepening breath. His hand ranged down the curve of her spine, seeking the loose hem of her shirt. A little gasp escaped her mouth as his fingers splayed on bare skin and moved up to find the clasp of her bra.

"If you're going to stop me, do it now," he muttered. "I want you, Tess. But I want you willing."

A dim inner voice whispered that stopping would be wise. But this was no time for wisdom. Tess was on fire. She raised her head for his kiss, her response telling him all he needed to know.

Her bra fell loose. The hand that had freed the clasp slid up to cup her breast, his thumb stroking her sensitive nipple. A moan formed in Tess's throat as she arched upward. Not until now had she realized how much she wanted him to touch her—how much she wanted to touch him.

Unbidden, she tugged at his belt buckle. Brock opened the way for her to find him. She gasped as her fumbling fingers closed around him. He was big and rock solid, heavy against her hand.

"Tell me where you want it, Tess." His voice was a whispered growl. "Tell me what you want me to do."

Leaning close to him, she spoke into his ear, using words she'd never thought she'd speak aloud. Just saying them aroused her.

He chuckled. "You've got it, lady, but not yet. We've got time." Removing her hand, he laid her on her back, stretched out next to her on his side, and unbuttoned her shirt to bare both her breasts. Her hands clasped his shoulders, fingers kneading his muscles as he sucked her. The sensation was slow, delicious torture.

"Please . . ." Her hips butted against him as the hunger welled in her. She wanted him. Now.

"Getting impatient, are you?" There was a teasing note in his voice. "Not that I mean to rush you."

"Blast you, Brock Tolman . . ." His kiss stopped her words. Skilled fingers reached down to unfasten her jeans and peel them down off her ankles, along with her panties and boots. His kisses worked their way down her belly until his face was buried between her thighs.

"Oh . . ." This was new, the pleasure so exquisite that she almost screamed. She gasped and shuddered, then lay trembling as he drew back, took a moment to protect her.

Braced on his forearms, he leaned over her. His dark eyes, reflecting golden sparks of firelight, gazed down into hers. "This is real, Tess. Whatever you're thinking, I want you to know that."

With one long thrust, he pushed into her, filling all the hungry, hollow places whose existence she'd denied over the years. She welcomed him with her whole body, her legs wrapping his hips, holding him deep. This was Brock, her adversary, her nemesis, the one man who could make her want him.

Their movement, when it began, was driven by urgent need, a wild, churning ride that carried her to a climax that was like the bursting of a thousand stars. He moaned, shuddered, and lay back, still holding her. For now, neither of them spoke. Words would only complicate things.

Tess sat dozing, her head sagging against Brock's shoulder. The late-night air was chilly. The inside of the Cessna was a little warmer, but there was nowhere to lie down and no way to watch for a passing plane. Earlier, they'd tried taking turns, one keeping watch and tending the fire while the other one rested, or tried to. But as the night wore on, they'd abandoned that plan and gone back to sitting together on the blanket with their backs against the fuselage.

Their conversation had been awkward, consisting mostly of small talk, avoiding the subject of where to go after their explosive lovemaking. It was as if they'd assumed a silent understanding—with so many dangers and troubles hanging in the balance, this was no time to chart the future of their relationship. Whatever was to happen would happen—even if it was nothing.

"Look—a falling star," Brock said.

Tess glanced up. "Oh—too late, I missed it."

"There should be more tonight. Yesterday I heard something on the news about a meteor shower. Are you up for watching with me? Or would you rather sleep?"

"I'll watch with you. Maybe I'll even make a few wishes."

He circled her shoulders with one arm. She nestled into his warmth as another meteor streaked across the sky and burned out over the distant hills.

"Did you wish on that one?" he asked.

"I didn't have time. They come and go so fast. I'll try to catch the next one."

"So what would you wish for, Tess?"

"First, I'd wish for Lexie and her baby to be all right. Then I'd wish for someone to rescue us. After that . . . maybe for you to find the person who's been causing so much trouble and stop them from ever hurting anyone again."

"Amen to that."

She sat in silence, enjoying his warmth and the smoky sage aroma of his shirt as meteors streaked across the sky. "What about your ex-wife?" she asked as the thought struck her.

"What?" He gave her a sharp, sideways look.

"Shane mentioned that you'd been married. Did your wife know about your past? Would she have any reason to want you hurt?"

Brock shook his head. "I met Ashley at a party, years after I'd gotten out of prison and changed my name. I never told her about my past—which might have been a mistake. She was a pretty little thing, more of an ornament than a partner. When I proved too busy to pay enough attention to her, she had an affair. We decided to end the marriage before things got ugly. I gave her a decent settlement. She remarried soon after that, and I lost track of her. End of story."

"So there's no way you'd suspect her?"

"Even if she had a reason, killing a bull and planting a bomb wouldn't be her style. She'd be more likely to come after me with a team of lawyers."

"So we can cross her off your list of suspects?"

"So far, I don't even have a list of suspects." He paused,

suddenly alert. "*Shhh*—there's something out there, beyond the light. Do you hear it?"

As Tess listened, her ears caught a faint but familiar snuffling, squealing sound. "Javelinas. They're probably just curious. Or they think we might have food."

Tourists tended to think the bristly, pig-like animals, who roamed like gangs of street toughs, were cute. But javelinas had sharp tusks, nasty dispositions, and little fear of humans. They were not to be trifled with—and these were coming closer.

"I'll see if I can scare them off." Brock bent to gather a few rocks. "Stay back—or get in the plane."

"Not on your life. I'll be right there with you." Tess glanced around for anything that might deter the animals. The orange plastic single-shot flare gun was lying on the blanket, loaded and within easy reach. It wasn't really a weapon, but if fired, the noise and the light might be enough to scare the four-footed hooligans.

She paused to toss a dry branch onto the smoldering fire. Then, gripping the flare gun, she hurried after Brock.

In the moonlit darkness, she could see the javelinas, five or six of them, milling a few yards outside the circle of firelight. They were big bruisers, numerous enough to take on anything, even a man. Maybe she and Brock should both have fled into the plane. But then they could be trapped in there for hours, unable to tend the fire or spot and signal a rescuer. They needed to drive the animals away.

"Hah! Get out of here!" Brock charged, flinging rocks that found their targets but did little damage. Tess ran alongside him, shouting at the top of her lungs. The javelinas scattered but soon regrouped a little farther away. Now they were not just curious. They were angry.

"Get back," Brock muttered. "If we build up the fire, maybe that'll discourage them."

"Try this." Tess had meant to pass him the flare gun, but

as she stepped backward, she stumbled over a twisted root. As she righted herself, her finger tightened on the sensitive trigger. The gun fired with a deafening bang. The flare shot skyward at an angle, bursting high above the javelinas like a holiday fireworks display.

Maybe the creatures had been fired at in the past and remembered. Whatever was going on in their little piggy brains, they must've decided not to stick around. Grunting and squealing, they stampeded off into the night.

As the dust settled behind them, Tess looked at Brock and began to giggle. "I'm sorry . . . They must've been as scared as we were."

Brock grinned and reached for her. They fell into each other's arms, convulsed with laughter. "Too bad we didn't have a video camera." Brock gasped out the words. "Me throwing rocks, you tripping and shooting off that flare . . . Oh, hell, stop me before I die laughing!"

She stretched on tiptoe to meet his lips. Their kiss was warm and deep, a joyful release.

No one could predict what would happen in the days ahead, Tess reminded herself. But here, in this brief moment, she knew that she loved him.

The remaining hours of the night passed peacefully. Sitting next to Brock while he took his turn dozing, Tess hugged her knees for warmth. By now the fire was little more than glowing embers. The heat it gave off was negligible. But the stars were already fading. Soon the sun would rise to warm the new day.

What would that day bring? Surely their rescue would come. But would she and Brock keep the closeness that had grown between them? Or would it be lost amid the clamor of danger, worries, mistrust, and rivalry that awaited their return?

She would have to be prepared for that—even to expect it.

By the time the eastern sky had paled with first light, they were both awake and stirring. They parceled out the last two water bottles and divided the remaining energy bar. After that, there was little to do except gather more wood and watch the sky.

It was full daylight when they heard the distant rumble of a motor—not a plane but some kind of vehicle. And the sound was getting closer.

Gripped by excitement, they scanned the horizon. At first they could make out nothing. Then a battered red pickup with oversize tires came jouncing over the top of a brushy knoll. Tess and Brock waved their arms. The truck's horn blared across the distance.

Tess blinked back tears of relief. This wasn't the rescue they'd imagined. But at least somebody had found them. Brock, however, seemed less confident.

"Get into the plane," he said in a low voice. "We don't know what kind of people are in that truck."

Tess did as he'd asked. Brock was right. Out here alone and unarmed, they couldn't be too careful. "You come, too," she urged him. "Maybe they think we've got drugs."

"I'll get in if I have to," he said. "First I want to see who these folks are."

Through the dusty windshield, she watched the truck pull into the clearing where the plane had landed. There were two people in the cab. A man climbed out of the driver's side carrying a hunting rifle. Tess could just make out the person who remained in the cab. It was a woman—maybe his wife.

Relief swept over her. They were Tohono O'odham.

Brock had raised his hands. "We're not armed, and we mean you no harm," he said. "If you've come to help us, we're grateful."

The man, forty perhaps, and dressed in work clothes, nodded and lowered the rifle. "We saw the flare last night. We thought somebody might be in trouble. But we have to be careful. There are smugglers out here."

"Are we on the reservation? That could explain why no one's found us yet."

"Yes, this is the reservation. My home is back that way." He nodded toward the hills.

Tess had climbed out of the plane. "Maybe you know the men who work for me—Ruben Diego and his son-in-law, Pedro."

The man's face broke into a smile. "Ruben is my uncle. Pedro is my wife's cousin. Are they well?"

"As far as I know. We were flying to Ajo when the plane ran out of fuel. We had to crash-land."

The man's wife, who'd heard everything through the truck's open side window, climbed out to give Tess a hearty *abrazo.* Tess paused her narrative to make introductions.

"I need to call my family, but there's no phone service here," she said.

"There is phone service in Sells. It's an hour away. We can take you—both of you."

Brock hesitated. "This is a valuable plane. If I leave now, I could come back to find it stripped bare." He slipped a card out of his wallet and handed it to Tess. "This is my insurance company. My policy number's on the back. Call them, let them know where I am. They'll take care of everything, including me."

"But I can't just go off and leave you!" Tess protested.

"Take this." The Tohono man handed Brock his rifle. "I've got another one at home. You can give it to Ruben or Pedro. They'll get it back to me. There's more ammo in the truck. I'll leave you some water, too."

"Thanks." Brock accepted the rifle, turned to Tess, and gave her a quick hug. "Get going. I'll be fine."

"Call me when you're safe." She tore herself away and, after pausing to grab her purse out of the plane, followed her rescuers to the truck.

* * *

Brock's gaze watched the red truck until it vanished over the knoll. Had he been too reckless, sharing his secrets with Tess and then making love to her? He'd sensed that if he held anything back, he would never win her trust. But his need for intimacy may have heightened the danger to them both. For her own protection, he'd be wise to put some distance between them.

At least for now, Tess would be safe—and so would he, if the platinum-level service policy he'd taken out on the plane worked as promised. If all went well, the rescue helicopter and the salvage crew would locate him and be here within a few hours of receiving Tess's call. Since the plane had almost certainly been sabotaged, the company would launch its own expert investigation into the fuel leak—all to the good, since they had technical tools and skills he didn't, and since he had no wish to involve the police.

Settling next to the plane, he laid the rifle beside him. He didn't expect trouble, but if it came, at least he'd have the means to handle it. Too bad he couldn't say the same for the mess that would be waiting for him when he got home.

At the fuel stop in Sells, Tess pressed enough cash on her rescuers to fill their gas tank and buy them a nice lunch. Then she called the number on the insurance card Brock had given her. Only after giving her ID and contact information and being assured that the company would take care of everything did she scroll to Val's number. Her pulse slammed as the phone rang on the other end. She braced herself for terrible news.

"Tess!" Val practically screamed into the phone. "Thank God! We've been worried sick about you. What happened?"

"It's a long story. First tell me about Lexie."

"She's fine. So's the baby. But she had a rough time. The doctor had to do a C-section, so she's pretty sore. But little

Jackson is a heartbreaker. I'm at the hospital with them now. Where are you?"

"I'm at the fuel stop in Sells. We had to crash-land on the res. There was no phone service. This morning some nice folks in a pickup came along and drove me here."

"But you weren't flying that plane by yourself," Val said. "Where's Brock?"

"He stayed with the plane to wait for his insurance people. I've already called them."

"So you spent a night together in the desert. I'm expecting all the juicy details, girl. Did you or didn't you?"

Tess felt the heat rush to her face. "Only you would ask that question. My answer is no comment."

Val chuckled. "I told you Brock had a thing for you. Sit tight. I'll be there in an hour."

Tess bought herself a hot dog drenched in mustard and a super-size Diet Coke. Grabbing a handful of napkins, she carried her purchases outside and sat down on a bench to wait.

She wasn't looking forward to Val's merciless grilling. She'd planned to keep the details of her night with Brock to herself. But no secret was safe from her sister.

At least Val could be trusted to keep a confidence. But never mind that. She had bigger worries—like how was she going to function as Brock's business partner after spending the night with him? Could she stand up for the interests of her ranch when, every time she looked at him, the memory of being in his arms washed away all common sense?

And what would he expect of her? A world of uncertainties waited for her out there. To deal with that world, she would have to be tough. She would have to take charge. Whatever happened, she couldn't let Brock take advantage of her. Not even if she loved him.

* * *

The plane crash wasn't a big story. But it had made the local TV news, complete with a drone shot of the wreck as a salvage crew rigged the craft for transport.

Casey watched the broadcast on the overhead TV at the gym. He was getting regular physical therapy on his ankle, but if he wanted to be ready for the PBR finals, he couldn't neglect the rest of his body. He was working his arms and shoulders on one of the weight machines when the news came on. He paid scant attention to the story about the plane crash until he heard the name of the pilot. When the newscaster moved on without offering any more information, he reached for his phone and called Val. She answered on the first ring.

"Casey, are you all right?" As always, the sound of her husky voice made his heart skip. They'd grown apart since their parting at the ranch. But that didn't change the way he felt about her. She was the only woman for him, and always would be.

"I'm fine," he said, "except that I just saw Brock's plane on the news. What happened? Is he okay?"

"Yes—and so's Tess. They crash-landed in the desert. Both of them walked away without a scratch."

"Tess was with him? There was no mention of that on the news."

"She said that Brock wanted to keep her name out of the press. He was flying her from Vegas to Ajo, to be with Lexie—oh, and Lexie had her baby. A perfect little boy."

The mention of a baby boy touched a nerve in Casey. But he knew better than to react. He also knew better than to tell Val what the detective had sent him. The pieces of the investigation were falling into place. He had names, dates, a former address, and even a blurred photo of the adoptive parents with their one-year-old baby. There was a real chance of finding his son.

Casey was burning to share the information he had. But

Val had been adamant in her refusal to take part in his search. Casey had promised to honor her wishes.

"That's great news about Lexie. Give her and Shane my congratulations," he said.

"I will. She's still in the hospital, but I'll pass on the word."

"And how are you, Val?" Casey struggled to keep the emotion out of his voice. He missed her so damned much.

"I'm getting by," she said. "For now, I seem to be the one holding things together while everybody else is in crisis. For me, that's a nice change. And I suppose you're getting anxious to get back in the arena."

"That's what I'm working on. The ankle's almost healed."

"I'm glad." She wasn't glad, Casey knew, but that couldn't be helped.

"I'll let you go," he said. "Again, give my best to Tess and the new parents."

"I will. Bye for now."

"I love you, Val." He spoke the words, but she'd already ended the call.

Casey finished the workout and drove home to his condo. Pleasantly tired, he popped a cold beer from the fridge and sat down at his desktop computer. The detective had e-mailed him some scanned documents related to their son's final adoption. They'd arrived a few days ago, including a photo. Casey had seen them earlier but now that he had time, he wanted to study them line by line, burning every detail into his memory.

Date of final adoption: April 26, 2012
Name of child: Matthew Randall Peterson, Age: 12
   months
Name of father: Phillip Clifford Peterson
Name of mother: Cora Mae Randall Peterson
Present address: 9854 West Baxter Drive
City, State and Zip: Palmdale, California 93510

The black-and-white photo of the family appeared faded, maybe from the scan. It showed a plain, wholesome-looking couple holding a toddler dressed in a miniature baseball uniform with a Dodgers logo. Did his son like baseball now? Casey wondered. Did he play, maybe on a Little League team? Casey had never cared much for team sports. For him, it had always been rodeo. But what did that matter? This was real. This was his boy.

The one missing piece of information was the present whereabouts of the Peterson family. They'd left Palmdale seven years ago. The detective was still searching records for their location. When he found it, his work would be done.

The rest would be up to Casey.

CHAPTER 14

THE CALL FROM THE INSURANCE COMPANY CAME TWO days later. Brock was in his office, about to go through the mail Jim had left in a neat stack on his desk, when the phone rang. Seeing the name of the agent, Ray Pratt, on the caller ID, he answered on the first ring.

"Brock, we just heard from the specialist who went over your Cessna," he said. "You told us it was probably a fuel line. You were right about that. The plane was sabotaged, but not by cutting. The aluminum was eaten away by hydrochloric acid—applied to the lines from both tanks. Whoever did the job was an expert. He—assuming it was a man—had to know exactly how much acid to use, where to put it, and how long it would take to corrode the lines."

"And to do that, he'd need access to the plane." Brock felt vaguely sick. "That airport in Vegas had security cameras. Did anybody check them?"

"Yes, but they didn't show much. There were at least a dozen mechanics going in and out of the hangars. Some

worked for the airport, others for the owners of the big jets.
Wearing coveralls and a cap, almost anybody could pass for
a mechanic, especially from the view of an overhead camera."

"What about fingerprints?"

"Only yours—and a few of your friend's on the door and
in the cockpit. Whoever tampered with your plane probably
wore gloves."

"Damn." Brock already knew that the damage was covered by insurance. But the expertise and boldness of the person—or persons—out to wreak vengeance on him was
almost overpowering. The worst of it was, the bastard had
him spooked. And Brock hated that. He hated that someone
else was calling the shots. Most of all, he hated feeling pow-
erless.

"The repairs will take some time—three or four weeks is
my best guess. We've lined up a good facility. We just need
your go-ahead."

"Tell them to get it shipshape and sell it for me. I'll buy
another plane, maybe one that doesn't fly itself."

"I'll give them the word."

Ending the call, Brock swiveled his chair to face the window. Looking out over the pastures, seeing the beauty of the
land and the animals, had always given him a sense of satisfaction. Now what he felt was worry and a quietly seething
rage. The trouble wasn't over. It wouldn't be over until he
found the cause and ended it—or until he was dead.

The phone was still in his hand. He needed to call Tess
and let her know about the plane. He'd only called her once
since the crash landing, and that was to tell her he'd been
safely picked up. They'd agreed at the time that for her own
safety, they would stay apart until the danger was past.

If the monster who was stalking him could kill his prize
bull, blow up an innocent old man, and sabotage a plane
with murder in mind, he wouldn't hesitate to harm the
woman Brock had come to love.

The decision was his best chance of protecting her. Still, Brock had his regrets. This morning he'd awakened in bed, aching to find her beside him and make love again. Other such mornings—too many of them—would pass before he could make her his.

He made the call. She answered after several rings, sounding breathless. "Sorry. I just helped deliver a pretty little heifer calf. Now I need to get out of the way before the mama becomes protective. Give me a second."

Brock heard faint rustling and bumping and the sounds of rubber gloves being stripped off before she spoke again. "There, that's better. What's happening, is there any news?"

"Yes, the plane was definitely sabotaged. Would you believe acid on the fuel lines?"

"Well, that's certainly creative." Brock could picture her in the pasture, shirtsleeves rolled up, hair fluttering in the breeze, sunlight on her beautiful face. "What now?" she asked.

"I'm still working on that," Brock said, thinking aloud. "But I'm reasoning it out. There has to be more than one person involved. I'm thinking maybe three—the boss who pays the money and gives the orders, a go-between who acts as a lookout and passes information both ways, and the criminal who's doing the actual dirty work—a cold-blooded professional who doesn't care about anything but the contract."

"That does fit what's been happening."

"If I'm right, it's the go-between I need to find. Get the rat, and he'll give me the others."

"Be careful, Brock. You're dealing with dangerous people."

"I understand that," he said. "But I'm sick and tired of looking over my shoulder, waiting for the next attack. I've got to do something." He paused, collecting his scattered thoughts. "I miss you, damn it. I want to make love to you again, all night, in a real bed."

"That's going to have to wait," she said.

"I know. But I'm not a patient man. Just take care of your-self, all right?"

He heard a noise on the other end of the phone, like someone calling. "Somebody needs me. Gotta go," she said. Then the phone went silent.

Brock lingered with the phone in his hand. He'd never told Tess he loved her. He'd been tempted to say the words before she had to end the call. But maybe that was just as well. The timing wasn't the best.

But their conversation had been just what he needed to organize his thoughts and move him to action. Someone was watching his every move. They'd known when he was pick-ing up the mail. They'd known he'd be flying to Vegas and where he would leave the plane. And they'd passed on the information to a hired killer. If that was true, the go-be-tween, as Brock had chosen to call him, had to be someone he trusted—someone working right here on the ranch.

Leaving the thought to simmer, he turned back to sorting the mail on his desk. A travel brochure and a tire sales ad were tossed into the waste basket. A bill for repairs to the mailbox and front gate was set aside. The last envelope was lying facedown. When Brock turned it over, his heart lurched.

The envelope was addressed in the same grammar school printing as the others. No return address. Same American flag postage stamp. But this time it appeared to have been mailed from Phoenix.

Brock used a letter opener to loosen the flap. As ex-pected, there was nothing inside but another age-yellowed newspaper clipping. Handling it with care, he laid it flat on the surface of the desk.

His gaze was drawn to the grainy photo at the top. Jeff Carpenter looked young and happy here. But even before he read the headline, Brock knew what to expect.

FORMER RIDGEWOOD RESIDENT
PRESUMED DEAD

Branson, MO, August 12, 2013

After a week, the search has been called off for the
body of Jeffery Wayne Carpenter, who vanished
from his fishing boat on Table Rock Lake, August 6.
A pistol with one shell missing from the magazine
was found in the boat, suggesting possible suicide.

Mr. Carpenter, who was a practicing attorney in
Branson, grew up in Ridgewood, the son of the late
auto dealer Chase Carpenter. He married Carla
Lundberg. They were later divorced. His former
wife, his father, and his younger sister, Mia, preceded him in death. He is survived by his mother,
Johanna Smith Carpenter, and his son, Jason
Carpenter. A memorial service, yet to be
scheduled, will be held in Branson.

Brock slid the clipping back into the envelope and locked
it into the wall safe with the others. At least he couldn't be
blamed for what had become of Jeff. But that didn't mean
someone else wasn't blaming him.

Brock hadn't spoken with Jeff since the night of the car
accident. But several years ago, he'd chanced to meet a man
who'd worked at the car lot. Over beers, the man had passed
on the story of how Jeff had started drinking, lost his wife,
and most of his clients. Not long after that, Brock had read
how Jeff had gone missing from his boat.

Tess had brought up the possibility that Jeff might have
faked his death and vanished to start a new life somewhere.
But Brock had dismissed the idea. Even if it was true, it didn't
make sense that Jeff would come back to kill him. He'd done
Jeff and his family a favor—hadn't he?

So why send the clipping about Jeff's death? Who would
save it and send it after all these years?

But right now, Brock had more serious concerns. He had

every reason to believe that one of his employees—men he liked and trusted—had betrayed him. He had to find out who it was, and who was giving the go-between orders, before someone else died.

Among his many talents, the man who called himself Jaeger possessed the gift of invisibility. His light brown eyes, olive complexion, and nondescript features lent themselves to disguises that could blend in with any crowd. When he was under contract, he'd learned to go unnoticed—to stay in cheap hotels and avoid the better restaurants, even though he could certainly afford them. He dressed in neutral colors—today a tan workman's jacket and a baseball cap that shaded his face. He spoke in low tones and never did anything to draw attention.

He was self-educated but keenly intelligent, with a photographic mind that remembered everything he heard, saw, and read. In various jobs, he had passed himself off as a pilot, a mechanic, a computer technician, a cowhand, even a doctor. It was all part of the package that made him one of the most sought-after hit men in the business.

He commanded high fees and could pick and choose his clients. But he was beginning to wish he'd taken a pass on this current contract. For one thing, the client, who had very deep pockets, insisted on paying him by check, mailed to a rental box. And this job wasn't a simple hit. He'd been instructed by phone that the target, Arizona rancher Brock Tolman, must be made to suffer—not just physically but mentally.

"Bring the man to his knees. I want him to feel pain, to feel fear and loss, and I want him to know why before you kill him."

Those were his orders, for double his usual fee. But Jaeger didn't like complications. All he wanted was to make the hit and move on to the next contract. That was why, after the bother and risk of killing some livestock, he'd decided to go ahead, take out Tolman, and be done—even if it meant cutting his fee.

But Brock Tolman was proving damnably hard to kill.

Any goon could shoot a man—quick but messy and likely to draw the police. Jaeger's specialty was setting up the hit so that when it happened, he'd be nowhere around.

His informant had told him that Tolman was picking up his own mail. But the carefully rigged bomb in the mailbox had killed an old man instead. And Tolman's early flight from Las Vegas had disrupted the timing of the acid on the fuel line, allowing him enough fuel to crash-land the plane in the desert and walk away without a scratch.

The client was getting impatient. Not only had Jaeger failed to kill Tolman but, according to the angry message on his phone, he had yet to make the man truly suffer. Before he died, Tolman needed to lose something—or someone—so precious that the loss would bring him low.

Brock Tolman had no family and, evidently, no close friends. That left just one possibility.

Somewhere, there had to be a woman.

Tess buttered a slice of toast, ate it standing, and washed it down with hot, black coffee. Then she strode outside to saddle her horse. Calving season was a busy time, and extra chores needed extra hands.

The sun was just rising over the mountains as she crossed the short distance to the stable. Bird calls rang on the cool morning air. Two ravens, lifelong mates, left their towering stick nest atop a dead saguaro and flapped off into the sky.

In the stable, she found Pedro forking out the stalls. That job was usually done by Shane, but he and Val had left early for Ajo to bring Lexie and the baby home. The ranch would be short-handed today, and probably for weeks to come. It was time to think about hiring some extra help.

Leaving the care of the bulls to Ruben, she rode her buckskin mare to the upper pasture, where the pregnant cows had begun to drop their calves.

Last summer, desperate for money and with the breeding window closing, Tess had arranged to trade a choice yearling for the services of a second-rate bull. Gadianton, named for a Book of Mormon character, had done his job. Almost all of the breeding cows and heifers were pregnant. But Tess had long since come to regret her choice. This spring's calves would have lackluster pedigrees. Most of them would be auctioned off as yearlings. The sale would bring in needed cash, but do nothing for the future of the ranch.

Reaching the pasture, she saw that several more cows had given birth in the night. Some of the calves were strong enough to stand and nurse. Others, still wet, were resting in the grass. The sun would warm them. Tess inspected them from horseback at a cautious distance. Cows, like most animal mothers, were fiercely protective of their young. Getting too close would be a mistake.

She would start planning now for the upcoming season, Tess resolved. Whirlwind and the other bulls who'd grown up on the ranch were too closely related to breed with the cows. Quicksand was young and had barely begun to build his reputation as a rank bull—which he would need to compensate for his missing bloodline.

That left Tess with two choices. She could invest in some new quality bulls or do what Lexie had urged her to do last year—buy semen to impregnate the best cows.

Both choices were expensive. Semen was like liquid gold. A single straw from a top bull, or even one of his offspring, could cost upward of a thousand dollars, plus the cost of the insemination. Even then, there was no guarantee that the procedure would work or that the calf would be a bull.

The Alamo Canyon Ranch didn't have that kind of

money to risk. If she wanted to improve her stock, she would have to swallow her pride and go to Brock for a loan.

Brock.

No matter where Tess's thoughts took her, they always led back to him. Her rival. Her antagonist. Her partner. The man she couldn't help loving.

She remembered yesterday's phone conversation and the new evidence that the plane had been sabotaged. Somebody ruthless and devilishly clever wanted him dead. They'd failed twice. That there'd be a third attempt on Brock's life was a given, not a question of *if* but *when*.

Tess had tried to put her worries aside and focus on her work today. But she was sick with fear. The hired assassin— assuming that's what he was—could strike without warning. If Brock were to drop his guard, or worse, try to draw the killer out . . .

Tess couldn't make herself finish the thought.

This weekend she'd be taking Quicksand and three other bulls to Prescott. Ruben would be driving with her. Brock planned to be there, as well, although they probably wouldn't get much time together.

Since he had no plane, he would probably drive one of his vehicles and leave the trucking to his cowhands. Tess might have argued against his going. He was bound to be safer on his ranch. But she knew better than to try. Brock was proud and stubborn. He would show up and spit in his enemy's face if need be, to show that he wasn't afraid.

Whether she liked it or not, Tess would have to accept that. When it came to fear, she had enough for them both.

When Val carried the breakfast tray into the bedroom, she found Lexie sitting up in bed, nursing her baby. Pausing in the doorway, she took in the sight of her sister, tousled and tired but still beautiful, with the small, dark head against her breast.

Val was totally happy for Lexie, but at times like this, she was stabbed by memories of her own baby, who'd been taken away before she had the chance to feed him. In the days after the birth, her milk-swollen breasts had ached for the tug of that hungry little mouth. But she mustn't think of that now. This was a time of celebration for the ranch family.

Lexie looked up and smiled. "Oh, you didn't have to bring my breakfast, Val. I was going to get up and come into the kitchen as soon as I finished feeding this little rascal."

"Don't even think about it." Val set the tray on a side table. "You almost died bringing that baby into the world. You've got a lot of healing to do before you're fit to be up and around. Maria says you're to eat every bite of this breakfast. She even brewed you some special herb tea. It's in that pottery cup with the lid."

"Oh, no!" Lexie pulled a face. "I had that yesterday. It was so bitter I could barely get it down. Please, Val. Pour it down the sink and don't tell her."

Val shook her head. "Maria's people have been living on this land for hundreds of years, maybe longer. They have their own medicine, and it's probably better than that factory-made drugstore crap. You're going to drink every drop."

"You were always a bossy one," Lexie said. "Between you and Tess, I never stood a chance. I still don't."

"And now you've got a new little boss." Val reached down and ran a fingertip over the baby's silky head. Her own baby's hair had been flame red. It probably still was.

The baby had finished nursing. Lexie lifted him against her shoulder and patted up a little belch. Then she handed him to Val while she closed her nightgown. "Have you heard anything from Casey?" she asked as if reading her sister's mind.

Val carried the baby to the bassinette, his warm weight and baby smell sweet in her arms. After laying him on his back, she picked up the tray and placed it across Lexie's knees.

"Casey's been extra quiet," she said. "I suspect he's onto something and knows better than to tell me about it."

Lexie speared a forkful of scrambled eggs with cheese. "How can you stand it, Val? If Jackson were somewhere out there in the world and I had a chance to find him, I'd never be able to resist."

"Not even knowing that even if you found him, you'd never be able to touch him or talk to him?" Val demanded.

"Not even then," Lexie said. "But thank heaven, I don't have to make that decision."

"Well, I did, and I decided not to try. If you want to know the reason, it's because seeing him wouldn't be enough. I'd never be able to stop myself from ruining lives. And what scares me is that if Casey finds our son, he won't be able to stop himself either."

"Oh, Val." Lexie reached for Val's hand and squeezed it. "I'm sorry. I wish things had been different."

"So do I." Val felt the tears welling. "I need a break. I'll be back to pick up the tray when you've finished eating. Promise me you'll drink Maria's tea."

"I'll do it now." Lexie picked up the pottery mug, downed the contents, and pulled a face. "Satisfied?"

"That's my girl." Val gave her a smile, walked down the hall and out onto the porch. She loved her sister and the baby, but her own memories were tearing at her heart.

Sinking into a chair, she gazed across the pastures, green with spring, sloping upward to the rimrock along the skyline. The bulls grazed beyond the high steel fence. A hawk circled in the distant sky.

Her child wouldn't be a baby anymore, she reminded herself. He'd be a growing boy with fiery hair like her own and, perhaps, Casey's ready smile. If her father had welcomed her home, she would have raised her son here on the ranch. By now he would be helping with chores, riding horses, and learning to rope. He would be surrounded by family who loved him—and maybe even a father.

Instead, she'd let him go to a life she and Casey couldn't share. She could tell herself that her son was safe and happy, and that Casey would come to find peace with the decision she'd made.

But today, nothing felt right.

Casey had missed his bullfighting teammates, Joel Hatcher and Marcus Jefferson. Catching up with them over prime rib dinners at their favorite Tucson steak house sharpened the need to get back into the arena and do his job.

"So how's the ankle?" Marcus asked. "Are you going to make it to the finals?"

"I hope so. The pain's gone, and I'm walking fine. As soon as the doctor clears me, I'm there."

"We'll be glad to have you back," Joel said. "Just make sure you're fit to dance at my wedding in June. And bring that hot redhead you keep hidden away. We haven't seen her since Vegas."

"Val doesn't like watching me work. She'd be happy if I quit. But then I don't know what I'd do with myself." Casey hadn't told his friends about the latest rift with Val over his search for their son. For now, he would keep that story to himself.

"Marcus wants to try freestyle after the finals," Joel said. "Maybe you can talk him out of it."

"Marcus is insane," Casey said, welcoming the change of subject.

"Hey," Marcus said. "Freestyle bullfighting's the ultimate rush. Take bucking bulls—they just want to toss their rider, maybe knock him around some, before they trot out the gate. But those black Mexican *toros*—they've got horns like daggers, and they're bred to kill. Out there in that little arena, you're facing your own mortality, man."

Casey had seen a couple of freestyle bullfighting events—a lone, unarmed bullfighter competing against the kind of bull whose ancestors had battled matadors to the death. For the bullfighter, the aim of the sport was to play tag with the bull, showing off his agility for points without getting gored and trampled. The bull's aim was to kill.

"The money's pretty good—especially if you're high point man," Marcus said. "Maybe you should try it, Casey."

"Not me," Casey said. "I'm too old and slow." And that was true, he realized. When he stepped into the arena with his team, he wasn't doing it for a thrill. His goal was to protect the bull rider. It was a job, like being a paramedic or a firefighter. He still enjoyed it, but he'd long since gotten past the youthful adrenaline rush.

"Have either of you given much thought to what you're going to do when you can't dodge bulls anymore?" he asked, wondering aloud.

"Hell, I don't plan to live that long," Marcus joked. "I plan to go out with a bang, at my peak, and give all the women something to cry about."

"My girl's already after me to quit," Joel said. "When we have kids, she wants me around to be a dad to them, not on the road somewhere getting my ass kicked by a two-thousand-pound bull. Her family's got a ranch. I'll probably end up there—maybe raise some bulls and hope for a winner. What about you, Casey?"

"That depends." Casey downed the last of his Corona. What plans did he have? Marry Val and leave her to go on the road? Get a job as a trainer or judge? Go to work for the Champions? "I guess I'm going to have to think about it," he said.

The meal was ending. He checked his phone. There was a text message from Seegmiller, the detective he'd hired.

News. Call me.

Casey's pulse leapt. But he didn't want to make the call here, in a noisy restaurant with his friends. And he didn't want to make it driving in evening traffic. He needed to be home.

"Sorry, urgent business," he said, excusing himself. "I'll see you at work—soon, I hope."

Driving back to the condo, Casey willed himself to stay calm. Seegmiller's news was probably just another clue or rumor. But what if it was more—what if he'd actually found his son's family?

Matthew, or maybe Matt. The boy had a name now. He was becoming more solidly real in Casey's mind. Just to know who and where he was, maybe see him from a distance, was all he could ever hope for. But even that would mean everything. He had a son. He was a father.

If only he could share what he knew with Val.

He pulled his pickup into the covered parking area, climbed out, and raced up the outside stairway to his condo. Inside, without bothering to turn on the light, he sank into a chair and made the call.

"Hello, Mr. Bozeman. I assume you got my message." Seegmiller, a former English teacher, was in his sixties with an old-school way of speaking.

"I did." Anticipation surged through Casey's body. "You said you had news. I hope it's good."

There was a pause. "I do have news. But I'm afraid it isn't good. Not good at all, in fact."

Casey's heart dropped. "Tell me," he said.

Seegmiller exhaled. "I was able to trace the Peterson family to Bakersfield, California. There was an address, but two years ago, somebody else purchased the home. I contacted the new owners to see if they might have a forwarding address. They said that the house had been vacant before they bought it. But a neighbor told them that the family who'd lived there . . ." Seegmiller paused, then continued, a catch in his voice. "I'm so sorry, Mr. Bozeman. The neighbor said that the Petersons had been killed in a terrible highway accident."

CHAPTER 15

CASEY STARED INTO THE DARKNESS, FEELING AS IF HIS heart had been ripped out, leaving a gaping, bloodless hole. Even if he could have voiced a response, there were no words.

"Mr. Bozeman, are you still there?"

"Yes." The word emerged half-broken.

"I've e-mailed a copy of the news article I found. It'll give you the details better than I can. After you've read it, take time to think about what you want to do next. Then call me with your decision." There was a beat of silence. "I'm very sorry for your loss."

"Thank you." Casey sat in silence for a long moment. Then he forced himself to get up and turn on the light. He had to deal with this tragedy—and ultimately, he would have to decide how to deal with Val.

Switching on the desktop computer, he brought up his e-mail. The message from Seegmiller was there. Steeling his heart, he clicked on it and opened the scanned file. There was no photo, only a half column of print from the back page of the local newspaper.

The Bakersfield Californian
June 2, 2019

DEADLY CRASH TAKES
BAKERSFIELD FAMILY

A Bakersfield couple, traveling with their young son, lost their lives last night when their Ford van cut in front of a semi-truck and was struck from the passenger side. The accident happened at 9:14 p.m. on Interstate 5 just past the Spicer City off-ramp. Phillip Peterson, the driver, and his wife, Cora Mae Peterson, were killed instantly. Their son Matthew, 8, was taken by ambulance to Memorial Hospital in critical condition. The driver of the semitruck was treated for minor injuries at the scene. An investigation is pending, but the driver is not expected to be charged.

Fighting the urge to cry out and punch his fist through the monitor screen, Casey read the item again, then reached for the phone and placed another call to Seegmiller. "What happened to the boy?" he demanded. "You must have checked, at least."

The detective sighed. "I did. I contacted Memorial Hospital. The clerk could find no record of him. The only suggestion she could offer was that he must've died in the ambulance and so was never admitted to the hospital. There's no record of his body being signed into the morgue, either. It's a dead end. He's gone."

Casey ended the call, slumped in the chair, and buried his face in his hands. His shoulders shook with silent sobs. *A dead end*, Seegmiller had said. But how could that be? How could he just give up and walk away without knowing what had happened to his boy? He had to find out. If it meant putting off his return to work, so be it. He would go to Bakersfield and search until he found whatever was to be found—even if it was only a grave or a name on a death certificate.

And he could only hope that Val would go with him.

Prescott, Arizona, claimed to have the world's oldest rodeo. The granddaddy celebration of them all—Prescott Frontier Days—was traditionally held in late June through early July. But there were other, earlier events scheduled for the outdoor arena. This one, sanctioned by the Professional Rodeo Cowboys Association, would have some high-ranking bull riders showing up to add to their point totals before the World Finals.

Tess was eager to show off Quicksand's prowess. But she was more than a little worried. The black bull had done well in the smaller rodeos, bucking off every rider and running up impressive scores. But this would be his first appearance before a big crowd, with all the noise and commotion that went along with it. Would he freeze and refuse to buck, or would he do the Alamo Canyon Ranch proud? Ruben had brought a bundle of white sage to burn in case the bull became agitated before his turn in the chute—not that it was guaranteed to work.

But Quicksand wasn't Tess's only worry. Brock had said he would be here—their first meeting since she'd left him at the plane. When they'd spoken on the phone later, he'd told her that, for her own safety, she should avoid being seen with him, or even having her name linked with his.

Tess understood or thought she did. Still, the situation worried her. What if Brock planned to walk into danger—trying to draw out the person who was after him?

There were personal issues, as well. Brock was hard to read, let alone predict. The man who'd made love to her in the desert could also be aloof, indifferent, even cold. This weekend, with danger lurking, she would be the least of his concerns, or even a dangerous distraction. She would be wise to do as he'd asked and keep her distance.

After a long night's drive, Tess and Ruben arrived before dawn and headed for the rodeo grounds. Prescott was an attractive town, capitalizing on its early western history. Its scenic setting, museums, shops, dining, and entertainment drew throngs of tourists. At this hour, the streets were quiet, but the pens behind the arena were already filling up as stock contractors unloaded their animals.

As they pulled into the lot, Tess glanced around for the big silver trailer with the Tolman Ranch logo on the side. She didn't see it, but the hour was early yet. And Brock rarely traveled with the stock trailer. Surely, after the sabotage on his plane, he wouldn't want to risk the men, the bulls, or the rig. Maybe he wouldn't be coming after all.

Tess and Ruben unloaded the bulls and settled them in a pen with food and water. Two bulls would be bucking tonight. Quicksand and the remaining bull would be bucking tomorrow night in the event final.

Tess had rented a cheap motel room with two beds where she and Ruben could crash, wash up, and change. It would be no more intimate than sleeping in the truck, which they'd done countless times before, and it would keep her from looking like a homeless vagabond the next morning. Tess didn't usually fuss over her appearance on the road—she would just jam her hat on her hair and go. But this time, she'd caught herself wanting to look presentable in case Brock showed up.

Silly woman! Why bother? she chided herself as she leaned against the high fence, watching her bulls. That night in the desert hadn't meant a thing to him; just a way to pass the time with a willing female. Brock probably had a stable of pretty, sophisticated women back in Tucson—models, socialites, the kind of ladies a man would enjoy showing off at some fancy party. She was more the type for sharing a platter of nachos in Lefty's Tavern.

But why did she have to be so blasted insecure? If she wasn't lady enough for Brock, that was his problem. She was who she was. If he didn't like it, he could go jump in the lake.

"Miss Champion?" The drawling voice from behind made her reflexes jerk. Tess turned to find a lanky man in high-end cowboy clothes with a press pass pinned to his vest. He was standing so close she could smell the breath mint in his mouth. She took a step backward.

"Tex Poulson, from the National Cowboy TV Channel." He flashed a photo ID card. "I was hoping we could set you up for an interview—about that bull of yours—the black one that nobody's ever rode."

Tess hesitated. She'd done interviews before. Mostly they were a waste of time. But the Cowboy Channel was national. Getting Quicksand's name out there could get her bull noticed by the right people—including Clay Rafferty.

"If we could do the spot now, it would run tonight," Poulson said. "That would stir up some interest and snag us more viewers for tomorrow's finals. So, are we good to go?"

Tess had been trucking bulls most of the night, and she could imagine how she looked. But the TV spot would be about Quicksand, so what did it matter? "Sure. Let's get it done," she said.

Poulson snapped his fingers, and a cameraman appeared with his equipment. Tess glanced around for Ruben, then remembered that he'd gone to get some breakfast. She was on her own.

"Let's get a close-up of the bull." Poulson directed the shots. When the cameraman came up against the pen and tried to shoot between the rails, Quicksand charged. The cameraman jumped back as the bull stopped just short of a collision.

"You mustn't get close like that," Tess said. "This bull's been traumatized. He's never seen a camera before. We're trying to keep him calm, but you're not helping."

"Sorry," the cameraman said. "At least I got a great shot of him charging."

"Traumatized?" Poulson pounced on the word like a chicken on a bug. "Traumatized? How?" The microphone was thrust into Tess's face. "Did it have anything to do with losing his horn?"

"No, he was found as a calf, lost in the desert, fighting off a pack of hungry coyotes. He's almost four now, but the experience stayed with him. He still spooks easily."

"Were you the one who found him?"

"No, it was a friend of mine. I traded another bull for Quicksand."

"A friend?"

"That's what I said." Tess didn't want to mention Brock's name on the air.

"I see the bull is wearing Tolman ear tags. Was it Brock Tolman who found the bull? Are you and Tolman . . . uh . . . close friends?" The innuendo was clear.

Tess cursed silently. She'd meant to replace those ear tags but had never gotten around to it. She scrambled to change the subject. "Let's talk about his bucking record—six outs, all buck-offs with scores in the midforties. And he's only a rookie bull in his first season."

"But this isn't really his first season, is it?" Poulson's gaze narrowed. "I did my homework before our interview. This bull froze the first time out last year. He refused to buck. Are you afraid he'll do it again? Would you care to lay odds?"

Tess held back a surge of anger. "We've done a lot of work with Quicksand, helping him overcome his fear. So

far, he's bucked magnificently. I'm extremely proud of this
bull. I believe he can go all the way. And now, Mr. Poulson,
I'd say this interview is finished."

The TV interview left Tess with a sour taste in her mouth
for the rest of the morning. Poulson, a well-known rodeo re-
porter, had controlled and manipulated her to get just what
he wanted. Now viewers would be waiting for Quicksand to
fail.

If she'd known Poulson was going for tabloid fodder, instead of talking about Quicksand's great performances, Tess
wouldn't have given him the time of day. The worst of it was
his bringing up her connection with Brock—something both
of them had reason to keep private. Wherever Brock was
now, she would need to alert him about the broadcast.

In the motel room, she sat on the edge of her bed and
composed a text, apologizing for the way she'd let Poulson
lead her on and warning Brock that his name had been mentioned. Brock wouldn't be pleased, but at least she'd let him
know.

Ruben lay on the opposite bed, fully dressed and snoring
like a diesel truck with a bad muffler. A smile tugged at
Tess's lips. She'd lost track of the times in the truck when
she'd drifted off to that sound. Ruben's snoring had always
made her feel safe.

She sent the text to Brock, not knowing how or even if
he'd respond. Then she took a few minutes to freshen up.
When she came out of the bathroom, Ruben was still snoring. Tess crossed the room quietly, let herself out, and
locked the door behind her. She would leave him to his nap,
check on the bulls, then maybe look for some fast food.

The arena was less than two blocks from the motel.
Stretching her legs, Tess covered the distance in a few minutes, arriving just in time to see the Tolman rig pulling
through the gate.

Two men sat in the cab of the truck. The driver was a cowhand she remembered seeing at Brock's ranch but didn't know by name. The passenger was Jim, the young man she'd met earlier.

Tess moved aside to watch as Jim, who'd climbed out of the cab, directed the driver to back the trailer up to the unloading chute. The rear door swung open. Three handsome bulls, wearing the Tolman brand and ear tags, thundered down the ramp to be herded into their pen.

As the truck pulled away and headed to a parking place, Jim gave Tess a friendly grin. "Nice to see you, Miss Champion," he said. "Did you bring that black bull that gave us so much trouble?"

"Yes, he's here," Tess said. "So far he's done great. No qualifying rides in six outs. But this rodeo, with the big crowd and the world-class riders, will be a whole new challenge. Wish us luck."

"You got it. We'll be cheering for him."

"Thanks." Tess turned to walk away, then stopped. "Oh, do you know if Brock plans to be here?"

He shrugged. "As far as I know. I haven't seen him yet, but when he shows up, I'll tell him you asked. Where can he find you?"

"When I'm not at the arena, I'll be at the Redrock Inn up the street. Room 116 if he needs to know. But never mind telling him. I'll probably run into him later."

Tess walked away, winding through the maze of chutes and pens to find her bulls. She probably shouldn't have asked the young cowboy about Brock. Gossip among the hired hands was never a good thing.

Her bulls appeared relaxed and contented. Even Quicksand had settled and was calmly chewing his cud. She curbed the impulse to reach between the rails and scratch his ear. Some bulls liked being petted. Quicksand wasn't one of them.

"You'll show them what you're made of tomorrow night,

won't you, big boy?" she murmured. "I know you will. You'll make us all proud."

By the time Tess caught sight of Brock, rodeo fans were pouring into the stands. She spotted him from behind, his broad shoulders and black Stetson just visible above the crowd. She curbed the impulse to catch up with him. If he wanted to find her, he would.

He disappeared in the direction of the press box. A few minutes later, she heard the text chime from her phone and saw his message.

Hilton 1138

The Hilton was the luxury-style hotel near the arena. The number had to be Brock's room. But what was she supposed to read into the message?

Was it a summons or an invitation? Did he plan to read her the riot act for allowing Poulson's interview? Was he inviting her to a business conference? Or did he simply want some private time together.

Tess wanted to believe that he was leaving the decision to her. She could come if she chose to, or she could stay away. Her finger hovered over the reply option. Then, with a shake of her head, she put the phone back in her purse. Part of her wanted to run to his arms. But this was no time for rashness. She would make up her mind later.

As usual, bull riding would be the final event of the rodeo. Tess studied the roster posted next to the gate to see which riders had drawn her first two bulls, Avalanche and Loose Caboose. She recognized the riders by name—a Texan and a Brazilian, both of them in the top fifteen. If her bulls performed as well as expected, the scores should be impressive. The riders for tomorrow night's championship round wouldn't be drawn until after tonight's semifinals. It would be tomorrow before she knew who'd be riding Quicksand.

As she turned away from the roster, a familiar figure strode past her, headed somewhere in a hurry. Seeing her, Clay Rafferty gave a brief nod before he disappeared in the direction of the bucking chutes. Tess took a deep breath as tension crept over her. With Rafferty here, it was even more important that her bulls do well, especially Quicksand.

She found Ruben with the bulls, looking fresh after his midday nap. The two bulls set to buck tonight had been herded into a holding pen, where he was giving them a final inspection. He glanced up as Tess joined him. "You look worried. Is everything all right, *hija*?"

"Fine. I just saw Rafferty, that's all. Our bulls had better be at the top of their game tonight."

"Ojalá." He grinned, using a Spanish expression that invoked hope and luck. "These two bulls, Avalanche and Loose Caboose, they know their jobs. As long as they're well taken care of, they'll get out there and put on a show. But that one—" He nodded toward the adjoining pen where Quicksand and the other bull, Rocket Man, awaited their turn tomorrow. "That black rascal—all we can do is pray."

"So far, he's been fine." Tess scanned the bustling pen complex for Brock's tall figure, but there was no sign of him. What was he thinking? Should she have replied to his text?

But never mind that, she told herself. Brock would be totally involved with his bulls and the business of the rodeo. He probably wasn't thinking of her at all.

When the time came for Tess's bulls to buck, everything went fine. The two riders qualified with scores in the high eighties and would be moving on to the finals tomorrow night.

Soon after that, the rodeo ended. As the crowds filed out of the stands, Tess checked her phone again. There was nothing from Brock except the text he'd sent her earlier. She hadn't seen him since his bulls had finishing bucking. Could he have slipped out of the arena early to wait for her?

It was decision time. But the decision had already been made.

"I have someplace to go," she told Ruben. "I may be coming back late. We both have keys to the room, so don't wait up for me."

"All right. I'll get some dinner and check on the bulls before I turn in. But be careful. Don't go wandering around alone."

It wasn't Ruben's place to ask where Tess was going. But he'd known her since she was a little girl, and he often treated her as if nothing had changed. Tess tolerated his concern, knowing that it sprang from a well of goodness in his heart.

"Don't worry, I'll be fine." She tossed back the words as she joined a crowd of well-dressed people walking down the street toward the Hilton. The night breeze was mellow, the distance only a few short blocks. Ruben had no cause to worry.

In the hotel lobby, she passed the desk without stopping and made for the elevators. She could feel her heart thudding as she pressed the button for the eleventh floor. Room 1138. She didn't need to recheck the number on her phone. She knew it by heart.

The elevator stopped with a slight bump. Tess followed the direction signs down a long, thickly carpeted hallway to the numbered door. What if he didn't answer, or even had company? What if she was about to make a fool of herself?

She rapped lightly. The door opened at once. Brock stood there in his jeans, his feet bare, the collar of his denim shirt open at the throat. "Come on in, Tess," he said, closing the door behind her and slipping the lock. "I wasn't sure you'd be here, but I took the liberty of ordering from room service. In case you're hungry, it arrived just a few minutes ago."

Walking into the room, lit by a single lamp, she saw the coffee table in front of the sofa set with a white cloth, napkins, silver, two crystal goblets, and a tray covered with a sil-

ver dome lid. The drapes were open. The floor-to-ceiling
window offered a west-facing view of the town, which spread
below like a mosaic of light and dark. From here, she could
see the arena. She could even see the street and the partial
roof of the motel where she'd rented a room.

On the wall opposite the sofa, a large flat-screen TV,
blank and silent for now, was mounted above a cabinet. The
sight of it triggered a harsh reminder. She glanced at the wall
clock. It was about time for the Cowboy Channel broadcast.
She forced herself to mention it.

"Hey, while we eat, we can turn on the TV and watch my
interview with Tex Poulson. You might as well see the worst
and get it over with."

Brock guided her toward the sofa with his hand at the
small of her back. The light pressure of his touch sent
rivulets of warmth trickling down her body. "Sorry, watching TV isn't what I had in mind," he said.

"It'll be on in a few minutes. Are you saying you don't
want to watch?"

"What I'm saying is, we're not going to see it." He turned
her toward him, looking down at her with one eyebrow
cocked in amusement. "What I mean is that the interview
isn't going to run."

She stared up at him, bewildered. "What do you mean it
isn't going to run?"

"Sit down." He chuckled as he eased her onto the cush-
ions. "After I read your message, I paid a call on Tex. He
and I go back a few years. I can't say we've ever been
friends, but I know some secrets that could damage his career. I hinted—just hinted—that if he didn't kill the interview, a few ugly rumors might raise their heads. He got the
idea."

"You blackmailed him!" Tess jabbed his chest with a finger.

"Would you rather have me pulverize his face or threaten
him with a gun? It's called damage control, sweetheart. No-

body got hurt, including you and me. Now let's forget it and enjoy the rest of our time together."

Tess sighed. "Please don't think I'm ungrateful. I just wish I understood you better, that's all."

Lifting her chin with two fingertips, he studied her face. "You're the purest person I've ever known, Tess. But I haven't had that luxury. I've lied, manipulated, hurt people, even broken the law to get where I am today. If I could change my past, I'd do it for you in a heartbeat. But I can't. I can't even change the person I am now. So if you have a problem with me as I am, you'd better get up and leave, because I want you, and I'm in this game for keeps."

He fell silent. A muscle twitched in his cheek. He'd opened his heart to her, leaving himself exposed and vulnerable. Knowing Brock's pride, it could be one of the hardest things he'd ever done.

Tess found her voice. "I don't know where or how this is going to end. I don't even know what's going to happen tomorrow. But I'm here, Brock. I'm here now."

In the next breath they were in each other's arms, devouring each other with kisses. With a strength that took her breath away, he scooped her up in his arms and carried her into the adjoining bedroom. The covers on the king-size bed were already turned down.

By the time he'd laid her on the bed, she was pulling his shirt off his shoulders in a frenzy of need. Tess had experienced desire, but unbridled lust, tempered with tenderness, was new to her. She was wild with wanting him.

While he stripped down and took a moment to protect her, she kicked off her boots, then lay back and let him peel off the layers of her clothes, kissing her as he removed her jeans, her panties, her shirt and bra. In the faint light from the other room, her gaze took in his glorious body, fit and hard, but mature, showing the first small signs of middle age. Perfect.

Their lovemaking was everything it had been in the

desert, but deeper, more passionate, more tender and lingering than she could ever have imagined. When it was over, they lay side by side, deliciously spent.

"I don't know about you," Brock said, chuckling, "but I've worked up an appetite. If you're hungry, we could eat and watch *The Late Show* before we turn in."

Tess stretched onto her side, facing him. "I'll have a meal with you. But it might not be wise for me to spend the night. I'm sharing a motel room with Ruben, and he might worry if—"

An explosive *boom* interrupted her words. The sound wasn't close, but it was loud enough to reverberate through the window panes. Tess bolted off the bed and raced into the front room. Through the windows she could see smoke and flickers of fire against the darkness, rising from the location of the motel.

"No!" She screamed the word again and again before she managed to get herself under control. Racing into the bedroom, she began pulling on her clothes. "Come with me, Brock! I've got to get down there!"

Jaeger watched the explosion from a laundromat parking lot, a few blocks from the Redrock Inn. His informant had told him about the woman looking for Brock Tolman—the two of them were friends, at least, he'd said. Maybe even lovers. And he'd managed to find out where she was staying. That was all Jaeger had needed to carry out his plan.

While the rodeo was in progress, he'd picked the lock on the motel room and set up the trap. Rigged to go off when the door was opened, the bomb was similar to the one he'd used on the mailbox at the Tolman Ranch—simple to make and easy to hide, but powerful enough to obliterate a man— or a woman—at close range. After setting the sensitive trigger, all that had remained was to bide his time at a safe distance.

Now, as the smoke fanned out on the wind and the wail of sirens echoed through the night, Jaeger counted his work as done. He never went back to check on a job. That was the way less experienced colleagues got caught. And in this case, whether the woman died or was only disfigured by her burns, the end result would be the same. Brock Tolman would suffer.

Jaeger would report the success to his client, clearing the way to close the contract by killing Tolman in the most efficient way possible. Then he would collect the last installment of his pay and move on.

Climbing into the tan Dodge Charger that was as invisible as he was, Jaeger drove out of the parking lot and headed for the highway.

CHAPTER 16

THE DISTANCE FROM THE HILTON TO THE REDROCK INN was about four blocks. With emergency vehicles cramming the street, running was the fastest way to get there. Tess plunged ahead of Brock, pushing her way through the onlookers that thronged the sidewalk. Wise, kind Ruben. His was the strength that held the ranch family together. Always calm and patient, always there.

Please, Tess prayed as she ran. *Please don't let him die!*

Ahead, she could hear shouting voices and see flashing lights—two police cars, a hulking fire engine, and an ambulance—that was where Ruben would be if he was alive, or even if he wasn't. She fought her way closer, through the milling crowd. Where the door to the motel room had been there was nothing but a scorched and gaping hole. But the units on either side, apart from shattered windows, appeared mostly intact. Had there been people inside them? Were they hurt?

A uniformed policeman stopped her at the yellow tape. "Get back, miss. This is a crime scene."

"Please!" Tess insisted. "The man in that room was my foreman, my friend. I have to know whether he's alive."

"All right. But only for a minute. And don't get any closer."

Brock had caught up with her. He stayed at her side as she passed into the taped-off area. Two medics were lifting a stretcher off a gurney to load it into the ambulance. Tess glimpsed a familiar, weathered face. The eyes were closed, the skin streaked with soot and burns. Pushing closer, she caught the paramedic's arm. "I know him. His name's Ruben. Ruben Diego. Is he alive?"

"He's unconscious." The Navajo paramedic kept working as he spoke. "He was on the ground, like maybe the blast blew him backward. Superficial burns. Shock. Concussion. Get back. We need to get him to the ER."

"What hospital?"

"Yavapai Regional. Willow Creek Road." He climbed in next to the stretcher. The door closed behind him. Seconds later the ambulance, lights flashing, siren screaming, was pushing through the heavy traffic. Still stunned, Tess stared after it.

"Come on." Brock tugged her arm. "We'll take my car."

They ran back the way they'd come. Brock's SUV was in the hotel parking garage. They both knew the way to the hospital.

"This is my fault." Tess was fighting tears. "If only I'd been there—"

"If you'd been there, you couldn't have done a damned thing," Brock said. "You'd probably have been killed. And this wasn't your doing, Tess. It was mine. Whoever rigged this explosion had to be the same bastard who blew up my mailbox. Now two fine, innocent men have paid for my past sins."

"But this bomb wasn't meant for you. And I can't imagine it was meant for Ruben. It was meant for me."

"Yes, but only because of our connection. I know we've tried to be careful, but there were people who saw us together and already knew you were important to me."

Brock gunned the engine to fly through a light that was just turning red. "But how could this monster know where you were staying? Hell, I didn't even know. Did you tell anybody?"

Tess searched her memory, struggling to calm her churning thoughts. Suddenly the conversation came back. "Oh my God!" she gasped. "Brock, I did mention the motel and the room to one person. It was Jim!"

In spite of its cheerful decor, the ER waiting room fit Brock's idea of a purgatory, where friends and families waited to hear the fate of their loved ones. Survival or death? Recovery or a disabled life? Eternities seemed to pass while they waited, scared and uncertain.

Some rodeo injuries were being treated behind the forbidding double doors. Brock had learned about them just by listening. A cowboy had been trampled by a saddle bronc. Sitting across the room, his young wife struggled to distract two crying children. An older couple, their son tossed by a bull, held hands in an effort to comfort each other.

For Tess, there was Ruben, who might or might not live.

She sat next to Brock, staring down at her tightly clenched hands. Brock ached to lay a comforting arm around her shoulders, but she was lost in grief and guilt. She would never stop blaming herself for having mentioned the motel and room number to Jim.

Jim Carson. So damned likable with his shy grin. So pleasant and helpful. But every time something had gone wrong, he'd either been there, or he'd known about what was happening—like who had begun picking up the mail, and where the Cessna would be left in Vegas. He'd probably put the rattlesnake in the trailer and pulled down that barbed wire fence. He could also have been the one to mail the news clippings from Tucson and Phoenix and leave the unposted one in the mailbox.

Brock cursed himself. Why hadn't he guessed sooner? How could he not have figured it out? If his theory about a team of three people was right, then Jim would be the go-between—the connection between the money person and the criminal. The picture made perfect sense. The only question was what to do about it.

Confronting Jim would be a bad idea. Without solid proof, he'd deny everything, warn his partners, and destroy any chance of the truth ever coming out. Keep him close—for now that was the only solution. Pretend to trust him, but watch his every move—especially any phone calls or other attempt to pass on messages.

A nudge from Tess alerted Brock. The doctor, who looked young enough to be in high school, had come out through the swinging doors. He was walking toward them, his expression unreadable.

Tess sprang to her feet. "How is he?" she demanded.

"His vitals have stabilized, and we've dressed the burns," the doctor said. "They're not fatal. But he's not out of the woods yet. The biggest worry is the concussion."

"So he's still unconscious?"

"Yes. We're prepping him for a brain scan. We'll know more when that's done."

"And you'll let me know what you find?"

"Certainly. But it's going to take some time. You might want to get some rest and come back."

"I'm not going anywhere," Tess said. "When he wakes up, I want to be with him."

"I understand," the doctor said. "We'll keep you informed as best we can, but it's bound to be a busy night." At the sound of his beeper, he turned away and disappeared through the swinging doors.

Tess was trembling. Tears welled in her eyes as she faced Brock. "I'm staying, but you don't have to," she said.

"What can I do for you, Tess?" he asked. "I'll stay if you want, but there must be ways I can help. Your bulls will need looking after. I can do that. What else? You'll want to call your family in the morning. Where's your phone?"

"Oh—it's in my purse. I left it in your hotel room. The keys to the truck are in there, too."

"I'll get your purse now. Meanwhile . . ." He slipped several bills out of his wallet and pressed them into her hand. "You'll need something to eat. And maybe other things, too. I'll be back as soon as I can."

"Make sure the rig is safe. Don't open any doors until you've checked."

"I'll keep that in mind." He gave her a quick, hard hug and hurried out to his SUV.

By the time Brock had found Tess's purse and returned it to her at the hospital, it was almost dawn. "Any news?" he asked her.

"Not yet." Her eyes were laced with red and framed in shadows. She looked exhausted, but he knew she wouldn't rest or leave the room until she'd heard from the doctor.

"Can I get you something from the vending machine?" he offered. "There's fresh coffee, and I think I saw a Danish with your name on it."

"Just coffee. Thanks, Brock."

He brought her a steaming cup. "When are you going to call the ranch?" he asked.

"Not until I know more about Ruben. I'm hoping for good news." Tears welled in her eyes. "I can't imagine our lives without him. Ruben is the glue that holds our family together."

And so are you, Tess, Brock thought. *Whatever happens, you're strong enough to pull them all through.*

"I'm going to look after your bulls now," he said. "Call me as soon as you hear anything."

"I will. And be careful. That awful person could still be out there waiting for you. There's a gun in the truck's glove box. If you don't have one, take it."

"I've got a gun, thanks. I'll call you after I've seen to your bulls."

The hospital registration desk opened early. On his way out, Brock stopped by long enough to sign the paperwork, naming himself as the responsible party for Ruben Diego's medical expenses. It was the least he could do.

After that, he drove to the arena and parked next to Tess's truck and trailer. As he inspected her vehicle for any attached devices, it occurred to him that the killer could've just as easily rigged the bomb here. But maybe the parking lot had been too busy and too brightly lit.

Looking down the row, he could see his own big silver trailer. The light was on in the sleeping quarters up front. Jim and Curtis, the other man who'd come along, were up and would soon be in the pens, taking care of the three bulls they'd brought to the rodeo. Brock warned himself to be prepared for anything.

Shouldering the bag of Total Bull chow that he'd found in the back of Tess's trailer, he passed through the gate into the pen complex. Tess's four bulls appeared to be fine. Brock filled their feed tubs and gave them fresh water from the nearby hose. Quicksand seemed to recognize Brock. He snorted and scraped at the sawdust with his single horn.

"Hello, you rascal," Brock said, chuckling in spite of his worries. "I see somebody's finally making you earn your keep. See that you put on a show tonight. I know a lady who needs good news."

The black bull lowed and tossed his head as Brock hefted the bag of chow and walked away. He'd already decided that if Tess wasn't able to manage her bulls tonight, he would do the job for her, but that matter could wait. He also needed to call and let her know her animals were all right. But first he had some business to attend to.

"Hey, Boss." Jim, the little Judas, greeted Brock with a friendly grin. "I saw you over there, feeding Miss Champion's bulls. Is she all right?"

Brock reined back the urge to bury his fist in that smirking face. "Miss Champion was sick all night. She thinks it must've been something she ate. I told her I'd take care of her bulls."

Jim wasn't quick-witted enough to hide the shocked expression that flashed across his face. "What about her foreman?" he asked. "I saw him last night. Can't he take care of the bulls?"

"He's sick, too," Brock lied shamelessly. "They both had marinated lamb kabobs at that Middle Eastern restaurant by the Hilton last night. I warned them that it might not be safe. They should've taken my advice."

"So . . . where are they now?" Jim's face had gone pale.

"In the ER. Neither of them could keep anything down. But they should be all right by this evening. Tess—Miss Champion—doesn't want to miss the chance to see her black bull buck at a big event."

Jim looked ill. "But she told me—" He cut himself off.

"She told you what, Jim?"

"Uh . . . nothing. I must've been thinking of another time."

"Well, I've got to go back. You and Curtis keep an eye on her bulls as well as ours," Brock said. "If anything happens to them, I'll hold you both responsible."

"Don't worry, we'll watch them." Curtis was older, a good cowboy and a trusted hand. Whatever was going on with Jim, Brock felt confident that Curtis wasn't involved.

Brock climbed into his SUV, backed out, and drove slowly down the row of rigs. As he passed his own trailer, he saw Jim standing in the morning shadow. He was talking on his phone.

On the way back to the hospital, Brock made a call to Tess's phone. She answered, breathless.

"Brock, I'm with Ruben! He's awake and talking! He's going to be all right!"

Brock could tell she was in tears. He breathed a silent *Thank you, God.* "I'll be right there," he said.

Ruben looked like hell, Brock thought. His head was wrapped, his skin covered with patches of dressing. Oxygen flowed through a clip on his nose, and a saline drip fed into a vein in his left hand. But his wrinkled, brown face was smiling.

"As soon as I touched the doorknob I could tell something was different," he said. "I jumped back and felt the blast. That's all I remember." He gestured toward his ear. "My head hurts, and I can't hear worth a damn, but the doctor says that will get better." With effort, he turned his head toward Tess. "I'm just glad it was me and not you, *hija.* And you"—he fixed his gaze on Brock—"don't you let anything happen to this girl. Hear? Or I'll come and take you out myself."

"I'll guard her with my life," Brock said, leaning close so Ruben could hear him or at least read his lips. "And I'm going to catch the bastard who did this and see that he pays."

"Good." Ruben sounded tired.

"The doctor wants to keep you a few more days," Tess said. "Then we'll bring Shane's van and take you home. I called Maria and my sisters. They send their love. Right now, you need to get some rest."

He caught her wrist. "Are you bucking your bulls tonight?"

Tess nodded. "I'll be helping her," Brock said.

"The sage is in the truck. Use it if you need to."

"I will. If you're awake, I'll come see you after the rodeo."

"Don't worry, I will wait for you," he said.

She gave him a smile and walked out of the room, with Brock behind her. As the door closed behind them, she sagged, quivering, against him. He wrapped her in his arms. "It's all right, Tess," he murmured against her hair. "You don't have to be strong all the time."

"What if he'd died?" she whispered. "Ruben's been like a father to me. And he was blameless. If I ever see the fiend who set that bomb, so help me, I'll kill him myself."

"Come on." He ushered her down the hall with a hand on her back. "Let's get some breakfast in the cafeteria. I'll catch you up on what's happening, and we can plan the rest of our day."

Jaeger gassed the Charger in Wickenburg, where he'd spent the night. Then, cursing, he pulled onto the highway and headed back to Prescott, the way he'd come. He'd reported the success of the explosion to his client and was enjoying a celebratory breakfast at Denny's when the call had come from the idiot kid he'd depended on for information. The Champion woman had been nowhere near the motel when the bomb went off.

Someone had triggered the device—maybe some fool who had the wrong room number, or a burglar trying to break in. Who it had been didn't matter. What did matter was that he'd reported a mission completed and requested another installment on his fee when, in reality, all he'd done was blast a hole in a motel room. As a man who took pride in being a professional, he couldn't let that stand. He had to go back to Prescott and finish the job—that would include offing the worthless twit who'd proven himself too unreliable to live and who already knew too much about him. Then he would take out Brock Tolman, collect his final payment, and enjoy a well-deserved vacation.

*   *   *

Val stood in the front yard watching a bank of roiling black clouds spill over the western ridge. Rain would be a blessing to the land. But in her present mood, the darkening sky loomed like a portent of trouble in her life and the life of the ranch family.

The morning had started with Tess's phone call about Ruben's being injured in an explosion. Ruben was alive, thank heaven, and was recuperating in the hospital. But Val had a feeling her sister wasn't telling the family everything. What had caused the explosion? Why had Ruben been involved? Was the danger over? So far, those questions had no answers.

Then, shortly after Tess's call, Casey had phoned Val, insisting that he needed to talk with her in person. "I'm coming to the ranch," he'd said. "Wait for me."

Much as she'd missed him, Val had sensed a painful confrontation ahead. "That's a long drive just to talk," she'd hedged. "Can't we deal with this now, over the phone? Or can't you at least tell me what it's about?"

"Not this time. Trust me, Val. I'll be leaving here in a few minutes."

So here she was, almost three hours later, gazing up toward the pass, waiting for his black pickup truck to come zigzagging down the switchback road. She had no idea what Casey had to tell her—just the premonition that her life was about to change forever.

By the time the pickup rolled into the yard, a stiff breeze had sprung up. The clouds were stampeding across the sky. Val had taken shelter on the front porch with the dog. When Casey parked and climbed out of the cab, the dog ran to meet him, wagging and dancing. Val did not.

He strode across the yard to give her a constrained hug. "Where can we talk?" he asked.

"How about here? It's too windy for a walk, and the whole house has become a nursery since the baby came home."

"Fine." He moved two chairs to face each other. "It's good to see you, Val."

"I'll decide whether it's good to see you after I've heard what you came to say." She noticed for the first time that he was carrying a thin canvas briefcase. "What's in there?" she asked, attempting a feeble joke. "If we were married, I might be expecting divorce papers."

"It's a record of everything I've gathered," he said. "You can look if you want, but I'd rather just tell you about it."

Val felt her stomach clench. "Casey, I can't deal with this. I told you—"

"Sit down, Val. Don't say a word until I've finished. Whether you want to or not, you need to hear this."

Val's instincts told her not to argue, even though what he had to say might break her heart. She sat, her hands gripping the arm of the cheap plastic chair as Casey's account unspooled, from the detective's early research to the adoption records and the names of the parents.

"Our son has a name," Casey said. "It's Matthew. Matthew Randall Peterson."

That isn't the name I would have given him. Val tried to keep silent, hoping the ordeal would soon end. But there were questions she couldn't hold back.

"Why do I need to know this, Casey? Why couldn't you just keep it to yourself and leave me alone?"

"Because of what I'm about to tell you," he said. "But maybe it would be better if I showed you." He unzipped the briefcase, took out a photocopied page, and handed it to her.

On the page was an enlarged image of a newspaper item. It was brief, not even a full column. But as she read it—the family in the terrible highway crash, the parents dead at the scene, the son, Matthew, taken away in critical condition—scalding tears welled in Val's eyes and trickled down her cheeks. Her throat felt tight and raw, as if she'd swallowed sand. "What happened to him?" The question emerged as a hoarse whisper. "Our son—did he die?"

"Nobody seems to know, Val. The hospital has no record of admitting him. There's no death record to be found. It's as if every trace of him has been lost."

"And you're going to Bakersfield to look for him."

"Yes, even if all I find is his grave. At least we'll have closure." Casey's eyes pleaded with her. "I can't just let this go and walk away."

She took a breath, so deep that her chest ached from it. "Then I can't either. He's my son, too. I'm going with you."

Tess's duffel, with a change of clothes and other personal items, had been destroyed in the explosion. After breakfast, on the way back to the hotel, they'd stopped at a Walmart. Brock waited in the SUV while she'd picked up jeans, a plaid shirt, some socks and underwear, and a few drugstore items.

"Shouldn't we go and check the bulls?" she asked as she climbed into the passenger seat and clicked her seat belt.

"I'll go later. But you should wait a few hours," Brock said. "When I saw Jim this morning, I told him that you and Ruben got sick after dinner and had to go to the ER. I wanted to see the look on his face when he found out you weren't at the motel—and to cover for Ruben's not showing up. I could probably have told a more plausible story—I was thinking on my feet. But, anyway, Jim bought it."

"And did you see it? The look on his face?"

"I did. It was only for a second, but he looked as if he'd been blasted in the gut with buckshot."

"That nice young man. I can scarcely believe it."

"As I drove away, I saw him on his phone, probably calling his bomber pal. We'll have to watch our step. If the bastard knows he failed, he'll be trying something else." Brock laid his free hand on Tess's knee. "I'm sorry. The last thing I ever wanted was to expose you to danger. It appears that whoever's putting money behind this doesn't just want to kill me. They want me to lose someone I love."

Tess's breath caught. Brock had never said he loved her. It was probably just a slip. Right now, she needed to look at the larger meaning of his words. "If that's true, maybe this person lost someone, and they blame you for it. They want you to suffer a loss, too—to feel what they feel before you die. Does that make sense?"

"Perfect sense. First, because I had no family, they killed my animals. When that wasn't enough, the hit man came after you. You should take your bulls and go home now, Tess, before that killer strikes again. I can look in on Ruben for you."

"No. Tonight is Quicksand's big chance. Clay Rafferty is here. If he likes what he sees, it could mean great things for the future of the ranch."

"You could take your other bulls. I could buck Quicksand for you and load him in my trailer for the trip home."

"No," Tess insisted. "Quicksand's accustomed to working with just two people—Ruben and me. I have to be here to handle him, or he might not cooperate. As for taking him with your bulls, in a strange trailer, that could undo all his training. I can't entrust him to anybody else, not even you."

"All right. But as soon as Quicksand's finished bucking tonight, I'm loading your bulls and taking you out of here."

"You're not going with me. I can make the trip alone. It's just driving."

"Don't argue. Curtis can drive my bulls home, with or without Jim. And I can send for my vehicle later. Right now, let's get back to the hotel. We could both use some rest before tonight."

Tess looked exhausted. Brock was tired, too, but he was too wired to close his eyes. He would use the time to do some long overdue research.

While Tess was in the shower, he set up his laptop and, using an app he'd purchased, requested a background check on Jim Carson, or James Carson. Several listings, most with photos, came up, none of them fitting the young man who worked for him. He narrowed the search, tried different parameters. Nothing.

Jim had to be using an alias.

So who was he? Brock thought about the clippings that had come in the mail, all of them connected to the rollover that had killed Mia Carpenter. The accident would have taken place before Jim was born. But there could still be a connection.

The original clippings were at home in his safe—the first one about the accident, the second about his own conviction, the third about the abandoned search for his late friend, Jeff Carpenter. Jeff had gone missing in Branson. Maybe he could find the same news item, or a similar one.

His search brought up an obituary. He skimmed it to the end.

Mr. Carpenter, who was a practicing attorney in Branson, grew up in Ridgewood, the son of the late auto dealer Chase Carpenter. He married Carla Lundberg. They were later divorced. His former wife, his father, and his younger sister, Mia, preceded him in death. He is survived by his mother, Johanna Smith Carpenter, and his son, Jason Carpenter. A memorial service, yet to be scheduled, will be held in Branson.

The old work colleague who'd told Brock about Jeff had also mentioned that Jeff's mother had suffered a stroke after her husband died and was confined to a nursing home. By now she'd be in her seventies and could be senile or dead. He could scratch her off his list of suspects.

But there was Jeff's son. His initials were the same as Jim's, and the age would be about right. Bringing up the app again, he entered the name Jason Carpenter.

After a few clicks, there he was—smiling photo and all. Without a doubt, the young man who called himself Jim Carson was Jeff's son, Jason.

But a world of unanswered questions remained. Jeff Carpenter's body hadn't been found. Could he still be alive?

Maybe Jeff wanted to get rid of the one man who knew about his secret guilt. Brock could understand that. But why not just kill him and be done with it? Why all the theatrical touches? The dead livestock? The bombs?

It was time he backed Jason Carpenter, alias Jim, into a corner and demanded some straight answers.

"What's this?" Tess had come up behind him. Fresh and damp from her shower and wrapped in the white terry robe provided by the hotel, she looked tempting enough to ravish on the spot. But this wasn't the time.

Brock showed her the screen. "So this is our young friend Jim," she said. "And goodness, look at his record. No arrests, not even a parking ticket that shows up here. And he's listed as a former student at Blessed Path Divinity College. The kid's a blasted saint!"

"But we know better, don't we?"

"What are you going to do?" She came around the sofa and sat down next to him.

"First, you're going to get some rest. Then, if there's time, we can pay a quick visit to Ruben before we go to the arena for the rodeo."

"Where we'll pretend to barely know each other, right?" she asked.

"We'll see. Whatever we do, I plan to keep an eye on you. Understand?"

"I understand. But what about Jim?"

"While you're napping, I'll go and check on the bulls. While I'm there, I plan to back our young friend against a wall and put some real fear into him. Before I'm through, he's going to tell me who he's working with, who's putting up the money, and why."

"I'll get dressed and go with you," Tess said.

"Oh, no, you don't." Brock stood, put an arm around her shoulders, and steered her into the bedroom. "You're supposed to be sick. It's too early for you to recover and show up at the arena. And you really could use some rest. But keep the door locked and chained. Don't open it for anybody but me. If you're hungry by the time I get back, we can order room service. Understood?"

"Yes, but do you need to be so bossy?"

"Bossy is my middle name. Especially when it comes to protecting a woman I care about." He gave her a quick kiss and left before her luscious body could lure him into bed.

He drove through the Saturday afternoon traffic, past Whiskey Row, where tourists strolled along the sidewalks and crowded into the bars, restaurants, and live music venues. The morning clouds had cleared. Sunlight glared through the windshield as he planned in his head how he would get Jim to talk. He knew better than to use physical force. But the threat of it, or the idea of going to prison, might be enough to loosen the young man's tongue.

Still pondering, he swung the SUV into the parking lot. His thoughts scattered like buckshot as he saw the two police cruisers and an ambulance pulled up to one of the arena's rear entrances. Uniformed officers were pushing back the crowds, stringing yellow crime scene tape.

Parking clear of the congestion, he climbed out of the vehicle and jogged closer. Just ahead of him in the crowd, he could see Curtis's lanky frame, red shirt, and straw Stetson. Brock edged his way through the pushing bodies to catch up with him.

"What's happening, Curtis?" he demanded. "Have you seen Jim anywhere?"

The face Curtis turned toward him was pale with shock. "Jim's dead," he said. "Somebody found his body in the men's restroom. Word has it the police are calling it a drug overdose. But you know Jim, Boss. Hell, that kid never took drugs in his life!"

CHAPTER 17

BROCK HAD LEFT HIS LAPTOP AND INVITED TESS TO USE it. Unable to sleep, she had dressed and was composing an e-mail to her sisters when she heard his knock and the sound of his voice.

"It's me, Tess. Let me in."

Setting the laptop aside, she flew to release the chain and open the door. As soon as she saw his face, pale with lingering shock, she knew something was wrong.

"My bulls! Are they all right?" It was the first thought that sprang to her mind.

"Your bulls are fine. I checked. But Jim's dead. A cleaner found him in one of the restrooms—a likely drug overdose, somebody said. But we know what really happened. He died the same way Cannonball died. Probably because he knew too much." Brock stepped into the room, picked up the remote, and switched on the TV. "I saw a press van drive up as I was leaving. Maybe we can get some breaking news."

He flipped through channels to a local station. "Here it is."

The screen showed a jam of onlookers and emergency vehicles, then a closer shot of paramedics carrying a covered body to the ambulance before the station went to a commercial.

"You're sure that's Jim?" she asked.

"Curtis saw the scene before the police arrived. It's Jim." He clicked off the TV. "The monster who did this is out there, Tess. He's close, and he's watching us. I've ordered Curtis to load the bulls and get out of town now. You need to do the same. I can follow you home to make sure you're all right."

"No."

"Don't be stubborn, Tess. He's tried to kill both of us. He'll try again."

"You heard me," she said. "You can leave if you want. But I've had enough of letting that murdering goon run my life. I'll be careful. I'll even carry a gun. But I'm not leaving town until Quicksand has had his chance to buck."

"Quicksand will have other chances. Damn it, I don't want to lose you, Tess. I love you."

Tears welled in Tess's eyes. She had ached to hear those words. But this was the worst possible timing. She glared up at him, letting him see her tears and her fury.

"Don't you dare play that card with me, Brock Tolman! I love you, too, but if you think that's going to change my mind, you couldn't be more wrong. I'm staying until my bulls have bucked. And if he comes after me, so help me, I'll kill the bastard myself!"

"You won't have to." He caught her in his arms and held her close. "I'm going to be right next to you the whole time, with my gun in plain sight. If he makes a move, and I recognize him, he's a dead man."

She pulled away and looked up at him. "That's the trouble. We don't know what he looks like. We don't know anything about him."

"We know how he acts. Staying invisible is part of his game. He doesn't want to be identified in any way, which is probably why he killed Jim. Our safest bet is to stay where there are people—in the pens and around the bucking chutes, where strangers won't be allowed. We know he'll have his eyes on us. But if he can't get to where we are without showing himself . . ." Brock's mouth tightened.

"He could still shoot."

"He could. But that doesn't sound like his style. A gunshot would draw too much attention. That's the one thing in our favor. He's a professional. He doesn't want to do anything that'll get him seen and caught."

"So how can we possibly know him?"

"Unless he gives himself away, we can't. So we'll need to keep a constant lookout and check our vehicles before we touch them. Damn it, I still wish you'd take your bulls and leave now. It's not too late."

"I've told you where I stand."

"Then heaven help us both. We're going to need it."

They ordered pizza from room service and ate it in front of the TV. Neither of them had much appetite, but they wouldn't get another chance to sit down and eat before the rodeo was over.

There was no more word about the death at the arena. The news channel had already moved on to other stories. "It could be a day or two before the folks at the crime lab figure out that Jim was murdered," Brock said.

"They should be able to tell that from the absence of needle tracks," Tess said. "But if they're backlogged, a supposed druggie might not be high priority."

"I'll give the police a call tomorrow and let them know that he worked for me. One way or another, that fact's bound to come out. Best if it comes from me. I'd do it now, but they might call me in. I don't want to be delayed at the station when I need to be with you."

"Will you tell them his real name?"

A beat of silence passed before Brock spoke. "Probably. How much I tell them might depend on what happens tonight."

"I promised Ruben that we'd come by after the rodeo. I'd really like to see him before we leave."

"I know you're a woman of your word, but that might not be a good idea. If we're still being tracked, a visit could put Ruben in danger, too. Our murdering friend doesn't appear too fussy about who he kills."

She sighed. "You're right. At least I'll plan on calling Ruben to give him the rodeo news. Oh, Brock, he didn't deserve this. Neither did Cyrus. Life is so unfair!"

Sadness, worry, and anger mingled in the expression that passed across his face. "Come on," he said. "Let's get back to the arena where we can keep an eye on your bulls."

By the time Brock had checked out of the hotel and driven to the arena, the Tolman Ranch trailer was gone from the parking lot. While Tess waited by her bulls, Brock left her long enough to arrange a replacement for the bull he'd sent home and to check the posted roster.

She felt safe enough in the pens, with security guards at both entrances. The faces of the cowhands and stock contractors were familiar. The chutes, as well, were off-limits to anyone who didn't belong there. She could breathe and enjoy the show. But somewhere, beyond this small island of safety, predatory eyes were watching. She could sense them, almost feel them.

On her way in, after Brock had checked her rig, she'd picked up the bundle of sage and a lighter. She would have taken the gun she kept in the locked glove box, but he'd discouraged her. He had clearance to carry the heavy pistol he wore in a shoulder holster under his vest. But she had no such permission.

Leaning against the rails, she watched her four bulls. The three experienced animals were calm. But Quicksand was restless, tossing wood chips with his horn, as if he'd picked up on the tension around him. She'd hoped that after a two-day exposure to the noise of a big rodeo—and the fact that the main grandstand was on the far side of the arena, a comfortable distance away—Quicksand would settle down. But something was clearly bothering the big black bull.

Brock returned a few minutes later, as the fans were flocking through the gates and into their seats. "I checked the roster," he said. "Good news. Cody Barnes will be riding Rocket Man."

"Great. He's young, but he's good. And what about Quicksand?"

"Even better news. He got drawn by Joao Reyes Santos."

"Oh, that's fantastic." Santos, a Brazilian ranking in the top five, had scored ninety-three points on Whirlwind the last time out. "Quicksand could give him a spectacular ride," she said. "Or even a spectacular buck-off." *Or nothing*, she thought, but didn't voice her fears.

Beyond the chutes, the rodeo started with the traditional parading of colors, the national anthem, and a prayer. Then the action began. After last night's elimination round, this was the final in which the cowboys and cowgirls would compete for buckles, prize money, and points to boost their national standing.

The open layout of the arena allowed a partial view from the pens. The first buckles were awarded in team roping, steer wrestling, and tiedown events. The young McKenna brothers took first place in bareback and saddle bronc. And the petite Cheyenne McKenna surpassed her personal best time to win in barrel racing.

After more events, it was time for bull riding. Excitement rippled through the crowd as the arena crew rolled out the safety barrels and the bullfighters, dressed in clown gear and makeup, took their places.

Rocket Man would be bucking fourth, Quicksand last of eight bulls. Brock shadowed Tess as her first bull was herded into the narrow pen and fitted with his flank strap. Rocket Man was an older bull, easy in the chute but a solid bucker. Tess had few worries as he entered the empty bucking chute without any resistance.

The first two bulls had bucked off their riders out of the gate. The third, a rank, spotted bovine named Monkey Business, gave his cowboy a six-second ride before hurling him in the dust, then wheeling in a head-down charge. The clowns sprang in to distract the bull, giving the rider a few seconds to scramble to safety. The crowd roared its excitement. Next it would be Rocket Man's turn.

The bull tossed his head as Cody Barnes dropped onto his back. Working above the chute to steady him while Brock pulled the young cowboy's rope, Tess was too busy to wonder whether she was being watched. Only after the ride had qualified with a good score of 87 and she was unfastening the flank strap did she realize her hands were shaking.

"Are you all right?" Brock asked as the bull trotted back down the passage to his pen.

"I'll be fine," she said. "Let's go get Quicksand ready for his big show."

By the time he was herded into the small holding pen to get his flank strap, Quicksand was behaving like an oversize toddler in meltdown mode. He was swinging his massive head and shoulders, banging against the thick steel rails. It was as if he was sensing Tess's own anxiety and acting on it.

Tess thought of the sage bundle she'd thrust into the deep pocket of her jacket. She should have lit it for him earlier. Now it was too late. By the time she and Brock maneuvered the soft, cotton strap around Quicksand's flanks and fastened it securely, the next empty bucking chute was waiting for him.

Quicksand was herded into the chute. His eyes were rolling, showing the whites. Was he afraid or angry?

As the current rider lasted eight seconds on his bull for the highest score of the night, cheers went up from the grandstand. The extra noise wasn't helping. Quicksand was bucking and slamming harder than ever.

Santos, a legendary rider, currently fourth in world standings, waited on the platform above the chute, dressed in a protective vest, long-fringed chaps, and spurs with blunted rowels, designed to help control the bull without hurting him. As the announcer boomed out the next ride over the P.A., mentioning that Quicksand had never been ridden, Santos lowered himself onto the bull's back.

When the rider's weight settled over him, Quicksand quivered and stopped struggling. As Brock pulled the rope tight and Santos wrapped it around his gloved hand, the bull became a massive ebony statue. Not so much as an ear twitched.

Watching from the platform above the chute, Tess felt her heart plummet. This was bad. More than bad. It was a nightmare. "Please, Quicksand," she begged in a whisper. "Please buck. I know you can."

The seasoned rider, seemingly unaware of the problem, shifted his weight behind his hand and nodded to the gate man. The gate swung open. Quicksand stood there, quivering, as if afraid to move.

Santos, as cool as winter rain, raised his leg slightly and kicked the bull's side hard with the blunted rowel of his spur.

Quicksand exploded like a shooting star.

As the bull flew out of the gate, starting the clock, Santos balanced with each move, back straight, arm high and pumping. Quicksand shot into the air again and again, twisting and spinning. By the time the clock had reached six seconds, the crowd was screaming. They were witnessing a great ride.

Then, at seven seconds, Quicksand made his move. A sudden direction change in midleap threw Santos off-balance. He flew to one side, landing on his feet in the dirt.

Wheeling in his tracks, Quicksand charged his rider. The clown who'd stepped into his path grabbed his single horn, only to be tossed high over the bull's back. A few wild seconds later, Santos had scrambled to safety. The clown was on his feet, and the roper was herding Quicksand through the exit gate.

The numbers came up on the big screen. No points for the rider, 96.5 points for the bull. An incredible score.

Tess, with Brock at her side, couldn't stop the tears as she unfastened Quicksand's flank strap in the narrow chute. "That was amazing!" she said, speaking to her bull. "I knew you could do it, big boy!"

"I knew he could do it, too." Santos stood on the other side of the chute. "He'd forgotten who and what he was. He just needed a nudge to remind him."

"I couldn't believe you knew what to do," Tess said.

The handsome Brazilian smiled. "In my time, I've ridden close to a thousand bulls, all different," he said. "As you Americans are fond of saying, this isn't my first rodeo."

"But you deserved to ride him for the full eight seconds. You were magnificent!"

"Quicksand was the magnificent one. It was an honor to be matched with such a bull." Reaching through the rails, Santos gave Quicksand's shoulder a pat. "We'll meet again, big boy. And then we'll see which of us is the boss."

As Santos walked away and Quicksand trotted down the passage to his pen, Brock put an arm around Tess and hugged her. This was a joyous moment, a brief celebration to be shared. But somewhere in the crowded arena, a cold-blooded killer watched and waited. Brock needed to get them both to safety.

With the rodeo at an end, fans were streaming out of the grandstand on the far side of the dirt oval. There was plenty of activity on the near side, too, with people leaving the VIP and competitor sections.

Keeping Tess close, Brock escorted her back through the chute area. Behind the pens, trailers were already backed up to the loading gates. Diesel smoke from idling engines permeated the dusty air. Animals, snorting and lowing, thundered up the ramps.

Brock let his vest front fall loose to expose the pistol in case anyone was watching. "We could be here awhile," he said. "We'll need to wait for loading space. And before we move your rig, we can't forget to check underneath for anything that doesn't belong there."

"That's a good idea," she said. "But meanwhile, I really need a pit stop before we get out of here. There's a restroom at the foot of the grandstand. I won't be long."

She started away, but he caught up with her. "No, you don't," he said. "I'm not letting you out of my sight."

"You can't go into the women's restroom."

"Of course, I can't. But I can walk with you and stand watch outside the door. I won't let anybody pass who looks the least bit suspicious."

"All right. But don't blame me if some little old lady starts beating you with her purse because she has to go and you won't let her in."

"Funny girl. Let's go. Lead the way."

He walked with her across the floodlit end of the arena, toward the neon restrooms sign. People milled around them, walking and chatting. Most were probably headed out to the main parking lot, but Brock found himself casting suspicious eyes at anyone who came close or even looked in their direction. This was a dangerous place at a dangerous time. The killer could be anywhere.

By the time they reached the side-by-side restrooms, the crowd had thinned. Two teenage girls came out through the door of the women's room, laughing and giggling as they walked away. As Brock posted himself a few steps from the door, a young mother, leading her little girl by the hand, opened the door and went inside. Tess followed them.

A short while later the mother and child emerged, the little girl wiping her hands on her pink princess T-shirt. Tess was still inside when a stocky gray-haired woman in a baggy dress, with a flowered tote bag slung over her shoulder, shuffled past him with her walker. Remembering how Tess had joked about an old lady beating him with her purse, Brock stepped out of her way as she pulled open the door and disappeared.

Glancing around, he could see no one who looked or acted suspicious. All the same, his danger senses were prickling. As soon as Tess came out through that door, he would rush her back to the stock pens, load her bulls, and hit the road. He couldn't get out of this town fast enough.

The floodlights cast a moving shadow from around the corner of the men's room. Drawing the pistol, Brock moved down the sidewalk and rounded the corner—only to find a teenage punk lighting up a forbidden joint.

As he saw Brock's gun, the young man dropped the joint and flung up his hands. "Don't shoot, mister!" he gasped. "I wasn't doin' nothin'."

"Just get out of here," Brock growled.

As the teen fled, Brock holstered the pistol and strode back to his place. A middle-aged woman in a rhinestone-studded cowgirl vest walked up to the restroom door and tugged on the handle.

The door didn't open.

* * *

There were three stalls in the restroom, including a larger one for the disabled. Tess had come out of a stall and was washing her hands when the door to the handicapped stall opened.

Reflected in the mirror above the sink, she saw an elderly woman with curly gray hair approaching from behind. Tess wouldn't have given her a second thought. But then, by chance, she noticed something.

The woman was wearing latex surgical gloves and holding something in her hand.

Acting on reflex, Tess spun around, feet kicking. The woman dodged the blows and lunged at her from the side. Tess's eyes caught the gleam of a long hypodermic needle, the kind used on large animals.

Stumbling, she made a break for the door, but a powerful hand caught her wrist and whipped her back in the other direction. A lifetime of ranch work had made Tess strong and fit. But she was no match for her assailant. No woman would have that much strength.

Her free hand flailed at his head, fingers catching the gray curls. The wig flew off, revealing close-clipped brown hair. The expression in the light-colored eyes that met hers was pure, cold evil.

One hand gripped her wrist. The other held the syringe high, poised to strike at a vulnerable spot, like her neck, where the needle could find a vein. To avoid the fatal stab, she had to keep moving. But she was already tiring.

As she struggled, she could hear Brock's voice and the sound of his fists beating on the steel door. The door had to be locked, the deadbolt needing a key on the outside. There was no way he could get to her. She was on her own.

Then a new thought struck her. Her enemy was wearing a dress. But he was a man. And there was one thing a woman could do to incapacitate a man. Bracing her back against the sink counter, she focused all her energy into one desperate kick. Her pointed riding boot flew upward under the dress, sliced between his legs, and found its target.

Yowling with pain and rage, he doubled over. His grip on her wrist had loosened, but he'd positioned himself between her and the door, and he still had the syringe. There was no escape—only brief shelter.

Twisting free, she plunged into the handicapped stall, slammed the door behind her, and slid the lightweight bolt into place. It wouldn't hold for long, but at least she had a moment to breathe and recover her wits.

She could hear him breathing hard, still hurting from the pain she'd inflicted. But pain wouldn't stop him from trying to kill her. Any second now, he'd be after her again—not just silent and cold this time, but seething with rage like a wounded beast. How could he get to her in the stall? There was an opening under the door, high enough to crawl through. But she could inflict a lot of damage kicking and stomping him. Climbing over the top of the door would put him in an awkward position.

He was strong enough to break the flimsy lock and rip the door open. But he was in a desperate situation, too. There was only one way out of here, and Brock was waiting outside the front door with a gun—the hit man would know that.

She forced herself to speak boldly. "Listen to me. There's a man outside with a gun waiting for you. Let me go, and I promise to walk away with him. You'll be safe to leave."

"I'm not going anywhere until I kill you, bitch." His pain-laced voice was a reptilian hiss. "Your boyfriend isn't the only one with a gun. I could shoot you, then shoot him on my way out. The rodeo's over. By now he'll be alone out there."

Was he bluffing? If he had a gun, she'd seen no sign of it. But it made sense that he'd be carrying a backup weapon. If he were to use it on her, Brock would hear the shot and be ready for him. The man would be smarter to kill her silently with the needle or even with his bare hands. That would give him a better chance of taking Brock by surprise when he made his escape.

But she was overthinking. With the brief standoff running out, there was only one thing to do—fight for her life.

Now, while he was still weakened by her blow, was the time to strike. She needed a weapon. Glancing around the roomy stall, she saw the plain aluminum walker that had been left next to the toilet—probably by the man who'd made it part of his disguise.

Picking it up, she twisted off the four rubber feet, leaving the hard metal edges. The stall door opened outward against the back wall of the restroom to make an easier exit for wheelchairs and other devices. She was as scared as she had ever been in her life. But she couldn't let that stop her.

Stooping, she glanced through the space beneath the door of the stall. She could see his feet, clad in the yellow Crocs that were part of his disguise. He was standing maybe four feet away, by the sink counter. Would he have the syringe or a gun in his hand? There was no time to wonder.

Raising the handles of the walker to her chest, so that the legs stuck straight out in front, she slipped back the bolt, kicked open the door, and charged.

The door slammed harmlessly against the wall. Tess saw the syringe as the metal feet of the walker struck his chest. Shoved backward over the sink counter, he grunted in pain but didn't lose his grip on the deadly weapon. His free hand flashed out, knocked the walker to the floor, and seized the front of her jacket, holding her fast. His ugly eyes bored into hers. "Time to end this, bitch," he snarled. "I'd enjoy keeping you alive and making you hurt. But you'll be dead by the time I pull the needle out."

In a desperate move, her hand groped in her pocket and found the sage. One end of it, the end made to be burned, was smoothly rounded. The other end was bundled sage stems, dry, rigid, and sharp. As the hand with the needle came down, aiming for her neck, she shoved the stems into his eyes.

He screamed, clutching his bloodied face with the hand that had held Tess captive. She spun away and raced for the front door. Her shaking fingers fumbled with the latch that unlocked the deadbolt from the inside.

Still gripping the syringe, he lurched blindly after her. He had almost reached her when he stumbled over the walker, where it lay on the floor. Thrusting out an arm in an effort to save his balance, he fell forward, facedown, and lay still.

As the door finally opened, Tess staggered outside and fell against Brock. Still holding the pistol, he caught her with one arm. "Are you all right?" His voice was harsh with emotion.

She nodded, pressing against him. "And him?" He glanced past her to where the hit man lay facedown on the blood-smeared tiles.

"I think he might be dead, Brock. But don't go in there. He could still be dangerous."

Ignoring her plea, he eased her gently aside. "Stay here," he said.

Still armed with the gun, he walked into the restroom, nudged the fallen man with his foot, then crouched beside him to check for a pulse. He shook his head. "You can relax. He's dead."

"Then I must've killed him." Her voice broke. "I know he was an evil monster, but I've never killed anybody before—never wanted to."

"Hold on." Brock stood and used the toe of his boot to raise the hit man's torso partway. "You didn't kill him, Tess," he said. "Looking at the damage, I'd say he fell on his own needle and injected himself in the heart." He let the body sink back into position. "He got what was coming to him."

Stepping outside, he holstered the pistol, gathered her into his arms, and held her tight. Tess could feel his body trembling. "When I realized what was happening, and I couldn't get to you to protect you, Lord, it was the worst feeling I've ever had. I never want to feel like that again. I never want to let you go. I love you, Tess." He kissed her, then released her. "Come on, let's get your bulls loaded and get out of here."

"Shouldn't we call the police?"

"Somebody else can do that. Right now, I just want to take you and leave."

As if summoned by his thoughts, two security men were walking across the field toward them. Brock motioned them to stop. "There was something going on in that restroom back there," he said. "You might want to check it out."

Brock led her on, his arm around her waist providing support and protection. "I can't believe he's gone," she said. "This nightmare is really over."

He kissed the top of her head. "It isn't over, Tess," he said. "It won't be over until I end it."

CHAPTER 18

VAL GAZED THROUGH THE TRUCK WINDSHIELD AT THE SUN-baked California desert. Rolling brown hills, dotted with scrub and scattered with cheap housing tracts, stretched endlessly along the freeway. The distance from the ranch to Bakersfield could be covered in one long day. But the drive seemed to be taking forever—especially when she thought of what lay ahead.

A glance at Casey, dozing in the passenger seat, softened Val's heart. They'd left the ranch before first light, the morning after his arrival. Casey had done most of the driving. But she'd spelled him every few hours to give him a rest. By now they were both tired.

Last night, for the first time in weeks, they'd made love with tender passion. She loved Casey more than life. But this trip could prove to be a dark turning point in their relationship. If they failed to find their son—or worse, if they found proof that he'd died, how could Casey not blame her, just as she would blame herself? It would be as if, in giving up her baby, she'd signed his death warrant.

Casey stirred and opened his eyes. "Hey, beautiful, how about a pit stop? Watch for the next off-ramp. After we've had a break, I'll take the wheel for the rest of the trip."

"Suits me." Tess saw an exit lane ahead. She pulled the black pickup to the right, swung onto the ramp, and headed down to the truck stop at the bottom. After freshening up, she walked outside and sat down at one of the shaded picnic tables. The sun was getting low in the sky. It would be in their eyes for the rest of the drive.

Casey came outside with cream cheese onion bagels and two fountain Cokes. Val forced a smile. He was a high-energy man whose body seemed to demand constant fuel. "Are we there yet?" she joked, mimicking a tired youngster.

"Not quite. Another hour maybe. By then it'll be getting dark. We can find a motel, get dinner, catch up on our sleep, and start fresh in the morning."

The thought of the morning and the search that would begin triggered a sudden tightness like a cord jerking around Val's throat.

"Are you all right?" Casey reached for her hand across the table.

She exhaled, willing herself to relax. "I'm scared," she said. "Scared of what we might find and scared that we won't find anything at all."

His fingers tightened around hers. "I'm scared, too. But we can't change what happened. We can only learn the truth. We owe him that much."

"I know." Val tried to visualize the young boy she'd known only as a baby. Matt. She was growing accustomed to the name. It had come to fit her idea of him. Slim and active, with Casey's twinkling blue eyes and her own fiery hair. Matthew. Matt. The thought that he might not be alive was breaking her heart.

She was his mother. If he'd died, wouldn't she have felt something, like a part of her being torn away?

"Oh, Casey." She blinked back tears. "I'm not hungry. Let's just go."

"Sure." He finished his bagel, scooped up hers, along with the napkins, and put them in the trash receptacle. "Want to take your drink? You need to stay hydrated."

"You're always looking after me." She picked up the cold soda and started for the truck.

"And I always will. So get used to it."

Val pretended not to hear. Getting used to Casey again was one thing she mustn't do. If their son had died, he would never forgive her, and she would never forgive herself. Their relationship would be over.

She sipped her ice-diluted Coke as Casey drove back to the freeway. Damn it, but she could use a drink. A real drink. Just enough to take the edge off her fear. But she knew better. Alcohol couldn't change reality. Nothing could.

By the time they drove into Bakersfield, it was dark outside. They checked into the first motel that looked clean and safe—a Holiday Inn with a Denny's next door. Val still didn't have much appetite, but she knew Casey was hungry, so she went with him and ordered French onion soup. He chose biscuits and chicken gravy.

A rack inside the front door of the restaurant held free brochures and tourist information. Casey selected a city map from the Chamber of Commerce and carried it to their table. They'd planned their first day with visits to the cemetery and the records section of the hospital. Where they went next would depend on what they found.

While they waited for their food, Casey studied the map. Val watched him—he was so focused, so intent. He had needed this, to be doing something that drove him even if it might lead to heartbreak.

They didn't make love that night. He spooned her as she

drifted along the edge of sleep, cloaked in his manly aroma and supported by his strong arms. His breathing told her that he wasn't sleeping either.

Toward dawn she sank deep enough to dream. She was in the cemetery with Casey, standing at the foot of two graves. There was another smaller grave between them. It appeared to be nothing but an empty hole.

From where she stood, she couldn't see the bottom of the grave. But she glimpsed something moving, like a shadow. Stepping to the edge, she bent forward, lost her balance, and toppled in. There was no bottom to the grave at all, only dark space that went on forever, and she was falling into it. Behind and above her, she could hear Casey calling her name. But she couldn't get back to him. She was falling over and over . . .

"Val! Wake up!"

Her body jerked. She could hear Casey's voice and feel his hand on her shoulder, shaking her gently. She opened her eyes.

"Good morning, sleepyhead." He smiled down at her. "You must've been dreaming. You were thrashing and twitching like a puppy chasing squirrels in his sleep."

"Yes. Crazy dream. Awful." Val rubbed her eyes. She could see gray morning light falling between the drapes. "What time is it?"

"Almost seven. The coffeemaker's brewing. I'll bring you some. I've already shaved and showered, so the bathroom's all yours."

"Thanks." Val yawned and took the Styrofoam coffee cup he offered her. Casey had always been a morning person. She loved him in spite of it.

Little by little, as she sipped the dark brew laced with hazelnut creamer, she felt her body coming awake. Would the day bring hope or heartache? She needed to be prepared for the worst.

While Casey watched the news on TV and checked his phone, Val showered and dressed in jeans, boots, a yellow blouse, and a black blazer. She fluffed her hair and added a dab of lipstick. Only her reddened eyes betrayed the distress she was feeling.

By the time they'd eaten breakfast, packed, and checked out of the motel, it was past 8:30. Casey had discovered a "grave finder" app on the website for Hillcrest Memorial Park, the largest cemetery in Bakersfield.

"I think I've found the parents in the directory," he said as they climbed back into the truck. "Phillip Peterson and Cora Mae Randall Peterson." He tilted the phone to show Val. "There's nothing about a child, but we can't be sure until we've seen the gravesite." He reached over the console for her hand. "Are you ready to do this?"

Val shook her head. "No, but let's do it anyway."

"Thanks, Val," he said. "I don't know if I could manage alone."

"I know I couldn't," she said as he backed out of the parking place and joined the stream of morning traffic. "But there's one thing I'd like to do first, if you don't mind indulging me."

"Anything."

She told him. He nodded. "Just let me know where to stop."

The cemetery, a private enterprise on the far side of Bakersfield, was a vast spread of grass, watered, cut, and shaded in some areas by trees. The headstones, laid out in neat rows, were placed flat at ground level to allow for efficient mowing. Narrow roads crisscrossed the landscape. Finding any grave here was as simple as finding an address.

Val gripped the bouquet of spring blossoms she'd bought in the floral section of a supermarket. They would probably wilt and be thrown out by the end of the day, but she wanted to pay this small tribute to the couple who had adopted, raised, and loved her baby.

Her legs shook as Casey helped her out of the truck. He held her free hand as they walked together to the graves. Val remembered the dream she'd had—the small, bottomless grave she'd fallen into. But as they drew near, she could see that there were only two graves, side by side, both names engraved on a single headstone. Phillip Clifford Peterson and Cora Mae Randall Peterson, along with their birthdates and the same death date. Their son wasn't here.

"Did you look for a separate grave under his name in the directory?" she asked Casey.

"I did." His voice choked with emotion. "It wasn't there."

Val bent and laid the bouquet at the base of the headstone. Did anyone else remember this tragic couple—maybe a relative who might have taken the boy? That remained to be discovered. So far, only one thing was certain. Their search was just beginning.

Casey drove back downtown and headed for Memorial Hospital. He knew that Seegmiller had already checked with the records clerk and found no trace of the boy. But they had to start somewhere. Any small lead would be better than nothing.

Beside him in the passenger seat, Val wept softly. Seeing the graves and learning that their son wasn't buried with his adoptive parents had undone them both. But the chance that he might be alive was still too precious and too fragile to mention.

The plump, graying records clerk at Memorial Hospital remembered Seegmiller's recent visit. "Like I told your friend," she said, "we have no record of the boy ever being here—and we're not in the habit of losing people. We track everyone who comes through our doors, alive or not."

"I believe you," Casey said. "But he's our son, and we can't stop looking until we know what happened to him. Can you give us any idea where to go from here?"

The woman paused, then slowly nodded. "There is one possibility. The news article claimed that the boy was taken in an ambulance to this hospital. But there's a chance the ambulance could've gone somewhere else. There could've been a traffic jam. Or the driver might have gotten word that our ER was full. With critical injuries like your son's, the patient would have been taken to whatever hospital was closest."

"And which hospital might that be?"

She shrugged. "Take your pick. There are seventeen hospitals in Kern County. You have a name and a date, that should be enough for a records search. If I were you, I'd make a list, start with the biggest ones that have trauma units, and work your way down. All I can do is wish you luck. You're going to need it."

As they walked out to the parking lot, Casey felt Val's fingers creep into his palm. "Well, at least we know what we'll be doing for the rest of the day," she said.

His hand tightened around hers. "Thank you," he said. "Somehow we're going to get through this and be all right. I love you, Val."

"And I love you." She meant it, but she wasn't so sure about being all right. They might never be all right again.

After the hit man's death, Tess had made a quick visit to the hospital while Brock had loaded her bulls. After that, she'd driven the loaded rig home, with Brock following in his SUV. At her urging, he had left her at the turnoff and continued on to his own ranch. They both knew she'd be safe enough driving the rest of the way alone.

The sun was coming up as she pulled into the yard. Pedro was waiting to help her unload the trailer. With his father-in-law in the hospital and Tess away, he'd carried extra burdens of worry and work. It showed in his usually cheerful face.

"I've got good news for you, Pedro," Tess told him as the pasture gate closed behind the four bulls. "Ruben's recovering well. We should be able to bring him home in a few days. And the people responsible for the bomb are dead. They'll never hurt our family again."

"*Gracias a Diós*. Maria has been frantic for her father. You can tell us everything over breakfast."

"And how have things been here?" They walked toward the house together. She'd only been away for a couple of days, but with so much happening, it felt more like weeks.

"The animals are fine. So are Shane and Lexie and the little one. But Val has gone with Casey to look for their son."

"Yes, I know. She sent me a text."

"Do you think they will find him?"

"Only with a great deal of luck. I fear they will come back with their hearts broken."

"Then I hope you are wrong," Pedro said. "But I must ask you another question. With Ruben needing to rest and Val perhaps leaving, there is more work on this ranch than one man can do."

"Yes, I agree," Tess said. "I've been thinking about hiring more help."

Pedro cleared his throat. "My brother has two strong sons. They are young, but good boys. They know horses and cattle, and they are looking for work."

"They could be just what we need. Get them here, Pedro. We'll give them a try. If they work out, they can stay."

"Good. I'll ask my brother to bring them in his truck. Maria and I will get the bunkhouse ready." Pedro grinned. "Did I mention that they are twins?"

"Now that does sound interesting." Tess gave him a smile as she mounted the porch and was welcomed by the dog, wagging and panting. She scratched his ears. It was good to be home.

Sitting around the breakfast table was almost like old times—except that Ruben and Callie were absent and Shane was there. Lexie had pulled her baby's stroller up to the table, where she could watch him. Young Jackson was filling out, growing round and plump. Looking at her sister's family across the table, Tess was aware that they would soon be leaving for Brock's ranch. Now that the danger appeared to be over, there was nothing to keep them from going. How was she going to manage without them?

As the conversation drifted around to it, she gave a watered-down account of the bombing, the discovery of Jim's body, and her own struggle with the hit man. Told in full detail, the story would have upset them all.

"There's one thing I don't understand," Shane said. "If the hit man was hired to kill Brock, why did he do so much damage at first? And why did he go after you?"

"It's complicated," Tess said. "The person who wanted Brock dead wanted him to suffer first—losing animals, property, and the one woman they'd seen in his company."

"And he still doesn't know who did the hiring?"

"Not yet." She would never tell anyone about Brock's secret past. That secret would remain between the two of them—as would other things that had happened.

Brock phoned her late in the day. He'd arrived home a few hours earlier and taken time to rest and catch up on events at his ranch.

"So how did things go at the ranch while you were away?" Tess asked.

"Surprisingly calm. No dead stock or broken fences. No threatening mail. I left Rusty in charge. He did a good job."

"And did you call the police about the dead hit man?"

"I did. They identified him from his prints. Fritz Jaeger, something of a celebrity in the underworld. There'll be an inquest, and you might need to give your testimony on Zoom. But anything you did was clearly in self-defense.

And you didn't kill him. He fell on his own needle—the autopsy will confirm that."

"More fun to look forward to." She made a wry joke.

"There's something else, Tess . . ." He trailed off, as if organizing his next thoughts.

"I know, Brock. You said this trouble wouldn't be over until you ended it. What do you plan to do?"

"Driving home, I did a lot of thinking. Everything started with that accident in Missouri, all those years ago. I need to go back, talk to people who might remember, try to find out who would hate me enough to hire a hit man."

"And who would have enough money to pay him."

"That too. I'll be leaving in the next couple of days. Just me. I know you'll be busy at your ranch, and I need to do this alone."

"I understand." And she really did. "But be careful. There's a woman here who wants you back in one piece."

She heard him chuckle. "Got it. And when I get back, I hope you'll let me pick up where we left off."

"Just come back," she said, thinking briefly of another man she'd loved—a man who hadn't come back. "I'll be waiting. I love you, Brock."

Making the rounds of hospitals was taking more time than Val and Casey had expected. Usually, it involved a wait until a busy clerk got around to helping them. Often it required filling out a form and showing ID. Once, after they were told to come back later, they sat and waited more than an hour instead, only to learn that there was no record of a Matthew Peterson in the hospital files.

The one flicker of encouragement came when they checked the death records in the Kern County building. Their son's name wasn't there.

"At least we know he didn't die." Val tried to boost their spirits. But there was no need to mention another possibility because they were both aware of it. An unconscious child with no living parents and no ID on him could have been classified as a John Doe and buried or cremated without a name.

By the afternoon of the second day, they were worn-out, discouraged, and barely halfway down the list of hospitals. Almost all the larger facilities, where the ambulance would most likely have gone, had already been ruled out. The places at the bottom of the list were more like clinics or specialty hospitals that were barely worth checking.

Needing a break, they stopped at a park, bought cold slushies from a vendor, and settled onto a bench with a playground nearby. Mothers and babysitters watched the children sliding, swinging, climbing, and running.

"One of those kids could almost be him," Val murmured.

"Not really. Our son would be too old for a playground like this. He'd more likely be skateboarding or riding a bike."

"Oh, Casey. What if we don't find him?" She sagged against his shoulder.

"Only one thing's for sure. We won't find him if we stop looking. But you're worn-out. We could take a break, maybe do a nice dinner and a movie, then start fresh tomorrow."

She shook her head. "No, let's keep looking. That's why we came here."

"All right." Casey glanced at his watch. "We've got time to try one more hospital before the records office closes. The next one on the list is Kern Medical. It isn't far from here."

"Fine." Val stood. "Let's go."

Kern Medical was the last of the larger hospitals they'd tried. They found the records office on the building directory board and followed the signs. To their relief, no one else was waiting to talk to the single clerk, a friendly looking middle-aged woman in a wheelchair behind a low counter. She gave them a smile as they approached the counter. The name tag on her pink jacket read LUCILLE.

"Perfect timing. I just finished my book." She held up the popular romance novel she'd been reading. "So how can I help you?"

Casey handed her a photocopy of the article about the accident. "We know the parents were killed, but we need to know what happened to the boy. He'd been adopted. But he's . . . our son."

Lucille read the article. Then she appeared to read it again. "Oh, my stars!" she exclaimed. "I remember this! Awful accident. Little boy with red hair. His name was Matt, right?"

Val's knees seemed to dissolve beneath her. Casey pulled up a folding chair for her. She sank onto it.

"I used to work the trauma unit as a nurse," Lucille said. "They transferred me down here when my legs gave out, but I remember that night like it was last week. When the ambulance couldn't get through the traffic to Memorial, they brought him here. We didn't even know his name until later. None of us expected him to pull through, but he was a little fighter. He just wouldn't give up." She studied Val and Casey through her glasses. "You say he's your son? I certainly see a resemblance."

"I gave him up as a baby," Val said. "I was young, desperate, and unmarried."

"But we plan to do something about that," Casey said, squeezing Val's shoulder. "So, do you know what happened to him?"

"Only that we kept him for about a month, while he recovered. He was quiet, hardly talked at all. We could tell he'd been traumatized."

"And then what? Where did he go?"

"We tried to find relatives. But nobody ever showed up to claim him. We had no choice except to turn him over to Social Services. They should have a record of where he's gone. You can find their offices in the county building. But you'll have to wait until tomorrow. Even if you were to leave right now, they'd be closed by the time you got there."

"We can't thank you enough, Lucille," Val said. "You can't imagine how much this means to us."

"You can thank me by letting me know how this all turns out," Lucille said. "I don't want to spend the rest of my days wondering what happened."

"You've got it. It's a promise." Casey gave her a grin, took Val's hand, and walked back outside with her, across the lawn toward the parking lot.

To Val, the whole world seemed to have changed. The low-hanging sun streaked the clouds with highlights of gold. A flock of blackbirds etched calligraphy against the sky. A sprinkler on the grass shot up watery jets that sparkled like diamonds. Her baby had lived, and they'd found a way to locate him.

But then the fear crept in, shattering her euphoria like a wrecking ball slamming a stained-glass window. So many things could still go wrong. After coming so close, the odds of finding the boy, let alone reclaiming him, were still against them.

"You're so quiet. What is it?" Casey asked.

"I'm just scared. So many wonderful dreams of mine have turned into nightmares. Anything could go wrong tomorrow."

"I know. I'm scared, too—scared that if things don't work out, I could lose our son and lose you, too." He led her to a nearby bench, sat, and pulled her down beside him. "Marry me, Val. If we get our boy back, he's going to need both of us. If something goes wrong, and we lose him, we're going to need each other."

Val gazed down at her hands. "Haven't I already said yes?"

"In so many words. But we need to make it happen. As soon as we get home. We can work out the details afterward."

"But that's just the trouble—the details. I'd have the choice of following you around the circuit with a suitcase, climbing the walls alone in your ugly condo, or staying on the ranch, which I'm already doing. And every time you stepped into the arena, I would die a little. I'm not brave and selfless like Lexie. I want my man in one fully operational piece—or no man at all, damn it."

Casey sighed and pushed to his feet. "Fine. We'll put it on hold for now. But I've laid all my cards on the table, Val. For now, they're still there. I can't promise they'll be there forever."

That night they ate takeout in their motel room and watched a succession of old movies until they were too tired to keep their eyes open. The strain was getting to both of them. For tonight, all they could do was get some rest.

When the county offices opened at 9:00 the next morning, Val and Casey were waiting at the entrance. Making an appointment with a social worker involved filling out another request and waiting to be called in. While they sat on hard-backed chairs and watched the clock creep from one minute to the next, Val's hand crept into Casey's. They'd had their differences last night, but right now, nothing mattered more than finding their son.

At last, a tall black woman with natural hair, glasses, and a bohemian blouse walked out. She introduced herself as Ms. Janna Michelob and ushered them into her tiny, cluttered office.

Motioning them to two chairs facing the desk, she took her own seat across from them. "So, you're looking for Matt Peterson. Is that correct?" she asked.

"You know him? You know where he is?" Val could barely contain herself.

"Yes, I handle his case. And if you're his biological mother, as you claim to be, I can certainly see where he came by that red hair. Would you like to see a recent photograph? Here."

She opened a manila file and slid it across the desk. Inside, clipped to some papers, was what appeared to be a school photo. The young boy in the picture was pale and thin, with a ghost of a smile that looked as if it had been coaxed from him by the photographer. But the blue eyes and thick, fiery curls were unmistakable. Val felt a hot surge of tears. She was looking at her son. He was alive. He was real.

"But where is he? When can we see him?" Casey demanded.

"He's in foster care. But don't get impatient. You can't just walk into a room, announce that you're his parents, and take him away. This boy is fragile. He lost both his parents in that terrible accident. Then he went through a painful healing process with nobody to love and support him but the hospital staff. And when we had to take him out of there, that was another separation. He's like a soldier with PTSD. He's afraid to trust anybody—afraid of being left alone again."

"Does he go to school?" Val asked.

"He does. But he's in Resource. Not because he isn't bright—he's actually very smart. But he has issues with communicating."

"Are you saying he doesn't speak?" Casey asked.

"He can speak," Ms. Michelob said. "But he rarely does. It's as if he's shut down. He's had therapy, and it's helped, but he has a long way to go."

"He's our son," Casey said. "We want him under any conditions. We'll do whatever it takes to give him a home. So how do we make that happen?"

"First of all, you need to understand what you'd be taking on. To help him heal, Matt needs total stability, with two parents, a home, and ideally, others—friends and family—who'll be part of his life. Before we let him go, you'll need to show the court that you can provide those things. If you think you can, you should consult a lawyer who specializes in cases like yours, where a parent has given up their rights.

There's a good one here in Bakersfield. I'll give you his card. I'll warn you, this is not going to happen overnight, but it can be done."

"Please," Val begged. "Can we see him now?"

"School is on break, so he's at home. I'll put in a call. But you'll have to follow the rules for a first visit. You can tell him your names, but not that you're his parents or that you might be adopting him. No touching unless the child initiates it. It has to be his idea, and Matt isn't much of a toucher. Fifteen minutes maximum, less if the child doesn't want to stay. And of course, I'll be there the whole time. Got it?"

"Yes," Val said. The rules seemed excessive, but she understood that they were there to protect the child from people like her who might want to grab him and hug him on sight.

"All right. The place is across town. Just let me call the foster parents. Then you can follow my car over there. I'll meet you out front."

They didn't talk much as Casey drove, following the red Toyota minivan through a maze of streets. Val didn't have to ask him what he was thinking. Now that they'd found Matt and learned about his special needs, he was faced with a painful choice—the career he loved, or the welfare of his son.

"We'll do whatever it takes to give him a home."

That was what Casey had said. Val knew he'd meant it. She knew the love and tenderness inside him, and she had little doubt what that choice would ultimately be. But he would have to get there by himself. This time she couldn't help him.

They were driving through a low-income neighborhood now. Homes with patched windows; kids playing soccer in the street. The red Toyota pulled up outside a house, larger than most, the color of its dented aluminum siding long faded. Casey parked behind Ms. Michelob, who was waiting for them at the curb.

"There are four foster kids here," she explained as they negotiated the cracked sidewalk and mounted the porch steps. "I know the place doesn't look like much, but Etta Price does a good job of keeping them clean, fed, and safe. They might not get much quality time, but Matt has done all right here."

She rang the doorbell. The woman who answered was overweight and tired-looking, but she had a kind smile. "Come in," she said. "Have a seat in the parlor. I'll send Matt in to meet you."

Val sat next to Casey on a sagging couch, while Ms. Michelob took a chair. The walls were bare of decoration, and the carpet was worn and faded, but the room was clean. From somewhere beyond the closed inside door came the sound of a television.

Then the door opened partway. Val's heart seemed to stop. She heard Casey's breath catch as a young boy in an oversize Marvel Heroes T-shirt walked into the room.

He was frail-looking, but a beautiful child, his fair skin lightly freckled, his indigo eyes shining with hidden intelligence. His fiery hair wanted cutting. It tumbled in curls over his forehead, into his eyes. Lifting a hand, he brushed it to one side.

"Hello, Matt," Ms. Michelob said. "Miss Champion and Mr. Bozeman have come to meet you. Can you say hello to them?"

"Hello." His lips shaped the word. It emerged as little more than a murmur.

"Hello, Matt. You're a fine-looking boy." Casey's voice rasped with emotion.

"Hello, Matt. I'm happy to meet you." Val's throat was so tight that it was painful to speak.

In the silence, the boy walked forward. Val held her breath as he reached out and touched her cheek with a fingertip.

Only then did she feel the wetness.

CHAPTER 19

Brock hadn't set foot in Ridgewood, Missouri, since the day when a dour county judge had sentenced him to three years in the state penitentiary. He'd left town cuffed and shackled in a prison van, his $100,000 fortune locked away in a safety deposit box in Branson.

As part of their agreement, Chase, who had some influence, had posted his bail so he could put the money away and take care of a few other personal matters. Then he had gone to trial, entered a plea of guilty.

Putting the cash in an interest-bearing account would have made him even wealthier. But he'd feared that Chase might find a way to access it and take it back, so he'd opted for security.

He'd kept one of two keys glued under the end paper of a Bible, the only personal thing he'd been allowed to keep in his cell. The other key, as a backup, had been buried in the earth alongside Mia Carpenter's headstone. Brock had never gone back for it.

Now, dressed in work clothes and driving the compact car he'd rented at the Springfield airport, he was back where so many things had begun.

As he passed the WELCOME TO RIDGEWOOD sign at the town limits, memories washed over him—working at Carpenter Motors, living over the garage, and making friends with Jeff; the wild Saturday nights, drinking and skinny-dipping in the lake; the willing girls; the midnight street races, and so much more. Life for a young man in Ridgewood had possessed an idyllic quality—until the night of the accident.

But he hadn't come here to reminisce. He'd come here looking for answers. If Jeff Carpenter had faked his death— and if he was out to destroy the one man who knew about his past—at least Ridgewood might give up some clues.

Now, as he drove down Main Street, Brock wondered if anyone would recognize him. Half a lifetime had passed since he'd called Ridgewood home. He had a mature face and body now and even a different name. The town had changed, too. The bar where he and Jeff had drunk that night before picking up Mia was gone. So was the drive-in. A chain supermarket had replaced the mom-and-pop grocery store. But the bank looked the same. So did the auto dealership, except for the name change out front. It was Ridgewood Motors now.

He made a right turn into the driveway, pulled into one of the customer parking slots, and climbed out of the car. The salesman who came out to greet him was a stranger— middle-aged but fit, with a thick black toupee. "Can I show you some good buys today, sir?" he asked. "We've got some great wheels for the best prices in three counties."

"Not today, thanks." Brock glanced around to make sure there were no customers waiting. "I'm from out of town, just making a trip down memory lane. I used to work here when it was Carpenter Motors. I washed and detailed the cars, moved them around, did all the grunt work. Chase Carpenter was a good man. He worked us hard, but he treated us right."

"So I've heard. But that was years ago, before my time," the salesman said.

"I've been trying to track down the family," Brock said. "If you've got a minute, maybe you can help me."

The salesman leaned against the side of a late-model Subaru Outback. "Well, like I say, I only know what I've heard. But people do talk. Most of that family came to a sad end."

"I get that impression, but if you don't mind, I'd like to hear your take on it."

"Sure. As long as no customers show up." The salesman rubbed his jaw. "Chase died years ago. It was cancer. But they say what really killed him was his daughter dying in a car wreck. The guy driving was drunk, rolled the car into a canal. He went to prison for it. Should've got the needle if you ask me."

"Too bad." Brock's expression was neutral. "What about his son—Jeff, was it? I remember him."

"He didn't do so great either. Got his law degree, married a rich society girl, had a son, and then it all went to hell. He started hitting the bottle, lost his family, ended up shooting himself and falling off the end of a boat at Table Rock Lake. No prints but his on the gun he left. Folks are still trying to figure out how he managed it. Almost sounds like a faked suicide, doesn't it?"

"It does. Was his body ever found?"

"Not for a long time. But this part I know for sure because I was here. The searchers had given up. Then, just a couple of years ago, a fisherman brought up some bones and rags. And would you believe it? It was Jeff. Down there all that time. The DNA test proved it."

Stunned, Brock willed himself not to look surprised. So Jeff's suicide had been real. He'd been dead all this time.

And the theory that Jeff was behind the clippings, threats, and murders was nothing more than dust in the wind.

He forced himself to speak. "You say Jeff had a son."

The salesman shrugged. "That's what I was told. Can't say I know where the boy is now. But the old lady—Chase's widow—is still alive. She's in an assisted living place out on the south road. Had a stroke that put her there. From what I hear, she isn't doing too well."

"So who owns the dealership now?" Brock's gaze swept over the lot full of shiny cars.

"Now that's an interesting story, too. Chase's widow inherited the place when her husband died. For a lot of years, she leased the business but kept ownership. I guess maybe she was saving it for Jeff if he ever turned up alive. When those bones were pulled up, she announced that she wanted to sell. She was bought out by some big franchise company for a pile of money—close to a million bucks if you can believe the rumor."

A car was pulling into the lot. The salesman straightened his tie and wiped a fingerprint off the Subaru's rear door with his handkerchief. "Gotta go," he said. "But you could try talking to the old bat. From what I hear, she got religion and went a little crazy, but you never know. Anyway, nice passing the time with you, stranger." He strode toward the newcomer, leaving Brock to climb into his car and drive back to the street.

Farther down Main Street was the city park. Brock found a shady spot on a side street, climbed out of the car, and sat on a bench gazing at the budding trees overhead. He needed time to weigh what he'd just learned.

The pieces of the puzzle had finally come together. The person providing the orders and cash behind two murders, four murder attempts, some serious property and stock loss, and possible extortion was Johanna Smith Carpenter—Chase's widow, the mother of Jeff and Mia, and the grandmother of Jason, otherwise known as Jim.

Those numbers didn't take into account the death of Fritz Jaeger, the hit man she'd hired to wreak vengeance on the man she blamed for destroying her family.

He could go to the police, but without solid evidence, they would never believe his story. Short of walking away, the only option that remained was to go to the nursing home and confront her.

There were some harsh truths that the woman needed to hear.

The Twilight Villa, a rambling, one-story brick structure, was overgrown with ivy and shaded by two drooping mulberry trees. It had been built after Brock left Ridgewood, but the place had long since taken on an air of age.

The smell of bleach, masked with cinnamon-scented air freshener, flooded Brock's senses as he signed the visitor log. Inside, the place looked clean and well maintained. The parlor, seen through a wide archway, was furnished in cushiony leather seating, where several elderly residents were watching an episode of *Petticoat Junction* on an oldies TV channel. Although the day outside was warm, a gas log blazed in the fireplace.

"Johanna is in her room," the receptionist said. "I'll send an aide down to let her know she has a visitor. We have to tell her your name. Does she know you?"

Brock nodded. "She hasn't seen me in years, but you might say we've been in touch."

A few minutes later, the aide, a young woman in scrubs, was back. "She'll see you, sir. Lucky timing. This is one of her good days."

He followed her down a long hallway to a room near the end. The door was slightly ajar. The aide motioned for him to go inside, then left.

Brock hadn't known what to expect when he stepped into

the room. The woman in the wheelchair was seated with her back to the window. The light behind her made it difficult to see her features except in silhouette. But he could make out a thin, erect figure with meticulously coiffed silver hair. Her legs were covered with a knitted afghan. A leather-covered Bible lay in her lap, cradled by her wrinkled hands.

"Close the door, Ben Talbot. Or is it Brock Tolman?" The low voice pricked his memory. He hadn't known her well, but he recalled her superior manner of speaking.

"If you want to sit, you can sit on the bed," she said. "Extra chairs just get in my way."

"I'll stand. And it's Brock Tolman." He closed the door.

"Yes. I saw you in a TV interview about bucking bulls. That's how I knew who you were."

He moved aside to escape the glare of the window. Now he could see more of the room. There was a closet and a doorless entrance to the ADA-compliant bathroom. Opposite the foot of the bed was a credenza with a TV on top. Lined up along one side were framed portrait photos of her husband, her son, her daughter, and her grandson.

He could see her face now. Johanna Carpenter had been a beautiful woman. Her elegant bone structure remained. But grief, hate, and ill health had aged her. The left side of her face was rigid, with a lopsided droop to her mouth, caused by the stroke she'd suffered. It might have been easy to feel pity toward her. But Brock felt nothing of the kind.

"I know everything, Johanna," he said. "Jason, the grandson you used against me, is dead. He was murdered by the hit man you hired to carry out your foolish vendetta. All for nothing."

He saw the shock pass over half her face. The other half remained eerily still. She slumped in her chair. Then, with an amazing show of strength, she seemed to pull herself together.

"It doesn't matter anymore," she said. "There's nothing

you or anybody, not even the law, can do to me. I have a terminal mass in my brain. The doctors have given me less than a month to live. I could die anytime."

She took a moment to glare at him, letting her words sink in. "I know I'll probably rot in hell. But I don't care. All I want is to die knowing that I've evened the score with the man who destroyed my family. An eye for an eye. A tooth for a tooth. Isn't that what the Good Book says?"

She opened the Bible in her lap. Her hand snatched up the small but deadly black revolver that was concealed in a hollowed-out space beneath the cover. Her eyes glinted with a fury akin to madness as she pointed the gun at Brock.

Brock froze where he stood. "Johanna, it wasn't—"

"Don't talk. Just hear me out." The gun was unsteady in her hand, but it wouldn't take much aim to hit a man standing three feet away. "Your killing my daughter was only the beginning. After the grief and shock, my husband had no strength to fight the cancer. And Jeff—Mia's death wrecked his life. He never forgave himself for letting you drive his car that night. In the end, it killed him, too.

"Jason was a good boy, and I take some blame for what happened. I offered to make him sole heir to my estate if he followed my orders. But if he died, it was because of you—because of what you did."

Brock measured the distance between them. He could try to take her by surprise, maybe push her chair over. But that would be too risky. She could shoot him in an instant. His best chance lay in talking her down or stalling until the aide came back and called security.

"Before you pull that trigger, you need to know the truth," he said. "Jeff was the one driving that car. After the wreck, he moved me to the driver's side and told the police I was at the wheel. Nobody bothered to take fingerprints."

"I don't believe that!" Her grip tightened on the pistol. "My son would never do such a despicable thing!"

"You know it's true. Jeff would never have let me drive his car, even when he was drunk. Chase knew what really happened. He gave me a hundred thousand dollars to take the blame and serve the prison sentence. He did it to spare you. You'd lost your daughter. He knew it would kill you to lose your son, too. He loved you that much. Think about it."

Her mouth quivered, but Brock went on talking. "I don't know what made Jeff start drinking and kill himself. It could have been anything—his marriage, his finances, we'll never know. But it wasn't me. I was the one who gave him a second chance after the wreck. I took the blame so he could keep his privileged life.

"You wanted justice, Johanna. But every person and animal you paid that monster to harm was innocent, including the woman I love." Brock held out his hand. "Now give me the gun, and we'll forget this ever happened."

"No." Her eyes had taken on a wild look. "I don't know if you're telling the truth, but I'll give you ten seconds to get out of this room. Any longer, and you'll be dead on your feet. Now go!"

Brock didn't argue. Keeping his eyes on her, he backed out of the door. As soon as he was out of her sight, he raced to the reception desk.

"Call security," he said. "Mrs. Carpenter has a pistol. She was threatening to use it."

The receptionist laughed. "Oh, we know all about that pistol. Johanna insisted on keeping it because it was her husband's. But we took all the bullets ages ago. Don't worry, the gun's harmless."

As she spoke the last words, the loud report of a gunshot echoed up the hallway, startling a flock of sparrows from the tree outside the window.

Before leaving town, Brock paid a visit to the city cemetery. After a brief search, he found what he was looking for—three graves at the foot of an ornate family headstone. The oldest one, on the left, was the only one he cared about.

Kneeling, he placed a long-stemmed pink rose on the grass below the name. "Sleep in peace, Mia," he whispered, thinking of the pretty, laughing girl who would never know life as a woman.

There were two other graves, with room to spare in the plot. Soon there would be two more. But Brock would not be coming back to see them. Instead he would look ahead to the future—to building a new family with the woman he loved and the other people he had come to care about.

Warm in the late-day sunlight, he walked to the car and started the engine. As he was driving through the cemetery gate, he remembered the key he'd thrust into the ground next to the base of the headstone. It could stay buried, like his past.

He would give Tess a call from the airport to let her know everything was all right. Then he would settle in and wait for the red-eye back to Tucson.

Morning, two days later

Sitting on the edge of her bed, Tess wrapped Mitch's photograph in the blue silk scarf he'd given her for her eighteenth birthday. After tying the ends securely, she rose, carried it to the cedar hope chest that had been her mother's, and tucked it beneath layers of fragrant linens. She had loved him dearly and mourned him for ten long years. But she had found someone new to love—someone warm and strong and passionate who thrilled her with his touch. Brock wasn't perfect, but he had laid his imperfections bare for her in open trust. She knew who and what he was—and she wanted a life with him.

As she left her room and walked along the hallway, it struck her how many things were changing at the Alamo Canyon Ranch. Now that the danger had passed, Lexie and

Shane were already organizing their possessions for the move to Brock's place. Although their absence would be sorely felt here, Tess understood that they needed to do what was best for their family.

But the family would be growing. Val had phoned last night. She and Casey had found their son. They were staying in Bakersfield until legal arrangements could be made for them to bring him home—wherever that home might turn out to be.

As she passed the kitchen, she could hear the sounds of Maria making breakfast and smell the aromas of bacon, coffee, and *chumuth*, the buttery, hand-made tortillas favored by her people. The enticing scent followed her outside as she opened the screen door and stepped out into the cool dawn.

Ruben was standing by the paddock fence, watching the bulls. He had come home yesterday, still needing rest but refusing to stay down.

Trailed by the dog, Tess walked across the yard to his side. The worst of his burn scars were still healing. On arriving at his trailer, he had taken off the gauze dressings and let Maria apply herb poultices known to his people since the dawn of time. Tess could see that the natural remedies were already working.

"Shouldn't you be taking it easy?" she asked him.

He shook his head. "What for? I can heal on my feet. It's good to be home."

For a time, they stood watching the bulls. Quicksand was already dominating the herd, standing a little apart, as if to guard his brother bulls from danger.

"I suppose you know that Lexie and Shane will be moving," she said.

"Yes, I know," he said. "Maria told me. Change is part of life. This old man learned to accept that a long time ago. You will learn to accept it, too."

"I suppose so. But things won't be the same without them."

"And what about you?" He turned to gaze at her with his wise, dark eyes. "Brock is a good man. A strong man. I think you love him. What will you do if he wants to marry you?"

"He hasn't asked me."

"He will. What will you do then?"

"I don't know, Ruben. This ranch has been my whole life. Who will take care of it if I go?"

"The ranch will survive. Right now, you must think of your own happiness. When is he coming here?"

"Today. He's already on the road. When he phoned, he did hint that he had something to ask me."

"Then you will know what to say. Your heart will tell you, *hija*."

EPILOGUE

Thanksgiving, the following year

*A*S THE BLACK ESCALADE WITH THE TOLMAN-ALAMO Ranch logo on the door crested the ridge, Tess reached across the cab and touched her husband's shoulder. "Stop right here. I've always loved this view of the ranch. I want to enjoy it again before we go down."

"Take your time." Brock switched off the engine, pulled the handbrake, and laid an arm around his wife's shoulders.

"Does it still feel like coming home?" he asked.

"The place has changed. It's still changing. But it will always feel like home—even though my home is with you now."

She looked out over her beloved Alamo Canyon Ranch. Yes, there'd been some changes. A modern prefab home stood on the spot where the old house had burned. Pedro and Maria were living there with Ruben. The two mobile homes that had stood next to the house had been hauled back to the reservation for other members of the family.

Thanks to a spring-fed watering system, the pastures were islands of green in the desert landscape. The beef cattle had been sold that fall, but the cows, calves, and bucking bulls were scattered over the rolling landscape, enjoying the fresh grass and the warm November sunshine.

Only Whirlwind was missing. Unable to part with him, Lexie had taken the silver bull with her to the Tolman Ranch, where he'd been reunited with his brother, Whiplash. But his earnings in the arena still went to the Alamo Canyon account.

Quicksand, whose strongest bond was with Ruben, remained here. But with the two ranches merged into a family corporation, it was Tess who managed his bucking events. The spectacular bull, still unridden, had bucked in last year's National Finals Rodeo and been chosen by Clay Rafferty for the new PBR season.

The merger between the two ranches had hit some rough patches at first, but by now it was working smoothly.

Shane managed the Tolman Ranch, with Lexie as breeding consultant. Casey, who'd given up the career he loved to raise the son he loved even more, managed the Alamo Canyon Ranch with Val's help.

Tess and Brock coordinated the bucking events, chose the bulls, and oversaw the general welfare of the corporation. The work kept them involved in the sport they loved. Today's Thanksgiving dinner would bring the whole family together.

"It looks like Shane and Lexie got here ahead of us," Brock observed. "I see their van down there in the yard."

"I hope Val and Casey have toddler-proofed the house," Tess said. "That little Jackson is a nonstop bundle of destruction. And oh—can you keep a secret?"

"You know I can."

"They're expecting another one. Lexie just found out."

He laughed. "Oh, good Lord. Double trouble."

Tess laughed with him, but the wistfulness was there. She and Brock had been trying for a baby of their own. So far it hadn't happened. But they hadn't given up hope.

He leaned over and kissed her. "Let's get going. They'll be waiting dinner on us."

As they drove into the yard, they saw Matt throwing a stick for the dog. The ranch had provided a perfect place for the boy to heal and blossom. Surrounded by loving people, animals, and life in the outdoors, his personality had emerged. He was bright, friendly, even talkative.

Matt's ambition was to be a cowboy. Casey was teaching his son to ride. Ruben was teaching him to rope. "But no bull riding," Casey had been known to say. "Not until he's old enough to know better."

As Tess and Brock climbed out of the vehicle, Matt waved, then wheeled and darted up the porch steps. "They're here!" he shouted through the screen door. "Let's eat!"

Today the dining room table had been expanded with extra leaves. A spare table from the bunkhouse had been placed at the far end to add more seating and make room for Shane's wheelchair and Jackson's high chair. The whole ranch family, including Ruben's clan, would be sharing the feast.

The meal, from the huge golden turkey to Maria's refried beans and roasted pumpkin, was a spectacular pageant of abundance.

"Heavens, this looks like something out of *Downton Abbey*!" Lexie exclaimed as she maneuvered the wriggling Jackson into his high chair.

"I think our food is even better than Downton's." Tess slipped into the chair that Brock held for her. "Maria and Val deserve a round of applause and"—she glanced around the table—"and a break after dinner while the rest of us clean up."

After the laughter and applause had faded, Casey, as host, said a simple grace. Then the ranch family began their feast to celebrate the joy of being together. Today was about all those who sat around this table—the work they'd shared, the dangers they'd faced, the sacrifices they'd made, and the future that lay ahead.

But most of all, it was about the love that gave meaning to their lives.

ACKNOWLEDGMENTS

Special thanks to Jeff and Wendie Sue Kerby Flitton of Bar T Rodeo for their gracious hospitality and invaluable help in researching this story.

Please read on for an excerpt from *A Calder at Heart*
by Janet Dailey.

CHAPTER 1

Blue Moon, Montana
Spring 1919

T HE PRAIRIE GRASS HAD LONG SINCE SPREAD OVER THE lonely hilltop grave. Even the headstone, fashioned from a slab of oak, was so weathered that the name and dates were barely readable.

But Dr. Kristin Dollarhide had no trouble finding the spot her sister-in-law had described.

Dismounting from the dun mare that had carried her here, Kristin dropped the reins and looped the riding crop around her wrist. The long grass swished against her boots as she walked toward the grave of the boy who'd been her first love. Her lips whispered his name.

"Alvar."

The wildflowers she'd stopped to pick along the way were wilting in her hand. But they were all she had. Kneeling, she laid the sad little bouquet at the foot of the headstone. Alvar

Anderson had been shot in a senseless fight between ranchers and immigrant farmers two days before Kristin had been
due to leave Blue Moon for travel and school. They'd said
goodbye the night of his death. But she'd been unable to stay
for his funeral.

In the ten years that had passed, there'd been other men in
Kristin's life, most of them killed in the Great War. But
Alvar would always own a piece of her heart—his memory
the last remaining part of her that was pure and good.

Maybe here, on the Montana land where she'd grown up,
that memory would help her find peace.

Her gaze took in the broad sweep of the prairie, rising to
wooded foothills and then to peaks that towered above the
tree line. The wheat fields she remembered were gone, the
immigrant homesteaders driven away by drought, locusts,
harsh winter blizzards, and finally the Great War in Europe
that had taken so many of their young men.

One of those young men had been Axel Anderson, Alvar's
younger brother, who would never come home again.

In the near distance, she could see the remains of the Anderson homestead—the foundation of the pillaged house, a
few fence posts, the toppled privy. Everything else had been
stripped for building materials made scarce by the war.

A white butterfly settled on Alvar's headstone, rested a
moment, then fluttered away. Kristin's gaze followed it as it
dipped and danced over the tiny yellow flowers that dotted
the grassland.

They had been so young, she and Alvar. Her one regret
was that they hadn't made love. Instead, her first time had
been a groping encounter with a fellow medical student she
barely knew, in the rumble seat of his Model T.

But why think of that now?

She was about to get up and leave when a shadow fell
over her, like a cloud passing across the morning sun. Turning, she gave a startled gasp. Silhouetted against the glare, a
tall, rough-looking man in trail-worn clothes stood a few

paces behind her. He had come up so silently that she'd been completely unaware of him.

The rifle she'd brought along for safety was on the horse. All she had was her riding crop. If the big man wanted to overcome her, the flexible leather rod with its flat tip wouldn't be much help. Worse, she could see that he was armed. But he made no move to draw the pistol that rested in a holster on his hip.

Scrambling to her feet, she faced him, the sun in her eyes and the crop in her hand. "Not a step closer, mister," she said. "Not unless you want a whipping."

"Take it easy, miss." He tipped his weathered hat. His speech—easy-paced, with a hint of a drawl—was pure Texan. "I didn't mean to scare you. I was about to speak when you turned around."

"A likely story." Kristin kept her grip on the riding crop. "Why didn't you say something sooner? Why did you sneak up behind me like that?"

"I wasn't sneaking, miss. But I was at a loss for words. I didn't expect to see a woman out here alone. I was as surprised as you were." He moved to one side, changing the angle of the sunlight. She could see his face now—features that could have been chiseled from granite. His short beard, peppered with gray like his hair, failed to hide the jagged scar that ran from his left temple to the corner of his mouth. His dark eyes had a haunted look—the kind of look Kristin had seen on far too many veterans who'd survived the war—as this man likely had.

But that didn't mean he wasn't dangerous. The horrors of combat had a way of twisting men's minds. Some, even those who'd come safely home, still saw the enemy everywhere. Driven by fear and delusion, this powerful stranger could hurt her, even kill her.

Kristin looked past him to the rangy buckskin horse that he'd left near her mare. She knew horses. That one showed quality breeding. Her danger senses prickled. Where would the stranger, who had the look of a vagabond, get a horse like that unless he'd stolen it—maybe even killed for it?

Fear crawled up her spine like a snake's cold belly. But she knew better than to let him see how nervous she was.

"This is private property. What are you doing here?" she demanded.

"I might ask you the same question."

"But I asked first. What's your business on this land?"

His mouth tightened. He nodded and spoke. "Actually, I was looking for a family. I have a map, showing the way to their place, but I must've read it wrong because there's nothing out here. I was about to ask you for help when you saw me and got the wrong impression—not that I blame you."

She exhaled, less afraid now but still keeping her guard up. "Most of the people who used to live out here have moved away. What was the family's name?"

"Anderson. I'm looking for the Lars Anderson homestead."

"You've found it." Kristin lowered the riding crop, relieved in spite of herself. "Their house stood right over there. You can see the foundation."

"So you know the family?"

"The eldest Anderson daughter married my brother."

"Then you must know where they've gone. I need to find them. It's important."

"They live in town now. Mr. Anderson homesteaded this land and farmed it for years. He wanted to leave it to his two sons. But he lost heart after both of them died—one of them years ago. He's buried right there." She nodded toward the grave. "The other one died in the war. He's buried in France."

"That would be Corporal Axel Anderson, right? He's the reason I'm here." Reaching into an inner pocket of his vest, he drew out a creased, stained envelope. "My name is Logan Hunter—Major Logan Hunter, not that it makes much difference these days. I was Corporal Anderson's commanding officer. He wrote this letter before he died in the Argonne

Forest. I promised to get it to his family. See—he didn't have an address, so he drew this map on the back."

The man's story rang true, especially with the letter as evidence. As Kristin's gaze took in the sealed envelope, something tugged at her emotions. The young boy she remembered had been so bright and full of promise. Axel's death must have broken his father's heart.

"I apologize for threatening to whip you, Major," she said. "I'm Dr. Kristin Dollarhide. I was stationed in France and posted to a stateside veterans' hospital after the war. I've just come home myself. If you want, I could give that letter to my sister-in-law for her family. It would save you the trouble of finding Axel's parents."

He slipped the letter back into his vest. "That's a mighty kind offer, but I'd rather deliver it in person. Corporal Anderson was a brave young man who died a hero's death. I'd like his folks to hear that from me."

"I understand. Lars Anderson works as a carpenter these days. Blue Moon is a small town. Anyone who lives there can tell you where to find him."

"Thank you, miss—or should I say Doctor?"

"Doctor will do. I've certainly earned the title."

"Then please allow a gentleman to see you back to your horse. No woman, not even a doctor, should be alone out here. It isn't safe."

"This *woman* killed two German soldiers who were trying to rape one of her nurses. I have a rifle on my horse. If trouble comes along, I know how to use it."

"And I've no doubt you're deadly with that riding crop, as well." His mouth twitched in the barest hint of a smile. "But if you'll allow me the pleasure . . ." He offered his arm. With a sigh of resignation, she accepted. Laying a light hand on his sleeve, she felt rock-hard muscle through the thin fabric.

"Will you be setting up a practice here?" He walked with a limp, favoring his right leg. The horses weren't far off, but he took his time.

"I hope so," she said. "The town needs a doctor, and I need to support myself. I've no intention of living off my brother."

"Well, then, maybe our paths will cross again." He stood by while she mounted the mare, then swung onto the tall buckskin, mounting easily despite his impaired leg.

Only then did Kristin notice something that jerked her back to full alert. The buckskin horse was wearing a distinctive brand—the well-known Triple C, for Calder Cattle Company, the biggest ranch in the state of Montana.

Acting on reflex, she whipped the rifle out of its scabbard, slid back the bolt, and aimed the muzzle at his chest. "Hands up high, mister!" she snapped. "Reach for that pistol and you're a dead man. We don't take kindly to horse thieves around here."

He raised hands. His face wore a thunderous scowl. "I don't know what you're thinking, *Doctor*, but nobody calls me a horse thief and gets away with it."

Kristin steadied her grip on the rifle. "Now throw down your weapon and ease out of that saddle. While you're doing it, you can explain why you're riding a horse with the Calder brand on it."

He made no move to drop the pistol or to dismount. "My mother was Benteen Calder's cousin. With my family dead of the Spanish flu back in Texas, Webb Calder is the only blood kin I have left. I wrote him, and he invited me to come here and settle. Webb lent me this horse, so you can put that damned rifle away. I don't like guns pointing at me. They make me nervous."

Kristin held the weapon steady. "Your being a Calder doesn't count for much with me or my family. And what about that letter you showed me? It strikes me as almost too much of a coincidence, your showing up here to deliver it when you're in league with the greediest land-grabbers in Montana. What's your real game, Major Hunter, or whoever you are?"

His expression darkened. "Only a woman could get away with calling me a liar," he growled. "A man would've been dragged off his horse and beaten to a bloody pulp. Now put that rifle away before I decide to take it from you. Every word I've spoken is God's truth, and that's all I'm going to say about it."

Wheeling his mount, he rode away at an easy trot, as if daring her to shoot him in the back. She wouldn't do it, of course. That would be murder.

Shoving the gun back in its scabbard, Kristin watched his tall figure vanish in the direction of town. Had she unmasked a criminal or insulted an honorable man? Either way, Kristin sensed that she'd made an enemy—maybe a dangerous one.

The Great War had ended with an armistice last November. But after talking to Blake, her brother, Kristin already understood that she'd come home to a different kind of war—a war between families—the Dollarhides and the Calders.

Visit our website at
KensingtonBooks.com
to sign up for our newsletters, read
more from your favorite authors, see
books by series, view reading group
guides, and more!

BOOK **CLUB**

BETWEEN THE CHAPTERS

Become a Part of Our
Between the Chapters Book Club
Community and Join the Conversation

Betweenthechapters.net